Mariah Kennec
Geelong, Victoria. She grew up on a small farm alongside three brothers, a sister, several dogs and her pet goat. Aged eleven, Mariah attended an international children's convention in Japan, which sparked in her a passion for social justice and youth advocacy, inspiring her to raise nearly $20,000 for various causes and run several youth advocacy groups. Mariah is currently a Young Ambassador for UNICEF Australia and loves sport, public speaking, drama, animals and playing guitar. In the future she hopes to study medicine or law and use her work to help break the cycle of poverty around the world.

*This book is dedicated to*
*all the children who suffer*
*and all the children who have the power*
*to change things*

# Reaching Out

## messages of hope

edited by Mariah Kennedy

ABC
Books

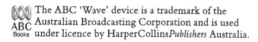 The ABC 'Wave' device is a trademark of the Australian Broadcasting Corporation and is used under licence by HarperCollins*Publishers* Australia.

First published in Australia in 2013
by HarperCollins*Children'sBooks*
a division of HarperCollins*Publishers* Australia Pty Limited
ABN 36 009 913 517
harpercollins.com.au

**HarperCollins*Publishers***
Level 13, 201 Elizabeth Street, Sydney NSW 2000, Australia
Unit D1, 63 Apollo Drive, Rosedale, Auckland 0632, New Zealand
A 53, Sector 57, Noida, UP, India
1 London Bridge Street, London, SE1 9GF, United Kingdom
2 Bloor Street East, 20th floor, Toronto, Ontario M4W 1A8, Canada
195 Broadway, New York NY 10007, USA

ISBN 978 0 7333 3192 3 (paperback)
ISBN 978 1 7430 9869 1 (e-book)

Cover design by Darren Holt, HarperCollins Design Studio
Cover illustration by Michael Leunig
Typeset in Baskerville MT Std by Kirby Jones

Printed and bound in Australia by Griffin Press
The papers used by HarperCollins in the manufacture of this book are a natural, recyclable product made from wood grown in sustainable plantation forests. The fibre source and manufacturing processes meet recognised international environmental standards, and carry certification.

# Contents

# Foreword

In 1989 the nations of the world came together to sign one of the most fundamental documents in the area of human rights, the Convention on the Rights of the Child. The Convention is the most widely ratified treaty in the world, and a very powerful affirmation of every child's right to survive, thrive, to be loved and protected, and to fulfil their full potential. The authors of this history-making document also included a very important clause — the right of children and young people to be heard, to express their views, and exercise their right to a voice. This anthology bears witness to that right.

My experiences through UNICEF have impressed upon me an overriding truism. Whether in the poorest regions of Southeast Asia or in areas of conflict in Africa, I find that same irrepressible and infectious optimism which enables children to live and think within the space of possibility, instead of within the limitations that society builds around them.

Future generations face enormous challenges, such as burgeoning populations, climate chaos, increased migration and an unprecedented pressure on natural resources. It is the optimism of children and their capacity to come up with creative solutions that are more important now than ever. Our children need to be heard. At UNICEF, we believe that children are the now and their voice and inclusion are essential.

If children are to have the future they aspire to, they need to be involved in creating that future — right now. We believe that children can participate in decisions that affect them and can be agents of real change in their world.

One such agent is Mariah Kennedy. Appointed in 2012 as a UNICEF Young Ambassador, Mariah embodies this positive outlook and active voice and has taken the incredible initiative of compiling this anthology — a collection of fiction and non-fiction pieces — with the aim of inspiring other young people to be the change they want to see in the world.

I hope that you will be moved by what you read here. There are pieces that will make your heart heavy — stories of sorrow, abuse, violence and injustice. However, there are also stories of young people who have seen the plight of others, and who have used their voices, skills and time to speak up against injustice and mobilise those around them to build a better world. As Mariah points out, apart from our human rights, the one thing we all have in common is a story. You create your own life story, and your story has the power to change the lives and stories of others.

For adults diving into this anthology, this book is a reminder of the capacity and the ability of young people to use their voices, skills and actions to change the lives of others. I encourage you to share the stories it contains and challenge you to rethink the way you involve and value young people in your life or your work.

I hope that you will be inspired and motivated to advocate for children's rights both in our own country and around the world. Mariah challenges each of us to adopt the irrepressible optimism of children and young people; to grasp the possibilities to ensure our future generations not only survive and thrive, but reach their full potential and in turn create the world that allows them to realise their dreams.

*Norman Gillespie*
*CEO, UNICEF Australia*

# Introduction

For the first five or so years of my life, I had a regular bedtime routine. After dinner, I would brush my teeth, hop into bed and my mum would tuck me in. And then she would read me a bedtime story. We must have made our way through hundreds of books, taking turns to read a page each. I loved to exaggerate character voices and act out scenes, and sometimes I'd add in dialogue or scenes of my own invention. A huge pile of my favourite books stood at the end of my bed — *Selby*, the talking dog, *The Magic Faraway Tree*, *The Famous Five*.

As I started school, I politely informed my mother that her assistance in reading was no longer required; I was a big girl and I could read by myself. My personal library grew as I immersed myself in *Nancy Drew*, *Heidi* and *Anne of Green Gables*.

These books were soon replaced, however, as my tastes continued to mature. I became obsessed with the *Percy Jackson* series, waited desperately for my letter from Hogwarts and threw myself with vigour into *The Hunger Games*.

Now that more years have gone by, my shelves sag under the weight of new favourites: *To Kill a Mockingbird, Jane Eyre* and the adventurous tales of the naturalist Gerald Durrell.

As you can see, despite my ever-changing tastes, books and stories have remained an important part of my life. They have helped me develop into the person I am today. Through literature I have discovered passions, adventures and ethics, and my view of the world has been challenged.

Literature is a unique and powerful tool for change. When reading, we become engrossed in a different world, for a short while experiencing the life of another. Their story comes alive through the pages and as we read we begin to see as they see, breathe as they breathe, live as they live.

Words can, and do, change the world.

Words have been used as tools for saving lives, and for destroying them. For waging wars, and for ending them. For inciting passion, and for cooling it. Whether we like it or not, literature influences the way that we think about things, reminds us of what's important and challenges our views and opinions. It was in this spirit that *Reaching Out* was developed.

One night at boarding school, I lay in bed looking at the books those around me were reading. Nightly, there is a half hour before lights out in which all students are tucked up in bed and engrossed in a book. Any disturbance during this time is quickly hushed, as all are immersed in their own little world. Each book is different, but the significance of the process is the same for all of us. Reading inspires us, focuses us and is an important part of our day.

The idea came to me the next morning. In class, daydreaming, it struck me. Surely, if I were to write to a few of these authors, illustrators and others who so inspired my peers, and if those role models were to write about the issues that are truly important in this world, young people might be encouraged to think about and discuss those issues. If they can, for a short while, walk in the shoes of those who suffer, those who aspire to make a difference, and those who have risen from adversity, they may in turn become inspired to make a difference themselves. Not only might such a collection interest and move youth, but what if it also helped to educate them? Made the issues they hear about in the news real by showing the human face of the statistics learned in geography class or the issues behind political arguments?

What if, by bringing together some of the most influential names in children's literature and some of the most inspiring young leaders of today, we were able to invoke real, positive change in the minds of young people — and thus in the world?

So I wrote to those with this power. And the response was overwhelming. Within a few months, almost thirty of my childhood literary and humanitarian heroes had agreed to contribute. What surprised me most was the passion of their responses: there was a universal desire to help change the world.

Over the course of the following year the contributions started flowing in, and every one I received was different. But, as you will find on reading this book, each is just as valuable as the next. Within this collection you will discover thought-provoking, humorous, inspiring, beautiful, and often moving depictions of the struggles facing youth around the world today. The range is impressive: from the thoughts of a former child soldier to the light-hearted tale of a group of children 'on strike' for peace and from the heart-wrenching sketch of an impoverished African child to poetry for peace-makers. Whether the perils at sea faced by an Afghani refugee or the story of a volunteer clown in African landmine country or the illustration of regrowth following disaster, the friendship of two girls from opposite sides of the globe or reflections from some of the world's greatest change-makers, there is something in this collection for everyone.

It is my hope that this book will help you to understand some important global issues affecting young people around the world every day. I hope that you will find something that resonates with you, moves you or causes you to look at a certain subject in a new light. Ultimately, it is my hope that you will be inspired.

It *is* possible for young people to make a difference. We need to communicate this to all around us. We need to spur the world into action and start creating the change that we all want to see.

Our generation is often criticised for our selfish and wasteful ways. We are told that we are out of touch with the world, spending too much time on things that don't matter. But what most people don't recognise is the extraordinary power of youth. We have energy, passion and belief in ourselves. We are not afraid to stand up and have our voices heard. This gives us the potential to create real change.

The challenge comes in mobilising young people. Too often, we are dismissed by adults. Our ideas and visions are seen as unrealistic or simply 'cute'. It's time we showed the world just how much power we have.

It can be overwhelming, I know. You may be wondering where to start or what you can do now, while you're still at school. So I've put together a five-point action plan that, from my experience, will truly make a difference.

1  Educate yourself. The first step to changing the world lies in knowing how. Reading this book is a great start. You could also sign up for newsletters for your favourite organisations, to keep up-to-date with their news. Watch TV programs, attend speeches, read articles — you can even play interactive change-the-world games, such as the Facebook 'Half the Sky' game.

2  Talk to others. Discuss issues with your family and friends; talk about them on Facebook or Twitter; give a speech at your school. Don't let what is happening be swept under the rug. Don't let faces be turned away, eyes be closed or opinions be hushed.

3  Express yourself. Make your voice heard: write to your local politician, to your local newspaper. Sign an action pledge online, at www.unicef.org, www.change.org or www.theoaktree.org.

4  Get involved:
   • Join or start a youth group for change.
   • Take part in events such as the 40 Hour Famine and Live Below the Line.
   • Attend a youth protest, such as the Vision Generation Mime Protest.
   • Sponsor a child through World Vision, Women for Women International or Plan International.
   • Wear a white wristband to Make Poverty History.
   • Sign up to the UNICEF Youth Advocacy program, which provides an opportunity to work alongside UNICEF to reach out to those in need, becoming a leader in your community.

5  Fundraise or give some of your own money. In a developing country, just $10 can provide 500 students with pencils, to help them write and learn at school. Raising $360 can provide a library of storybooks to help a whole school learn to read and $1800 can

provide a school or village with a 30,000-litre water tank, for clean, healthy water every day. It's such an empowering feeling to know that your donation or hard work has actually achieved something; that you have directly — and dramatically — improved lives.

I often hear it said that the world is too big, the problems too immense and immovable for us to ever make a difference. I believe that an important fact is overlooked: for every child living in poverty, for every child living through war and for every child who simply deserves a better life, there is someone who can help them. And you are one of those someones. Wherever you go in life, whatever you do, please don't ever be scared to be loud; to be heard; to stand up for what is important. You'll be surprised at how many will stand with you.

I discovered this truth shortly after I began work on this book. I applied for the role of UNICEF Young Ambassador and, much to my surprise and delight, I was successful. The work that I've been doing since my appointment has been a constant source of inspiration and wonder to me. I have had the privilege of working alongside impassioned and energetic young people from around Australia and the world. I've visited schools to talk to and work with the students, worked alongside others on youth campaigns, and reached out to many more via social media and the online world.

One thing that I've learned is that, no matter how diverse our background; no matter which country or city we have grown up in; and despite differences in upbringing, culture, and even language; we share a connection. We share a passion.

We, as young people, will one day inherit the world. But the world we want to inherit looks very different from the world we live in today.

We want a world that has a place for the 25,000 children who die of preventable diseases each day.

We want a world that doesn't ignore the pleas of a desperate mother whose newborn baby is starving in her arms.

We want a world in which our children can be taught about poverty in history class, not geography class.

We want a world in which each child can grow up without the pain of witnessing a brother or a sister killed by a landmine while playing a friendly game of soccer.

We want a world in which peace is more than just a dream; we want a world in which peace is a reality.

We want our future back.

We need to harness this want and turn it into change.

Throughout the past few years, both through personal travel and through my work with UNICEF, I've had the honour to meet some inspiring children from many different backgrounds. The determination, resilience and burning, passionate desire for change in each of these children never fail to astound me.

During a recent visit to Myanmar, I sat down to tea with a young girl called Yoha. At fourteen, she's not much younger than me. Yoha lost her father to malaria the previous year, and her mother to an unknown cause only months later. Newly orphaned, she and her three sisters have moved in with her grandma. Despite all the difficulties she faces, Yoha has only one dream: to finish school, go to university and become a tour guide. Her English is impeccable and she has already begun to study local and national history, supplying me with a ready stream of facts over our tea-break. To attend university, she has to pay a $300 entry fee, half of which she has already earned in her afternoon job of selling her sister's lacquerware to tourists. Somehow, despite such hardship, Yoha retains hope, optimism and her bright, infectious smile.

I found another example of this amazing fighting spirit while taking part in a three-day trek through remote Burmese mountainside villages. Most of these villages have little access to the surrounding countryside, let alone the bigger villages and towns. On spending time with the children there, I was struck by the one thing for which each of them seemed eager. Rather than asking for money or sweets, they possessed a tremendous thirst for education, asking me if I had pens, notepads or old textbooks that I could pass on. Overjoyed to receive anything, even something as basic as a small pencil, they sang, laughed and held my hand. These children face extreme poverty, experiencing things that no child should. Yet they remain some of the most inspiring humans I have ever been fortunate enough to meet. Their desire to improve their lives and future is real and it gives great promise to an impoverished world.

I'm sure we all agree that every day the world faces some big problems. We are living through an age that has more pain and suffering, more hunger and more injustice than any other time in history. In no war or act of genocide past or present have so many people died per minute, per hour and per day as those killed by hunger and poverty today.

Fortunately, we have the research, technology and opportunity to change things. This knowledge — this power — will go to waste if we simply stand around doing nothing.

But we don't have to do nothing; we have a choice. You could walk away today, go back to your normal day-to-day life and forget about those living desperately in poverty or caught in the middle of a violent civil war. Or you could decide to be part of a movement to save lives. You could fight for what you know is right.

In the past, dramatic change has come about as a result of the hard work, energy and passion of a single generation. And we can do it too. It's within our power to rewrite history and it's exciting to be a part of a generation which can achieve that.

It all comes down to one question: do we care enough?

If the answer is yes, then *anything* is possible.

To change the world, we don't need a revolutionary leader, we don't need a new scientific breakthrough and we don't need a miracle. We simply need each other.

I'd like to leave you with a quote from one of my dear friends.

I met Pon, an eight-year-old girl living on the street, during a recent trip to Cambodia. Every day after school, Pon would walk with her carton of flowers to the road where my hotel was situated, to sell her wares to tourists. Her English was flawless, and I would often sit with her and we would chat, or take a walk together through the crowded streets of Phnom Penh. It was during these times that I learned about Pon's life — the strict teachers at her school, the games she played with her friends during break-time, the friendly tuktuk drivers who would buy her ice-creams on Sundays, and the latest escapades of her three-year-old brother.

We became good friends. Evenings were our 'special time', spent racing each other down the street, playing 'I Spy' with local shopkeepers, or working out cheating strategies for 'Scissors, Paper, Rock'.

At the end of my stay, it was difficult to say goodbye. On my last night in Cambodia, I stood on the steps of the hotel, blinking back tears as Pon instructed me to 'Come back soon, and bring all your friends'.

It was then that she handed me a single white flower and, standing on tiptoes, whispered into my ear: 'You and me, my friend. Together, we're going to change the world.'

*Mariah Kennedy*

# Dear Olly

*by Michael Morpurgo*

Olly was painting her toenails, light blue with silver glitter. She stretched out her legs and wriggled her toes. 'What d'you think?' she said. She answered herself, because no one else did. 'Amazing, Olly, I think they're just amazing.' But her mother and Matt had not even heard her. She saw they were both deeply engrossed in the television. So Olly looked too.

It was the news. Africa. Soldiers in trucks. A smoky sprawling city of tents and ramshackle huts. A child standing alone and naked by an open drain, stick-like legs, distended stomach, and crying, crying. A tented hospital. An emaciated mother sitting on a bed clutching her child to her shrivelled breast. A girl, about Olly's age perhaps, squatting under a tree, her eyes empty of all life, eyes that had never known happiness. Flies clustered and crawled all over her face. She seemed to have neither the strength nor the will to brush them off. Olly felt overwhelmed by a terrible sadness. 'It's horrible,' she muttered.

Matt wouldn't look at her as he spoke. 'I'm going to be a clown, Olly, I mean a real clown. And now I know where I'm going to do it. I'm going where the swallows go. I'm going to Africa. Do you see that girl on the news with the flies on her face? There's thousands like her, thousands and thousands, and I'm going to try to make them happy, some of them at least. I'm going to Africa.'

Everyone did all they could to stop him. Matt's mother told him again and again that it was just a waste of a good education, that he was throwing away his future. Olly said it was a long way away, that he could catch diseases, and that it was dangerous in Africa with all those lions and snakes and crocodiles.

Aunty Bethel told him in no uncertain terms just what she thought of him. 'What they need in Africa, Matt,' she said, 'is food and medicine and peace, not jokes. It's absurd, ridiculous nonsense.'

Every uncle, every aunt, every grandmother, every grandfather, came and gave their dire warnings. Matt sat and listened to each of them in turn, and then said, as politely as he could, that it was his life and that he would have to live it his way. He argued only with his mother. With her, it was always fierce and fiery, and so loud sometimes that they would wake Olly up with it, and she'd go downstairs crying and begging them to stop.

Then one morning, when they called him down for breakfast, he just wasn't there. His bed was made and his rucksack was gone. He had left a letter for each of them on his bedside table. Olly's mother sat down on his bed and opened her envelope.

'He's gone, Olly,' she said. 'He's gone. He says he's taken out all his savings and gone to Africa.'

People, thousands upon thousands of people living in a ramshackle city of huts and tents, a refugee city, spread out all over the valley from the foothills to the lakeside, a place of wretchedness, a wasteland of human misery that echoed with the howling cries of the hungry and the sick, the lost and the grieving.

The new girl, just brought in that morning — Matt couldn't remember her name — sat cross-legged at his feet, beaming up at him. She had gappy teeth, and Matt remembered Olly being like that, and all the business of the tooth fairy. Home seemed a million miles away, on another planet. The swallows on the wall reminded him that it wasn't.

Matt was busy enough by day about the orphanage, working alongside Sister Christina and the dozen or so nurses and nuns, helping out wherever he could — in the kitchen, cleaning down in the dormitories and the hospital, sometimes teaching under the tree in the courtyard.

In the few months he had been there Matt had become the great fixer, their handy handyman. As Sister Christina once told him teasingly: 'You understand all the truly important mysteries of life, Matt — generators, Land Rover engines, wiring, plumbing, drains.' Matt had made himself quite indispensible about the place. And he had never been so happy. For the first time in his life he felt completely fulfilled at the end of each day. Dawn to dusk, he worked his heart out and loved every moment of it. But dusk was best. 'Matt's happy hour', as Sister Christina called it, or 'Funny Man time', to the children.

And so it was, an hour of clowning antics and joking and juggling and story-telling in the courtyard before the children were taken off to their dormitories for the night. Settling two hundred children to sleep is difficult at the best of times, but as Matt was discovering daily, all these children had lived through unimaginable horrors and terrors, and the coming of night seemed to be the time when their memories returned to haunt them, the time they most missed their mothers and fathers.

For Sister Christina, too, and for everyone who worked at the orphanage, 'Matt's happy hour' had become the one time of the day they could all look forward to. No one liked to miss it. They laughed because they rejoiced to see the children so happy and bright-eyed, but also because Matt somehow managed to touch the child in each of them. Day in, day out, they were dealing with children so wounded in body and soul, that it was sometimes very difficult for them to keep their own spirits up. To them 'Matt's happy hour' was manna from heaven, a blissful haven of fun at the end of the day. They loved him for it, as did the children, and for Matt the warmth of that love meant everything.

With the story over, the children drifted slowly across the courtyard to their dormitories. Matt had one on his back and half a dozen more clutching on to his hands, his arms, his baggy red check trousers, in fact anything they could hang on to. He helped settle them into their beds, cuddling where a cuddle was needed, whispering goodnights, calming fears. As he had expected, it took longer than usual that evening, for the air was heavy and humid. But that was not the only reason. That afternoon they had heard an explosion. It was some way away — probably another landmine, Sister Christina had told him — but close enough to send a shiver of apprehension through the orphanage. All the children knew well enough what such sounds meant, and what horrible damage such sounds could do to the human body.

Matt came at last to Gahamire's bed. He was sitting up, waiting for Matt as usual. Gahamire grabbed him by the hand and pulled him down beside him. He snatched off his battered bowler hat, put it on, mimicking one of Matt's sad faces, and then bursting into laughter.

The transformation of Gahamire had been dramatic and wonderful. Only two months before he would do nothing but sit and stare vacantly at Matt as he clowned and frolicked in the courtyard. He would spend all day sitting on his own, rocking back and forth, never speaking a word to anyone. Then one day, as Matt was flat on his back under the Land Rover changing the oil, he felt someone squatting down beside him. It was Gahamire. Matt reached out and touched his nose with an oily hand, and Gahamire's face cracked into a smile. 'Funny Man,' he said, and he'd stayed to watch.

Since then, Gahamire had latched on to Matt, and would never go to sleep at night until he had been to say goodnight to him. Matt had a whole routine.

'We'll do gorillas again, shall we?' said Matt. Gahamire nodded and waited. 'Well,' Matt went on, 'you know where they live, don't you? On the top of that mountain. They're up there now, going off to sleep just like you. We'll go up there one day and see them, shall we? And how does the big gorilla say goodnight?'

Gahamire beat his chest and the two of them made gorilla faces at each other and giggled.

'And how does the big gorilla scratch himself?'

Gahamire rolled on his back on his bed, and grunted and groaned and scratched himself.

'And how does the big gorilla pick his nose?'

And Gahamire stuck his finger up his nose and wrinkled up his face in disgust.

'And how does the big gorilla go to sleep?'

Gahamire snuggled down at once and closed his eyes.

'Night, night, big gorilla,' said Matt and he got up to go. But Gahamire still had him firmly by the hand and wouldn't let him go.

'What is it?' said Matt.

'My home. My home is by a mountain, a big mountain,' said Gahamire. 'I go. I go up the mountain to find my mother.'

'Of course you will, Gahamire. Sleep now.'

Matt was strangely restless that night. His thoughts rambled and raced. He thought of Olly, of his mother. He should write more often. They'd be worrying. He'd write a card tomorrow. He thought of Gahamire, and wondered if his mother could possibly be alive. So far as anyone knew, both his parents were dead. Such happy reunions did happen. Not often, but they did. He fell asleep, smiling in the hope of it.

It was at breakfast that they discovered Gahamire was missing. As the others were searching through the compound, Matt made his way to the Land Rover, got in and drove off. Sister Christina called after him. 'Matt! What are you doing? Where are you going?'

'To the mountain. He's gone to the mountain. I'll find him.' He roared out through the gates and was gone up the dusty track before anyone could stop him. Matt was quite sure of it. Hadn't Gahamire told him he would go looking for his mother? And like an idiot, hadn't he dismissed it as mere wishful thinking?

He took the most direct route to the mountain, the way he thought Gahamire must have gone, across the road and up the steep rutty track beyond. Here, he stopped the Land

Rover, turned off the engine and called out. There was no reply, only his own echoes dying in the trees all around. Ahead of him the mountain rose steeply on either side of the track, thickly wooded all the way up. He couldn't see the top as the whole range was covered in a blanket of mist. Matt drove on slowly, his eyes peeled, stopping every now and again to call for him, to listen for him. 'It's me, Gahamire. It's Funny Man. Are you there? Are you there?'

For an hour or more he drove on like this, stopping and calling, and starting again. But still no voice answered him. And then, out of the corner of his eye, a sudden shiver of movement. Matt stopped the Land Rover. A shadowy face, then eyes, wide white eyes in amongst the trees. He had found him. He turned off the engine. Gahamire was cowering in the undergrowth, rocking back and forth and moaning, his face wet with tears. Matt approached him slowly, talking as he came. 'It's all right, Gahamire, it's only me. It's Funny Man.'

Gahamire looked up at him. 'The men, they come to my village. They kill and they kill. My mother hid me under the altar in the church. Then she went away —'

But Matt never heard the rest of what Gahamire said, for that was the moment the landmine exploded under his foot.

Matt came to consciousness only a few moments later. His head was full of pain and noise. He tried to sit up, but couldn't. Gahamire's face seemed to be swimming in amongst the trees above him. Matt couldn't decide if Gahamire was wailing or humming. He couldn't work out what he was doing lying there.

'I'd better get up,' Matt said. But Gahamire held him down hard by his shoulders. 'You stay still, Funny Man. You stay still.' Matt tried to fight him, but he seemed to have no strength. He felt himself being swirled away down into a murky darkness and wondered if he would ever wake up again.

When he did, some hours later, he was in the Land Rover. He knew the smell of it, the sound of it. He felt no pain, only bewilderment. All about him was a haze of faces and voices. Then Sister Christina was talking to him. Her voice sounded far away.

'Matt. Matt. You're going to be all right.' Gahamire was beside him, holding his hand. 'Don't you worry,' Sister Christina was saying. 'We'll have you in hospital in just a jiffy. It's the French hospital. It's not far.'

It was the look on Gahamire's face that told Matt it was serious. He panicked then and struggled to raise himself to see what he could, but Sister Christina held him fast where he was. It took all her strength to do it. She tried to calm him, to reassure him. Only then did it occur to Matt that he might be dying. 'You'll tell my mother?' he said. 'You'll tell Olly?' Then he knew nothing more.

When he woke, he could feel a dull ache in his leg. He was covered in a white sheet. There was a nurse at his bedside.

'Hello Matt,' she said. She spoke in a heavy accent. 'I will fetch the doctor for you.' Matt's head was swimming. He felt himself drifting off to sleep. When he opened his eyes again the doctor was standing by his bed. He had long black hair and a beard. Matt thought he looked like a pirate. The nurse took his hand and held it, and Matt wondered why. The doctor spoke almost perfect English, but he seemed uneasy.

'You came through the operation very well. How do you say it? Strong as an ox? You'll be up and about in ten days.'

'What's the matter with me?' Matt asked. 'What happened?'

'A landmine,' the doctor said. 'I have to tell you, Matt. Your right leg. We did all we could, but I'm afraid we could not save it. It's not so bad, Matt. They'll make you another one, not so good as before, maybe, but you'll be able to get around, do what you want, live a full life. It will take time, though.'

'But I can wriggle my toes,' said Matt. 'I can feel them.'

The doctor crouched down. 'I know you can, but it's not real, it's in your head. I'm very sorry, Matt.'

'And my other leg?' Matt asked. 'Is my other leg all right?'

'It's fine,' said the doctor. 'Everything else is fine. You had a bump on the head. So you've got a wonderful black eye, that's all.'

When the time came for Matt to leave the hospital, the ambulance took him on a short detour back to the orphanage, so that everyone could say their goodbyes. The whole place had been decked out with flags and bunting, and everyone was singing: *For he's a jolly good fellow.* Then Gahamire came up and presented him with his battered bowler hat. 'You come back, Funny Man,' he said. Matt found he could neither answer nor smile. All he could do was wave. Then they closed the ambulance doors and drove him away to the airport.

Alone in the aeroplane, Matt cried at last — for his lost leg, and because he was being torn away from the orphanage, from Gahamire and the children, from the place and the people who had made him so happy.

As she had promised, his mother was there at the airport to meet him. There were tears, of course, but Matt made her laugh in the end. 'It'll be cheaper on shoes and socks, Mum,' he quipped. 'Come on, cheer up. It's only one leg. I've still got the other one.'

With every passing day now he grew stronger. He felt the shadows of despair lifting, and was more and more at peace with himself.

One afternoon, he turned up to meet Olly at school, for the very first time with no walking stick, his eyes bright with excitement. 'Well?' he said, holding out his arms and pirouetting proudly.

Olly played at being unimpressed. 'So you can walk on two legs.' Then she hugged him tight. 'Clever you.'

'There's something else I've got to tell you and it's even better,' Matt went on. 'Come on, I'll show you when we get home.'

He took her at once up into the sparrow hide. 'Watch,' he said. 'Keep your eye on that one, the father. You watch him when he perches.' It was some time before either of the parent birds took a rest from feeding the young. When at long last one of them did, Matt whispered, 'You see? The father bird, he can't use his right leg. Look at him. He's like me.'

'So?' said Olly.

'Well, he manages, doesn't he?' Matt went on. 'One leg or not, he's flown all the way here, and come the autumn he's going to fly all the way back to Africa again. And that's just what I'm going to do. I'm going back, Olly, back to Africa.'

'Not for a while, please,' said Olly.

'Not for a while, Olly,' he replied. 'Not till the swallows fly.'

# The rules for smiling

*by Neil Grant*

The dog lay on the ground with its nose weeping blood into the snow. Gradually the blood spread until it looked like a map of Afghanistan: the panhandle of the Wakhan Corridor seeping into the Valley of the Five Lions, through Parwan Province to Bamiyan — the heart of the country, the homeland of the Hazara people. The dog didn't know any of this; it was oblivious to the greater geography of this country and the world.

It knew the town of Bamiyan, but only the outskirts. It had never seen the bazaar across the river with its sheet-metal workers, *chaikhanas* and fruit stalls. Sometimes the winds would cross from there and lift the smells of the settlement high up to the village where the dog lived. He would breathe in the chalky odour of newly slaughtered chicken and the musk of sawn poplar from the timber mill.

He was a fighting dog — a huge mastiff with trimmed ears and a boxlike head. They had bred him for this work and he did it well. But now there were grey hairs on his muzzle and his eyes were clouding. In the mornings it took him longer to rise and the pain in his hips would have made him yelp if that had been in his nature.

The man who kept him fed him well on scraps of lamb, rice and bread, plenty of fat to help him through the long winters. But he had never known tenderness, not even as a pup. He had been taken from his mother at six weeks and trained for violence. He had been ignored and punished, chained to a lump of fractured concrete in the baked-earth yard. And he had grown big. And he had grown strong. So strong that his master feared him. He could see it in the man's eyes as he dropped food near the end of his chain and retreated. But the master had done his job — the dog would never rise up and attack the man, no matter how much he beat or shouted at him.

The small group of houses — you could hardly call it a village — where the dog stayed was past the niches where the giant statues stood. Some people lived in the caves burrowed into the hill, the smoke from their fires circling inside the stone until it found an exit to the sky. But the dog's master was one of the lucky ones. He had not been displaced during the long series of battles that had torn apart the country. Many had lost their homes during the Russian invasion and the Mujahiddin uprising that had followed. The battles had been fierce, and eventually the Russian had fled. The dog knew nothing of this. He was oblivious to history where it did not touch him personally. He remembered his birth, the exile from his family and each of his many fights; this was his history.

At his first fight, he had gone watery with fear. The other dog had been huge. But it was also old and therefore slow. The dog had used this to his advantage. Afterwards, the master had sewn his cuts with cotton and given him a sheep's heart as a reward. He had won his next fight and then two more, then ten. Soon, dogs were brought from the surrounding provinces to do battle with the legendary Bamiyan warrior.

But as the fights grew many, they also blurred into one another — a mess of tearing and snarling, of fur and fury. The dog licked the blood from his paws, nursed chipped teeth and torn ear nubs. Scars on his muzzle interlaced to produce a complicated arrangement of symbols, a story only he could read.

The cold was coming up through the dog's belly fur now. He knew he would die soon and was glad it would be over. His life had been harsh and he deserved nothing more than this ending.

It was then he remembered his mother's softness, the sweet taste of her milk, her nose curled to her tail, and now he nuzzled in with his siblings. He allowed himself a small whimper. That memory hurt more than every fight combined.

\* \* \*

Freshta had gone to the top of the hill to escape the smoke and anger of the cave. Since her father had died there had been little joy. Her older sister had been married two weeks before to a man from Daikundi. She would never see her again. They were not a wealthy family.

Freshta's mother had always been a capable woman but the death of her husband had broken her. He had not died a hero's death; his toe had found a Russian landmine while he was grazing their sheep in the high pasture. This was their first winter without a man in the house and it was hard. Their baba — a grandfather whom she had never met — was due to arrive from Mazar in a day or so. She hoped he would be as kind-hearted as her father but she doubted it. It was as if she was coated in an oil that prevented luck from sticking to her.

The climb up the hill was steep but it warmed her. Her breaths came in satisfying clouds that she broke into as she walked. Near the top, she paused for a rest. The town of Bamiyan was below. The irrigation streams were frozen now, the poplars bare, and beyond the chaotic strip of wooden shops and shipping containers rose the ancient citadel of Sharh-e Ghulghula — the City of Screams — where Genghis Khan had made the rocks turn red with blood. Freshta wondered if these lands would ever be free of war.

She had heard that a new invader was coming from the south. The people in the bazaar called them *talibs* — students — and said they were so devout that their bodies defied bullets. Whole cities were falling to them, men laying down arms. They were a ghost army, undefeatable. Freshta wondered what this would mean for her. Sometimes she felt like a twig pulled this way and that in a river swollen with melted snow.

She continued her journey to the top of the hill. There was the Koh-e Baba — a chain of grand mountains covered in snow, even during the hottest months. When she was younger, she would lie in the wheatfields and trace the sharp outlines of the mountains with her finger. Today the sky was as blue as the chador her mother would wear to the bazaar. That chador was kept by the door of their cave. Soon Freshta might need her own. The country was changing and she was moving from the life of a child to that of a woman.

The cave was the only home Freshta had known. Before she was born, the Russians had flattened their home in Qala-e Dokhtar with a tank. The Mujahiddin had been hiding in the village granary. Her family was one of many caught in the middle. It was not all misery, however; there were paintings in the cave in soft colours. Centuries old, her father had told her, painted by holy men who worshipped a god called Buddh. Freshta had uncovered them by picking the mud from the wall above her bed. They were of slender-waisted women and men with shining crowns. Freshta believed they watched over her in her dreams. Her own private angels.

Her father had named her Freshta. It meant angel and her mother had said they clipped her wings at birth so she would not fly from them. She believed this for years, complaining that her shoulders sometimes hurt, feeling for the buds where the wings might sprout at any time.

The dog lifted its grey muzzle from the ground. Someone was approaching. He hoped it was not village boys out for sport. They would throw stones or sticks; worse if they knew he was wounded. They were always brave when he was on the end of a chain.

He could hear the crunch of snow underfoot but couldn't turn to see who it was. The noise stopped and the dog could hear the person panting. It was a young one, maybe a girl. He let his head flop back to the ground. He closed his eyes. Even though he could be in danger, he no longer cared. Let it come and let it be swift.

When Freshta saw the object in the snow, she thought it was a rock. Then it moved, turned a huge grizzled head until she was almost in sight. She stopped, dead still, trying to hold her breath. No use; she had to breathe. It was a dog. She had always been told dogs were bad. Best to stay away. Even the pups in the bazaar carried disease. Then they grew up to growl and bite.

She edged closer, despite her fear; she was her mother's daughter after all. Closer still, until she could see the fur on the dog's back, thick with ice crystals. Closer, until she could smell him and see the pool of blood spread like a map of Afghanistan in front of him.

He raised his head again, and she wanted to run. She stilled her heart, willed her feet to remain where they were. Her breath came in steaming explosions from deep inside. She crept even closer. The dog growled — a low rumbling, so slow that it seemed like the ticking of a clock.

*Easy, old man. Quiet now, Baba-jan, my dear grandfather.* The words tumbled from her. They had little meaning, or so she thought, other than pure sound — an antidote to the dog's growls. *I am not here to hurt you. Be calm.*

The dog continued to growl. Freshta was an arm's length from him now. Within striking distance. She would be badly hurt if the dog turned on her. She had seen such wounds and they took a lifetime to heal.

*Are you hurt, Baba-jan?* He plainly was. The blood had frozen solid around his nose. *I can help you. Let me help.* The dog's growls moved around her like an earthquake. She could feel them in the meat of her legs and in her stomach. *We can be friends, you and I, Baba-jan.* His growls slowed further, then stopped. His head flopped back to the snow.

The dog wished the girl would finish him. Maybe she did not have the courage. But there was something in the girl's voice that soothed him, made him want to hope. He had never heard such softness. Why did he still resist death even at the end?

The snow was cold on his head. And still his heart pumped life into his body. He closed his eyes and dreamt of spring.

Freshta reached out and touched the dog. He flinched. She grew bolder and ran her hand the length of his body, brushing away the ice that had formed there. His pelt was thick but she could feel his ribs. She knew what she must do.

In springtime, the fields were full of sweet clover. Birds rushed out of the wheatfields. If only he were allowed to run and snap at them. The sun was warm and the nights were bliss. The dog would lie soaking up the warmth and storing it for the colder days ahead. There were fights to be had, sure, but there were also moments like this where there was no business at hand other than the pure pleasure of being.

The dog could taste fresh naan on his tongue. The bread was warm and fresh, just the slightest crispiness to its surface. He loved this taste above all others — wheat dough baked slowly in a tandoor, the smoke still clinging to it. Who would believe a dog could experience such things? Who would care?

His master would not feed him before a fight. His stomach would lurch and knot, he would be crazy with hunger by the time of the contest.

He dreamed on, further and further into his memories. And his body became light. So light, that finally, it floated from the ground.

When Freshta returned with Abdul, she knew the dog was dead. But they lifted him anyway and, placing him on the cart, rolled him down the smooth path that ran from the rear of the hill. Here the snow was thickest. It pulled at the cart's wheels and made the going hard. Their tracks fled from them in two stark lines.

Abdul and Freshta lugged the heavy body up to the cave.

*If the dog is dead, Freshta, remind me why we are taking it to your home?*

Freshta ignored the question. Eventually, they got the dog to the cave and, turning the goat out from her pen, laid it gently on the straw.

Baba arrived in the middle of a snowstorm. He had walked from Shashpul after the van he had been travelling in ploughed off the road. It was a long way in the cold for an old man. Freshta's mother made him a glass of hot *chai sabz* and sweetened it with a spoon of precious honey. She rubbed his hands until they turned from blue to red. It seemed a lifetime since Freshta had seen her mother this happy.

Freshta sat in the corner. She didn't know this man — her mother's father. Even the stories of him seem distant.

He beckoned her to him. *I have a surprise for you*, he said. He handed Freshta a crumpled photograph of a small girl standing among the doves at the Blue Mosque in Mazar-e Sharif. The girl looked so familiar. She was around Freshta's age and wore a bright green headscarf. She was laughing as the birds swooped around her.

Baba-jan said, *You know if a grey dove joins the flock at the shrine, it will turn white within forty days?*

Freshta took the picture and examined it closely. There, at the girl's right shoulder, was a grey dove. *Thank you for the picture, Baba-jan*, she said.

*That's your mother*, he said, pointing to the girl in the photo.

They sat in silence for a moment then she spoke again.

*Baba-jan?*

*Yes, Freshta.*

*I have something to show you, too.*


Freshta's mother had grumbled when she had given the goat pen over to the dog. But Freshta had found another small cave nearby in which to house the goat. She had sat with the dog until he had grown stronger. She had fed him slabs of leftover naan and strings of fat begged from the butcher. The dog's eyes had slowly brightened and the tip of his nose had become wet once more.

*He's a brute*, said her grandfather as they entered the pen. The dog growled as if he understood.

*That's not nice, Baba-jan*, said Freshta.

*It may not be nice but it is true*, replied her grandfather.

*Excuse me, Baba-jan, I would never be that rude to you.* Freshta blushed into her scarf. *The dog is also called Baba-jan.*

*The dog has my name?*

*I am sorry, Baba-jan. I didn't think.*

*Well, we must do something about it. A new name is needed. Something regal. How about Delawar? That means warrior. Or Jahangeer — world conqueror?*

Freshta moved from one foot to another. She didn't want to disrespect her grandfather but neither did she want such a warlike name. The dog's fighting days were over.

Freshta's baba looked at her carefully. He took her chin between two smooth fingers. *I think Salaam would be a good name.*

*I don't know if it fits him*, said Freshta.

*But it means peace. Also, it is what we say when we greet someone. Surely that is the friendliest of names.*


Freshta walked Salaam on a rope every day. Sometimes Baba-jan would go with them, across the streams and up by Sharh-e Ghulghula to the Kakrak Valley. As the days grew warmer, the farmers began to work their fields, ploughing them and redirecting water through the complex system of ditches. Salaam would taste the air and wag his tail, tentatively at first, at passers-by. Baba-jan could hardly believe the change in the old dog.

But Freshta's mother did not like the animal. She begrudged him the scraps that Freshta fed him and the walks that took Freshta away from her chores. She distrusted him. *He will turn to his old ways, Freshta. Fighting is part of his soul. I hear that his owner is looking for him. He may offer money.* But Freshta had been encouraged to be strong-willed. She would not give the old battle dog over.

The leaves were dropping from the trees. Winter would be upon them soon. Baba-jan slept longer during these colder mornings but Freshta was eager to greet the day. If she waited until her mother got up, there would be no time for herself. She took Salaam's rope from the door of the goat pen and rubbed the dog under the chin. He yawned, his great pink tongue almost forming a complete circle inside his mouth.

The dog allowed himself to be led down the rubbly slope towards town. He moved slowly, the cold inside his bones making them ache. But he looked forward to these walks, the smells and sounds of the town. Perhaps he had this in him all along — this joy for life hidden beneath all that violence.

They crossed the river by the two-plank bridge, the girl moving ahead of him. The planks bowed to the river and the dog shuffled nervously. He hated this crossing. The bridge was propped in the middle with an island built of stone. Every flood washed it away but it saved a ten-minute walk upstream to use the road bridge.

As they were stepping onto the second flight of planks, the dog saw the man. He recognised him at once, and it triggered a growl so low and full of hate that the girl froze on the bridge.

*Salaam alaikum*, said the man.

Freshta didn't reply. The man wore a dirty brown shalwar kameez and had a scarf wrapped untidily around his head.

*I like your dog*, said the man.

Freshta moved backwards, stepping on Salaam's paw. He kept up his steady growl.

The man continued. *He looks familiar. How long have you had him?*

Freshta did not want to talk to this man but he blocked her way. Salaam could not move backwards on the bridge or turn around. She drew her scarf over her face. *I have not had him long*, she said. *He was a fighting dog.*

*He still is a fighting dog*, replied the man. *I can see it in his eyes. I lost a dog like that a few months back.*

*This isn't him*, Freshta replied hurriedly.

*How do you know? It looks like him.*

*It isn't him!* yelled Freshta. *Leave us alone.*

*You should respect your elders, young girl.* The man reached for Freshta's arm and pulled her from the bridge. He brought her close. *This dog needs to fight. It is in his nature. Thinking otherwise will only bring both of you unhappiness.*

It was true that the dog's nature was to fight. He had been bred and trained for only this. But he had also been taught to love by the girl. To say that he thought this through while the man was hurting the girl would be to place too much weight on the dog's ability to reason, but something went on deep inside him as he watched. When the man twisted the girl's arm back, he lunged at him.

A two-legged creature is much easier to knock to the ground than a dog. And the neck, so long and thin, is open to the world.

It would be nice to think there could be a happy ending to this story. But Afghanistan is not such a simple place. It would be nice to believe that the dog was allowed to live and that he never fought again; that a lifetime of violence could be changed by several small acts of kindness. And maybe it is so.

It would be nice to ignore the Taliban's arrival in the town and the years of brutality that ensued.

But the Taliban did come to Bamiyan — that much is known. They posted rules on the shattered walls banning kite flying, the playing of music and schooling for girls.

But when Freshta peered from the slit in her chador and read the latest rule, she smiled.

It is important to remember that there are rules for smiling too. And that they will never be governed by men with guns. A smile can show happiness or sadness, or a mixture of both. A smile changes a human face and a human heart. But when a smile is hidden it goes unshared.

No one could see the smile behind Freshta's chador. Or the complicated arrangement of emotions behind it. The sign on the wall read:

No dog fighting.

# Travels with teddy

*by Deborah Ellis*

'It's on the floor again.' The bossy lady across the aisle was talking to Juanita again. It was too dark in the bus to see, but Juanita knew the lady's eyes were looking from her to the fuzzy pink bear in the aisle.

*So pick it up yourself if it bothers you*, Juanita thought, but didn't say. She didn't know enough English words, and she didn't want trouble. She leaned over and felt among the old gum and boot dirt for Teddy.

'Somebody's going to trip,' the lady said, 'and then where would we be?'

*Still here with you*, Juanita thought. 'Thank you,' she said, the foreign words still unfamiliar in her mouth.

'Your brother can't hold on to his toy; maybe you should take it away,' the lady went on.

Juanita didn't understand all the words the lady was saying, but she did catch the disapproval and she was not in the mood for it. It had been a long trip, and the bossy lady had been on their case for four States. Juanita closed her eyes, hoping the lady would shut up. The lady did.

Juanita's little brother, Sam, was asleep between her and Mama. Juanita was small, even for ten. She took after her mother. The three of them could easily sit in a seat meant for two. Juanita was glad this wasn't a bus where the seats had arm rests fixed in the middle. When they were on that kind of bus, one of them always had to hold Sam, and he didn't like to be held.

Juanita tucked the stupid bear firmly under her arm, where it wouldn't slip. From habit, she gave it a squeeze. What had been put in there was still inside. Of course it was. It wouldn't have gone anywhere since the last time she squeezed the bear to make sure.

She didn't blame Sam for not liking the thing. It was a very ugly pink, with a hard plastic face that was more frightening than charming. Sam had taken one look at it when Carlos had handed it to him, and with a scream had flung it across the room. He'd gotten the back of Carlos's hand before Mama could snatch him out of harm's way.

'He will love that bear!' Carlos yelled at Mama. 'You will make him love it or you will deal with me!'

'He will be fine,' Mama said. 'He's just tired.' Then she tried to talk to Carlos about money for the trip. Juanita could have told her not to bother. When Carlos was angry, what little generosity he had went down the drain.

'You'll get paid when you deliver. You'll have your bus tickets. What more do you need?'

'Just for food,' Mama said, with the pleading sound in her voice Juanita hated. 'A cup of coffee at a rest stop. Something to eat for the children.'

Carlos made several horrible suggestions of how Mama could earn money for a rest-stop coffee. Juanita clamped her hands over her ears so she wouldn't have to hear. Carlos laughed at Juanita and started looking at her in a way that was nasty. Mama stopped pleading and pulled Juanita away. From the groceries Carlos had brought to their motel room she made snacks to take then borrowed ten dollars from one of the other motel families for coffee and milk on the trip.

Juanita tried to go back to sleep but couldn't get comfortable in the bus seat. Her right leg kept wanting to jump and dance, and she had to scrunch up her toes to make it behave. If she could turn on the light, she could practise writing English words with the pen and pad of paper she'd taken from the motel room, but she couldn't reach the ceiling light without standing up and stretching. That would be sure to wake Sam, who wasn't as good a traveller as she was. And anyway, the bossy lady could complain that the light was bothering her.

Juanita adjusted the stuffed bear so that its face peeked out from under her arm. Occasional passing cars lit up its plastic eyes. It almost looked like the bear was winking at her.

'Don't wink,' she whispered. 'We are not friends.' She squished its face away again. Her brother stirred and whimpered. She stroked his hair and quietly sang a song from their grandmother's village near Durango until he was asleep once more.

When Juanita closed her eyes again and tried to rest, all she saw was the endless desert, her father collapsing and not getting up, and their coyote, their smuggler, demanding payment while her mother bent over the dirt grave saying the rosary and weeping.

'My husband already paid you! He told me that he paid you!'

'Do you have proof? Do you have a receipt? Your husband made a bargain. In return for money, I will take your family into the United States. No money, no bargain. Why should I take a risk for you for nothing? Why shouldn't I leave you all to die with your husband in the desert?'

'The children!' Mama had cried. Juanita was so scared she forgot about being hungry and thirsty and so very tired. 'I will pay you — I promise. I am a hard worker. In America I will work hard and pay you everything. You will get your money. If you leave us in the desert, all you will get will be our dead bodies.'

The coyote pretended to consider. He might have been fooling Juanita's mother, who was so desperate she wasn't thinking straight, but he didn't fool Juanita. He was a very bad man, and he wasn't considering anything. Juanita didn't know what he was up to, but she didn't like him.

The smuggler must have realised this because, when her mother was on her knees, weeping with gratitude and relief, he caught Juanita's eyes. She was staring straight at him, the way you stare straight at someone you catch cheating at games or telling a lie. His lip curled into a sneer. He knew that she knew, and he didn't care. He didn't have to.

They crossed the Rio Grande that same night, plunging into the dark, raging river, Sam strapped to his mother's back with a cloth over his mouth so he wouldn't cry out. They had to move between swoops of the searchlights.

Carlos was waiting for them.

Two days staying quiet in a tiny motel room, not even being able to look out the window at this great new land, this America, that had held such magic when Papa talked about it. Two days of eating strange food without flavour, and Mama afraid with every car noise that it was the immigration police coming to arrest them. Two days of Carlos appearing and reappearing, asking them questions about their home village and the family they'd left behind in Mexico.

Juanita watched television. They had to keep the sound down, but the television also kept Sam quiet. He stared for hours at the flickering lights and pictures of happy American children having such fun and eating so much. Juanita practised her English. She already knew some

English words from her teacher back home. She could say, 'Hello, how are you? I am fine. America is a beautiful country.' From the motel TV, she picked up, 'Who will be the next American Idol?' and 'This is CNN Breaking News.' It seemed easier to remember words when there was music attached.

They left on their first bus trip the morning of the third day.

'Wear these,' Carlos told her mother, giving her a plastic padded thing to put around her waist. 'Wear it under your clothes. There's one for your daughter, too.'

'Not my daughter. No.'

'She can wear it or she can stay here with us until you get safely back with our money.'

Juanita had worn it. She put it over her undershirt, so the plastic wouldn't make her skin sweat and itch, but under her other clothes. Carlos had given her a new shirt, yellow and loose, and a red undershirt. Juanita liked having new clothes but the colours didn't go well together. She was afraid people would laugh.

'No one will care how you look,' Carlos said, 'unless you do something that makes them notice, and if you do, I'll find out.'

Carlos tried to strap something onto Sam, too, but Sam simply wouldn't co-operate. It was almost funny watching this big, scary man having an argument with a two-year-old. The two-year-old won. They had to think of something else.

That was the first bear.

It was brown and furry and had a sewn-on smile that was happy and friendly. Sam loved it, and cried like crazy when it got taken away at the end of their journey.

The second bear was black and white. Juanita knew it was supposed to be a panda, but it didn't really look like a panda. Sam liked it, though, and talked his little Sam-talk to it all the way across America. He cried even harder when it was taken; its belly was slashed open right in front of Sam, the plastic bag full of white powder pulled out, and the dead teddy carcass was kicked to a corner of the room.

By the third trip, and the pink bear, Sam was wise.

'We have made two trips,' Juanita's mother told Carlos. I think we have paid you back.'

'You think wrong,' Carlos said. 'Who pays for your bus tickets? Who pays for your motel room? You think these things are gifts? I'll let you know when you've paid me back.'

'Do you think I don't know what is in these bags you strap to us?' Mama asked.

Even Juanita knew. Well, she didn't know exactly, but she knew it was bad.

'We will be caught by the police. I know we will be caught.'

'Who will suspect a nice mother and her two nice children? And if you are caught, you will still owe me. Like I said, I'll let you know when your debt is paid.'

Carlos could make them travel, and he could make them keep his secret, but he couldn't stop Juanita from looking out the window as the nation passed by. He couldn't stop her from watching all the different types of people who took the bus, or listening to all their different ways of speaking. She picked out words she could recognise, and said new ones she heard, over and over to herself. Americans didn't speak English the way she had learned it in Mexico. 'May I have a glass of milk, please?' They ran everything together, leaving words out, moving words around. She supposed that's how she talked, too, when she spoke her own language in her own country. Back home, everyone understood, just the way these Americans seemed to understand each other.

She closed her eyes, thought about words, and was almost asleep when the bus gave a sudden lurch to one side. The tyres screeched like a scream, and then everything fell apart. Juanita was tossed from her seat. She bounced off one wall, then another. She hit people and baggage and heard windows smashing. There was one terrible last skid, and then the bus came to a stop.

Juanita was buried under people and their belongings. 'Mama!' she cried, but her cry was only one among many. She pushed her way up, what she hoped was up, digging her way through the rubble the way a mole digs its to safety.

'Give me your hand!' the annoying lady was saying. Juanita recognised her voice. 'I'll pull you through the window.' Then, maybe 'cause Juanita wasn't obeying, she said, 'Hecho, por favor.'

You're saying it wrong, Juanita wanted to say, but instead she stuck out her hand. Someone grabbed it and pulled at her. She felt gravel, then grass. She was outside.

'Mama!' she screamed. She heard her brother crying — she'd know that cry anywhere — and got to her feet and grabbed him even before she realised that she was okay, she could still walk, nothing was broken.

'I smell gas,' someone yelled. 'Everyone — get away from the bus!'

'Mama!' Juanita yelled again, but Mama was already there, pulling at her, taking Sam from her arms so they could run faster.

And then there was a sound, louder than any sound Juanita had ever heard. She was facing away, but she could still see the light from the fire and the explosion. She could feel the heat and the force of the blast that pushed them forward, kept them running, running.

They ran into a thicket of trees then collapsed among the branches. Juanita looked back. The fire from the bus made everything bright like day. She could see a lot of people still running. She hoped they all got away, especially the woman who had bothered her across four States then helped her escape.

Sam cried and cried.

'Is he hurt?' Juanita asked. Mama checked him all over.

They checked themselves, too. They all had bumps and scratches, but nothing worse.

Police cars, ambulances, television trucks, all came to the scene. Mama said the rosary, and Juanita joined in. It seemed like a good time to pray.

Juanita and her family stayed in the trees while the night went away, and the daylight revealed a bus with its wheels in the air, a dead creature, burnt out and empty. They watched stretchers loaded with body bags being wheeled into the backs of wagons.

No one came to look for them.

'The bear,' Mama said. 'I forgot about the bear. I must go and get it!'

She started to get up. Juanita pulled her back.

'It burnt,' she said. 'It must have. And if it didn't, are you going to go to the police and ask for it?'

'I will never get my debt paid,' Mama said, almost in a whisper. She leaned back against a fallen tree trunk. 'Carlos will not accept this. I will have to pay him back for the bear.' She looked at Juanita with panic in her face. 'We can't even go home to Mexico because he knows our village, he knows who our family is.'

Juanita looked at the rising sun making the sad wreckage gleam and sparkle. She saw the victims being taken away.

'Maybe we died on the bus,' she said.

Mama was busy trying to soothe Sam so she didn't hear her at first.

Juanita said it again.

'Maybe we died on the bus. If we died on the bus, Carlos can't come after us.' She reached under her shirt and yanked off the plastic belt full of whatever bad powder Carlos had put in there. 'If we died on the bus, then this died with us. And we can bury it.' She picked up a stick and started pushing away leaves and debris. She dug a hole and dropped the belt into it.

Mama passed Sam to Juanita, took off her own belt full of drugs, and dumped it into the hole as well. They filled it in together, making the ground look like there was nothing buried there.

'I miss Papa,' Juanita said.

'Me, too,' said Mama.

Mama picked up Sam. Juanita took her hand and they walked through the other side of the thicket to whatever was ahead. Juanita knew from riding the bus that El Norte was a big, big country, with many roads, wide and narrow, that led to many different places. They'd cross this field, and maybe another one, and soon they'd come to a town where someone might have a job for Mama, and food for Sam, and a place where Juanita could practise her English and maybe even go to school. They'd take new names and make a new life.

Juanita squeezed her mother's hand.

'Welcome to America, Mama,' she said, and they got busy walking.

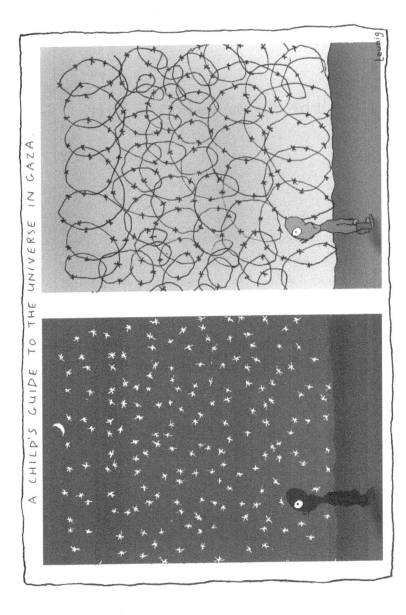

# The cheetah and the hare

*by Danielle Gram*

[*Editor's note:* The following story is based on the experiences, lives and stories of the child soldiers and child 'brides' throughout Africa and in particular northern Uganda.]

April is my favourite month. It is when the fiery sun and thirsty sky of dry season become covered by big, puffy rain clouds that make shapes like wild animals chasing each other across the vast blue sky. After weeks of tempting passers-by, the branches of mango trees droop low, burdened by the weight of sweet, ripened fruits. In April, school closes for a month-long break and my friends and I pass the day away outside before running for cover from afternoon downpours.

For most of my life, my village was an idyllic and peaceful place. Like a natural playground, we had branches to swing from, insects to race, and footballs to construct by wrapping and tying dried grasses until we had the perfect shape to kick and chase. After a long day of play, I could retire to my family's plot and find comfort within one of our huts.

My father made our home with his very own hands. He needed ox-like strength to carry the heavy mud bricks and stack them one on top of another to make our home's thick, circular walls. My mother helped by collecting wooden branches and tall grasses, which she piled upon her head and carried to our home site. These materials eventually made a thatched roof, protecting us from the elements and muting the sound of April's heavy rains.

Like most families in northern Uganda, we lived far from cities and towns, with our closest neighbours a several-minute walk away. Twelve family members shared our three huts, with one housing my mother, grandmother, auntie and four sisters and another for my father, three brothers and me. The remaining hut was used for cooking savoury smoked goat's meat; greens mixed with peanut butter; beans and *posho*, a food made from maize flour which we eat with almost every meal.

My brothers and I could play hide-and-seek for hours amid the tall maize stalks and grasses that surrounded our home. One time, my youngest brother, Oketa, hid so well, lodged between a termite mound and a tree trunk, that he drifted off to sleep for two hours while the rest of us searched for him!

At day's end, I used to love sitting at the feet of my father, listening to stories about our tribe — the proud

Acholi people — and the folk stories his father, the chief of the Palwo clan, once taught him.

For hundreds of years, Acholis had lived in the remote northern lands of Uganda, herding, farming and generally living in peace. When threats did come, from rival tribes or bloodthirsty wild animals, Acholi men were known to be fierce warriors.

I loved hearing about how my grandfather once saved our whole village from raids led by Karamojong warriors. The Karamojong tribe lived in northeastern Uganda, and would frequently enter the land of others to steal cattle and take war prizes.

I imagined wartime as something for Acholis to be proud of, a period when our people would confidently defend our land, women, and children. I never imagined that a war would come that would target children like me, and I especially didn't think our own tribesmen would lead the effort.


I first heard whispers about Joseph Kony and his Lord's Resistance Army at school one day in mid-May. An older boy, about fifteen years old, was sitting under a flowering jacaranda tree, sharing stories about Kony's magical powers.

'The Ugandan army will never find him because he can transform himself into a snake and slither away, or burst into flight like a hawk,' Oryem told the others. 'One time, more than a thousand soldiers cornered Kony and thirty of his militiamen, yet when it came time to fire their guns, Kony used magic to make the bullets disappear.'

From what Oryem shared, it was hard to know if Joseph Kony was part of fact or fiction — another heroic warrior of folktales or a real threat to Ugandan people.

When the following March drew to a close, I prepared to leave school. For those children lucky enough to attend school, leaving at the end of the term was always bittersweet. On the one hand, I looked forward to going home to my village so I could play with my brothers and sisters, help my parents dig in our garden and eat the delicious food my mother and grandmother prepared. But at the same time, I knew the value of education. My family was large and poor, and of my seven siblings, only one had completed primary school in town. Apart from me and my younger brother, Otim, the others remained at home because my family did not have the money to pay the fees required for boarding school.

Our arrival back to our village from school was greeted with celebration. My mother cooked two chickens to celebrate the return of two of her sons to the home. I was especially congratulated because I had placed second in my class for the term. We ate and drummed and danced well into the night, all proud of our education and thankful to our elders for sacrificing the money needed for school.

Three days after returning home, my brother Obua and I decided to go exploring down by the creek an hour's walk from our home. We spent the afternoon crafting nets out of sticks and reeds and launching them into the lazy water below.

With our small catch in tow, we took our time walking back home. Obua, two years older than me and much taller, carried the fish in a bucket upon his head and every now and again, would sneak an arm behind me and drop a slimy fish down my back. I would try to get back at him for this, chasing him and throwing dirt his way, but somehow, he always seemed to have the upper hand.

Suddenly, Obua stopped at the side of the road.

'Karabunga, did you hear that?' he asked me.

'What? All I've heard for the last hour is your big mouth!' I answered.

'No, I'm being serious. I thought I heard the sound of gunfire. You know, we must be very careful these days. I've heard rumours the militias of Joseph Kony will come to our region and that when they do, they will take the children and kill the women.'

'It's impossible,' I reassured my older brother. 'What would they want with the children? We would just be a burden to a military, always complaining for more food and sleep.'

Obua laughed, agreeing that if *I* were taken, they surely would desert me as soon as they knew how much beans and *posho* I could consume in one sitting.

That night, after eating the supper our mother had prepared from our fishing catch, my family sat around the fire ring outside of our huts. My father told stories as my brothers and I listened intently and the women sat off to the side, braiding each other's hair and humming praise hymns. On this night, my father told the story of the hare and the cheetah. The hare was usually my favourite character in our culture's folktales, always wise and crafty and avoiding trouble by using his brain. In this story, the hare caught a water buffalo which he intended to bring home to his family for supper, but on his way, he encountered a hungry cheetah. The cheetah, the fastest animal of the savannah, approached the buffalo with such speed that he could have easily outrun the hare with his supper and taken the hare for dessert. Understanding the mess he was in, the hare tricked the cheetah into believing the buffalo was intended as a gift for the chief, a figure whom all of the animals respected. The cheetah wanted to see for himself and followed the hare all the way to the chief's hut with the buffalo, protecting the hare and his catch from a lion and hyena along the way. When they arrived, the hare requested to enter the chief's hut alone to inform the honourable man of his gift. The hare entered the hut and changed his voice, first mimicking the voice of the chief, then responding normally. The cheetah listened carefully from outside of the hut, believing the hare's performance. When the cheetah heard confirmation that the chief wanted the buffalo as a gift, he disappeared into the bush, leaving the buffalo to the crafty hare.

The hare was like that: no matter what situation he found himself in, he could find a way out that left him better off than before.

With the sun long gone and the thin crescent moon covering our home in shadows, we retired to our huts for the night. I drifted off to sleep thinking about how I could become more like the hare.

At around midnight, I was startled awake by the sound of pounding fists on the metal door of our hut.

'Open up!' a man shouted. 'We need to speak to the head of this family.'

My father quickly threw off his blanket and stumbled to the door, whispering to my brothers and me to stay calm and remain inside.

He opened the door a crack and squeezed himself out, shutting it behind him.

'Yes, what can I help you with?' I heard him ask.

'We want food and we want money,' a man said sternly. From the sounds of the footsteps walking around our huts, it seemed like the spokesman was joined by at least five others.

'I think we have some food left over from supper,' my father answered calmly. 'I am a man of humble means and have very little money, but I might be able to find a bit to give you.'

'A bit? We'll see about that. Men, search the huts!'

Before my father could do anything, a foot flew through the door of the hut where I had been sleeping.

'Get up, get out! The rebel's voice sounded young, and from the little of his face I could see in the faint moonlight, he appeared only a few years older than me — perhaps he was sixteen, if that.

My brothers and I assembled quickly and stood in a line outside of our hut. My sisters, mother, auntie and grandmother were similarly forced out of their hut and now stood a little away from us. A man with a gun stood over my father, who was kneeling by the embers of our fire.

What happened in the minutes following still brings me too much pain to recount in detail. As my father looked on helplessly, three men went through our huts and took out anything they saw that might be of use to them. When one came out carrying the colourful decorative beads of our mother — a valued possession in Acholi culture — my grandmother cried out for him to stop.

I looked away as a militiaman dragged my elderly grandmother off into the grasses behind her hut. I would never see her again.

After our huts had been robbed, the group's commander brought his face close to each of my siblings and me, asking us to stand one by one so he could have a look at us. A wide scar marked his cheek and his piercing stare sent a shiver down my spine. He grabbed Obua, two of my sisters and me and left the others kneeling by our father.

He ordered us to carry heavy trunks upon our heads and to march off into the bush. We struggled with the weight but did as we were told. I heard my mother's pleading cries as we headed into the night, 'Please don't take my babies. They are only children! Take me instead! Take me and I will carry and cook for you.'

Her cries met deaf ears.

For hours, I followed closely behind Obua, and my two sisters trailed me. We marched all through the night, fighting the urge to rest our aching legs and tired minds.

'I'm afraid, Karabunga,' my sister whispered to me.

'Just focus on each footstep and nothing more,' I told her, masking my own anxiety about where we were going and what lay ahead.

By dawn, we reached a militia encampment. I couldn't believe what I saw; it could have been a school yard. There were nearly fifty children there, both boys and girls. The boys were being trained as soldiers and held heavy guns, strapped across their chests. The girls served the men and boys, working as cooks and porters. Some, still young enough to play jump rope in a school yard, had been selected as wives for the commanders and best performing soldiers.

After a short rest, my siblings and I were awoken by our commander.

'Stand up, it is time to go,' he told us.

Outside of our hut, three groups of youth had formed. Our commander split my sisters up and sent my brother and me together to a platoon of boys. It was clear they would force us to be soldiers and that staying together as a family would not be an option. I was happy I would remain with Obua but feared greatly for my sisters' safety.

That afternoon, Obua and I were taken for training. We were both given guns like we had never seen before. Mine was a rifle, while Obua, older and stronger than me, was handed a machine gun and a string of bullets that curled around him like a snake.

Mangoes were set upon tree trunks for us to practise our shooting. I held my rifle as the older boys had demonstrated and pulled the trigger. The force of the shot propelled me backward and I nearly fell to the ground. Everyone around laughed except the two younger boys next to me, who knew the same would happen to them when their turn came.

For a week, we trained in the clearing of the bush. When it rained, we all fought for cover under the shea nut and acacia trees as narrow flowing streams of muddy water overtook our training base.

At night, the commanders told us stories of Joseph Kony, the founder and leader of the Lord's Resistance Army for which we now trained.

'He's a prophet of God,' a senior soldier said. 'He has the power to defeat any enemy by calling the spirits of our ancestors and using the magic they give him. When you fight for him, you fight for God. Even if you die, you do not lose because you are on the right side.'

'He even has a cure for AIDS,' a child soldier whispered to me.

'How do you know? Have you ever seen someone cured?' I asked.

'No, stupid. Kony only meets with a few of his most trusted advisers. The rest of us hear of him through our commanders,' he replied.

I heard many reasons for why we were being trained — to replace the Ugandan government with Acholi leadership, to make a government based upon the Ten Commandments — but none seemed to explain why the militia targeted our own tribesmen and abducted children. The vast majority of us who fought did so not because we believed in the militia's cause but because we were taken from our homes and given no choice.

On our last day of training, Obua and I were sent to separate platoons. For the past week, I had prayed every day that no matter what happened, God would keep me with my brother, even if that meant we would die together. I hid my tears from the other soldiers as I hugged Obua goodbye.

My commander was a twenty-four-year-old man named Mwaka, who had been taken from his family to fight when he was fifteen. For the past nine years, he had done everything asked of him: stealing, killing, torturing and working toward Kony's version of a righteous nation. He was muscular and wore stylish sunglasses like the rap singers I'd seen in music videos. He kept his hair twisted into long dreadlocks, smoked cigarettes and played the latest Acholi music from his battery-operated radio. Sometimes, he would make the girls in our platoon dance as he would sip *waragi*, the local alcohol.

When I first met him, I thought I wanted to be like him, strong and cool, and then I saw his darker side, his anger that came like lightning and struck down anything it encountered.

My first mission was in Kitgum, a district bordering South Sudan. Every day, we conducted raids on homesteads to steal food, money and any supplies we needed. I often thought of the night this happened to my own home, and prayed for the soul of my grandmother, who died trying to protect our property.

The worst raids were those that took people. Sometimes, we stole so much food and gear that we needed more people to help us carry our load. Often, young boys were taken, but when Mwaka said he had been given special instructions from Kony to gather more wives for commanders, young girls were taken.

One night, we abducted a girl named Akena after burning down her home and leaving her parents badly beaten. As we left her family's plot, I was instructed to follow her closely and make sure she didn't try to run away.

Akena was twelve years old like me, and as feisty as any girl I'd ever met. She followed orders, but had a brain that allowed her to escape her daily duties through rebellious thoughts. Most days, she had to join the other two girls of our eleven-man platoon in the tasks of cooking and cleaning.

While the boy soldiers were discouraged from interacting with girls, Akena and I quickly became friends, forming a relationship we tried to hide from Mwaka. We quietly told each other stories as we marched, imagining faraway lands where children didn't need to kill people or work as forced labour. We both had excelled in school and quizzed each other during long marches. I was better in mathematics, so I drilled Akena in arithmetic, while her English was as good as a teenager's.

One morning, Akena didn't wake with the other girls to prepare our breakfast.

'Where is she?' Mwaka demanded of the two girls busily preparing the morning porridge.

Both girls looked up, but neither answered.

'Where is she?' he asked again, this time separating each word in a tone that sent a shiver down my spine.

Again, the girls failed to answer.

'That's it,' Mwaka shouted, kicking over the pot of porridge, sending boiling liquid into the girls' laps.

He stomped over to the hut where Akena had retired the night before and forced his way inside. A few minutes later, he emerged with Akena, who didn't dare look up from the ground.

'You girls have betrayed me by refusing to answer my questions,' Mwaka shouted at the two girls near the fire. 'Fifty lashes for you both! Karabunga, make a switch.'

I hated to do it, but I knew how Mwaka could become when angered. I gathered grasses and twisted them together to make a firm rope. At the ends, I tied sharp rocks.

'You will do it yourself, Karabunga,' Mwaka said, 'I've seen how you like to make friends with the girls.'

The two girls kneeled on the ground before me and looked up with eyes that silently begged for forgiveness. I drew my arm back and released the first hard hit, wincing as it struck. Fearing further beating, neither girl made much noise as I hit time and time again. They lay helplessly as their blouses turned red with blood, and I followed orders.

With empty stomachs, we all lined up to begin our day's march, silent from anger and sadness from what had occurred earlier in the day. I was ashamed of my actions and cursed Akena for not leaving her hut that morning.

Years later, I learned that Akena had become a woman that day. She knew that made her capable of becoming a soldier's wife and preferred to stay in her hut rather than catch Mwaka's eye.

Months passed by slowly. Our routine was generally the same: marching, training, abducting, killing and stealing. Occasionally, we encountered troops of the Ugandan national army sent to destroy our rebel efforts. When numbers were in our favour, we fought them. More often, we retreated further north, using the tall grass for cover.

Eventually, we reached Sudan with a platoon that had grown to eighteen boys, three adults and seven girls. Like Uganda, Sudan had been fighting a war for many years which also took children from their homes and made them do monstrous acts with weapons.

Rains did not fall the months we were in Sudan. The dirt cracked, forbidding life from growing. For a short while, we continued our village raids. We entered round mud huts of transient Acholi and Nuer tribes, beat their inhabitants, stole goods and left the houses burning behind us. I hated doing it, but forced by the rebels, I had no choice. Soon, even the huts we entered had little or no food. The boys and I were sent to catch desert rats with our hands in order to preserve our scarce bullets.

We formed circles when it came time to sleep, sitting back to back with a partner, taking turns staying awake. We listened carefully for the rustling sound of animals in the bush. The night was infamous for smaller children being carried off into the darkness in the mouth of a hungry lion.

Day after day our bodies grew thinner, exposing our ribs and making our shoulders poke out like sundials toward the sun. When we didn't have water, we drank the blood of the animals we killed, and often became too weak to move and delusional from dehydration. If we spotted a bird's nest in a tree, we helped each other climb its branches and ate the eggs raw. If we saw anything scurry across the dry ground, we chased it: snake, rodent or mammal.

Often we encountered people who appeared to be resting against tree trunks but had fallen asleep and never awoken, betrayed by the drought that stripped the land of vital streams and vegetation. We braved the swarming flies and stench to gather what we could from the dead, sometimes weapons, ammunition or clothes. For our poorly supplied army, anything we could find was worth the discomfort of stealing from the dead.

Akena and I continued to tell each other stories to take our minds off of our growling stomachs and families' fate. I told her stories my father had shared about the hare, and she and I began to talk about how we could become as wise as the animal of our folk stories, outsmarting our companions, escaping and finding our way home.

Three days passed without any food. Already five members of our platoon had died — one from a stray bullet, two from sickness and two from thirst or starvation — and in our weakened state, it became clear we would all soon die if we did not find something to eat.

Mwaka devised a plan. Six of the boys would be sent to raid a Dinka encampment and would bring back the spoils for the rest to enjoy.

The Dinka were infamous throughout northern and East Africa for their merciless practices during war. They were said to never lose a battle, protected by their ancestors, and to be excellent at aiming weapons. We all knew that sending six children to beat the Dinka was a suicide mission.

Mwaka reviewed the remaining boys in his platoon and made his selection. I would go along with five others ranging in age from eleven to sixteen. We picked up our guns and marched off into the distance.

As we approached a clearing, we spotted the fire rings the Dinka use to cook their cattle meat. Even during a drought, the Dinka had food to eat because of their sizable herds.

'Let me go first,' said Acan, the youngest boy among us. 'I saw my family die and have no reason to return.'

'I want to go, too,' said Anywar. 'I would rather die than continue another day in this desert.'

After some discussion, we agreed to let the two boys go before us, Acan leading the way, and Anywar following close behind. I crouched low in the high grass and aimed straight ahead, just beyond the backs of my friends toward the heart of the Dinka encampment.

Acan and Anywar moved swiftly. When they made it to within five metres of the first hut, we heard a sudden uproar. Fifteen Dinka men jumped out from behind the huts with guns drawn, as if they had been expecting us. Acan and Anywar fell instantly.

The remaining boys and I fired off rounds as we attempted to run away. The Dinka were faster and better shooters. They shot one of my companions and captured another. I can't even imagine what became of the one captured, surely a fate worse than death.

I managed to get away and eventually reunited with Olang, who had run quickly but lost his gun as he fled. We both walked in silence the rest of the way back, afraid of returning without our friends or food, and less five guns.

Mwaka was waiting impatiently for us back at the camp. The girls had prepared the last bit of tea they could manage from water we had collected several days before.

'Where is the food?' Mwaka shouted. 'Why do I see only two of you?'

'The Dinka almost killed us,' I responded softly. 'The others are likely all dead.'

'But you survived. Why didn't you continue to pursue the food? Surely dying would have been better than leaving us with your mouths to feed!'

I looked down at my feet, more exhausted than upset.

'Olang, where is your gun?' he asked, noticing what I had hoped he would oversee.

'Sir, I lost it,' Olang said. 'I had to drop it so I could run faster.' Olang shrank before my eyes from a tall fifteen-year-old to the stature of a cowering child.

'That gun is worth more than you are! It is worth more than both of you put together. I've had enough of your nonsense!' Mwaka screamed. He reached to his side and grabbed his gun. In an instant, Olang was dead.

Olang's death was more than I could take. It was bad enough to lose friends to the Dinkas, but to have our own commander take the life of one of the few we had left was too much to accept.

I spent the rest of the afternoon by myself. I closed my eyes and imagined my father and mother back home. I no longer knew if they were alive, but I talked to them anyway. Lying under the hot Sudanese sun, I dreamed of my mother cooking on her mud-brick stove while my father sat rocking his chair back and forth by the night's fire.

'Son, do you remember the story of the hare?' my father asked.

'Of course, Father. I listened to your stories a hundred times,' I answered.

'Then why haven't you begun thinking like the hare? Be like the hare, and you will find your way home.'

'But how?' I asked.

As quickly as the vision had come, my father vanished. I tried and tried to get him to come back to me, asking questions and pleading for answers. Eventually, I gave up and returned to the others.

The next day, Mwaka received word that we would join two other platoons returning to Uganda, who had enough food for a grand feast. Normally, this would be news worthy of celebration, but all of us had lost interest in soldiering on.

We ate the meat of an elephant a soldier had managed to

kill. At eighteen, the soldier became a hero to all of Kony's child soldiers attempting to survive Sudan's drought.

After eating and drinking all our weak bodies could manage, I found Akena.

'Meet me at nightfall, one hour after everyone goes to sleep,' I whispered to her.

Akena nodded and we both returned to the feast.

When nightfall came and everyone seemed asleep with stomachs full, I quietly exited my hut, telling the night guard I needed to use the latrine. Leaving would not be as easy as just running away. Soldiers were always positioned with the order to shoot even at the slightest suspicion of desertion.

Fortunately, Akena kept time like the sun and arrived at our meeting spot just after I did.

'What is it?' she asked me.

'My father appeared to me in a dream yesterday urging me to escape this terrible life,' I said.

'But escapes so often end in death,' replied Akena.

'Whether escape ends in death or life, both are better than being forced to steal and kill. I am leaving tomorrow and I want you to come with me,' I told her.

Akena stood silently for a moment and then responded. 'Okay, tomorrow we will think like the hare and find a way home.'

The morning began uneventfully. Akena joined the other girls in making breakfast porridge and I made small talk with the men. It was when the marching started that we began to hatch our plan.

The day was hot and dry, with wildfire winds. Sweat dripped down our backs as we marched, soaking our shirts and making our guns stick to our backs.

Around midday, we stopped in a clearing to rest.

'I'm feeling horribly ill,' Akena complained, excusing herself from the group. Throughout the hour we sat, she disappeared into the grasses, making sounds as if she were sick to her stomach.

We had witnessed several children die this way. Drinking dirty water often caused bad stomach sickness and for children marching at our rate, dehydration quickly followed.

We had become so used to death in our platoon that Mwaka had become ruthless. Someone too weak to continue would simply be left to die alone, no matter how young a child or good a soldier.

When it came time to march on, Akena feigned a fever. The heat of the day covered her body in sweat like the rest of us and she shivered with chills.

Mwaka assessed her condition and decided she would be left to recover until the platoon returned after nightfall.

Akena's plan had succeeded and now it was my turn to attempt escape.

The hare's greatest advantage is that it understands other animals' vulnerabilities. For nearly a year, I had followed Mwaka, spending all day and night in his presence. If I knew anything about him at all, it was that he had an insatiable appetite for riches.

'My auntie lives not too far from here,' I told Mwaka, making my way to the front of the marching line.

'So, do you want me to pay her a visit?' Mwaka said with an evil grin, clutching his gun and pretending to shoot.

'No, no, but I do know of a man who lives in her village who once lived in Europe and now has a home filled with jewellery and cash.'

'Go on,' Mwaka said.

I continued to speak about this man of my invention while Mwaka planned our raid.

When we approached the edge of the village, I told Mwaka to wait behind so I could scout the home and bring back information. At first, Mwaka refused, insisting on sending another person with me. Finally, he relented, agreeing that if anyone saw me alone, they would assume I had come to visit my auntie.

I walked down the village's orange dirt road until a cluster of huts hid me from Mwaka's view. Then I ran, faster than ever before, leaping like a hare chased by a lion.

At first I ran with no direction, going as far as my legs would take me until I knew I had achieved a good distance. Then I ran like a free man, giving thanks with each long stride that took me closer to Akena.

When I arrived back at the clearing, I found Akena sitting under a tree. She looked at me with tears streaming down her face and threw her arms tight around my back. I cried too, seeing in Akena the struggles my sisters must have faced and the uncertainties which still lay ahead.

Few child soldiers talk about their time as abductees, but most will tell stories of their escapes. Maybe these will be the heroic folktales of my generation, passed down with cautionary messages of peace to our children and grandchildren.

The truth is: escaping is only the beginning. Many child soldiers have no homes to go to after running away, with their family members dead and little chance of re-entering school.

Akena's return revealed that both of her parents were killed by rebels, and for care her siblings had been scattered among her aunties living in refugee camps.

I fared slightly better. My father died of disease while I was away and one of my sisters was killed in the war. Back at home, I found my other two abducted siblings — Obua and my older sister — had both managed to escape. My family members were all happy to see me when I arrived back, but a short time at home revealed how much had changed. Obua no longer jokes like he once did and often wakes in the middle of the night screaming from bad dreams. My sister had been forced to become a commander's wife and returned home with a small baby. None of us talk about what we did or saw in the bush and prefer to focus on each day that lies ahead.

The hardest part for me is knowing I will never again attend school. The war stole me from my studies and took away my family's income. With my father dead, my brothers and I have to work in the fields to gather food for the family, with no spare time or money for school.

Still, I have hope for a brighter future. I have hope that children around the world will hear our stories and pledge to end the use of child soldiers. I have hope that they will share our message and support our return to school so that we may forgive what we have lost and have a chance at a brighter future. I have hope that someday soon, childhood will be respected in every corner of the earth and children may grow up knowing peace and being peace.

*Author's note*

Between 1988 and 2008 alone, Joseph Kony's Lord's Resistance Army abducted more than 60,000 children. The abducted children were and are forced to serve as soldiers, porters, cooks and 'wives' for the militias, missing out on their childhoods and witnessing or committing atrocious acts that haunt many of the children years later.

According to UNICEF estimates, 300,000 children are currently active in thirty conflicts worldwide. A Council on Foreign Relations publication states that an additional half million children are believed to be active in militaries not currently at war, and that forty per cent of the world's armed groups have children in their ranks.

To find out what you can do to help, visit:
www.helpchildsoldiers.com

# Refuge

*by Jackie French*

The sky was grey. The sea was grey too. It shivered. The
sea filled the world, its fingers slapping at the tiny boat with
its grey timbers and a grey metal framework at one end.

Australia was somewhere behind the darker grey line
where sea met sky. It was hard to believe in Australia, here
in this universe of grey.

Even the faces of the other passengers were grey. Faris
had counted thirty-four, apart from himself and Jadda: men
in trousers and kurtas; women in scarves or burqas; and
two children, younger than him, sitting by their mothers as
though they were used to waiting — as though waiting had
been their entire lives.

Only Jadda was bareheaded, her grey hair held back
with two clips. Jadda had flung off her burqa as the boat
cast off from the ramshackle jetty in Indonesia.

For a while she and Faris had used the fabric as a thin
cushion between them and the splintered deck of the

boat. But as the wind rose, and the foam and spray spat in their faces, the burqa had grown sodden. Now it lay in a small wet clump, next to the one small plastic bag the two men who crewed the boat had allowed them to bring. Everything else Faris owned was wrapped in more plastic bags hidden around his waist — his birth certificate and other papers that Jadda said were the most important things he owned.

There hadn't been much to leave behind. There had already been so many leavings in the past year, since the phone call that ripped the night, ripped his life. The 'friend' saying urgently that the police were coming to their flat, just as they had come for his father five years earlier. The sharp voice on the phone had said that Jadda must take him now, at once, to safety.

He'd had time to thrust two shirts, a pair of trousers, his mobile phone, two books and even his laptop into his school bag. He had clutched the bag to him as they huddled in the back of the truck driving them across the border.

They had sold his laptop in the first week at the refugee camp, for there was no electricity, at least not in the long rows of tents in which they lived.

But he kept the phone, tied around his waist in one of Jadda's old stockings, where the camp toughs wouldn't notice it, turning it on only once a week to save the battery, at the time his father called from Australia, his voice a stranger's now after five years away.

'I'm sorry,' his father had said on that first phone call to the camp. 'I am sorry that I have led you to this.'

Faris said nothing. He wanted to yell: 'What have you done? Why did you do this to us?'

But he couldn't.

'Don't ask,' Jadda had told him, on that night five years back when his father had staggered home, blood on his jacket, his face like someone had smudged his eyes with black polish. His father had shaken his head when Faris tried to hug him, and vanished to talk urgently to Jadda in the kitchen. Faris could hear their muttered voices.

Jadda had come out. 'Go to the pictures,' she said, pressing money into his hand. 'Now!'

Faris had never gone to the pictures at night. He had never gone to the pictures alone. He peered into the kitchen, where his father sat, with that white blank face.

When Faris got back, his father had gone. Blood stained the kitchen table.

Jadda's face was cold marble. 'Pack,' she said. 'We have to go.'

'Where? Why?'

What had happened to his father? His father was an important person now, a doctor at the hospital. Jadda had given him a gold-plated stethoscope to wear around his neck. His office had his framed certificates all around the walls. Trouble came to other families. Not to men like his father!

'The police have taken your father. Don't ask more, Faris. You can't tell what you do not know. Trust me. It is safer if you can say truthfully, "No one told me anything." Now pack. Fast!'

Faris packed. Jadda made phone call after phone call. At last friends arrived to help them move what they could to a small flat over a carpet shop. Faris wondered if it would be harder for the police to find them there: to question them or torture them, to see if a rebel's family knew where other rebels might be.

How could his father be a rebel? Rebels shouted, and drew slogans on the walls. Rebels plotted. They didn't live in houses with fine gardens, with rich carpets on the floor. Their sons didn't go to good schools.

He had not gone back to his good school. Jadda had not gone back to the academy where she had taught English literature and language. Had the schools asked them not to come, the son and mother of a rebel?

He didn't know. He didn't ask.

Jadda sold her jewellery, piece by piece, so they could live. She taught him his lessons at their tiny kitchen table. Friends avoided them, or perhaps they avoided friends.

They lived like that for three years, waiting for the police to drag them off for questioning, or even, like a miracle, for his father to come grinning through the door, in his good jacket, with the bloodstains gone. It had all been a mistake; he wasn't a rebel at all.

Neither happened.

And then the call from his father two years earlier. He had been freed, perhaps to see if he would lead the police to real rebels. But he hadn't come to see his son and mother. He had hidden in a truck, had reached a refugee camp over the border.

Now he was in a place called Australia. He could call them each week. He was trying to save money, was trying to find a way for them to come to Australia too. He would call again.

Jadda cried that night, deep gulping sobs, when she thought Faris was asleep. But instead he sat with his laptop on his bed, looking at Australia.

It was beautiful. A rich country. Bright fish swam on its Barrier Reef. Tourists wandered on golden beaches. Its Opera House gleamed under the blue sky. Faris was glad his father was near an opera house, where he could hear the music that he loved.

After that, his father phoned at the same time each week for a few minutes only, talking mostly to Jadda. Phone calls were expensive. There was little jewellery left.

Every night Faris looked at the tourist sites for Australia. Big breakfasts of pineapple and melon. Infinity pools that rippled towards the sea. Beaches, beaches, beaches, where gold sand met blue sky and turquoise sea or forest.

And then the urgent call, not from his father: the one that sent him and Jadda into hiding. The police were coming for them, to force his father to come back, to give them information. He and Jadda scurried through shadowed streets to a waiting car, hid under blankets in the back, trying not to look at those who helped them.

You could not tell what you didn't know.

The car took them to a warehouse. In the warehouse was a crate. They stepped into the crate. Faris heard the lid go down, heard a truck's engine, felt the bump as the crate was loaded on it.

The drive seemed short. It also seemed to take longer than his whole life so far.

The truck stopped. The back opened. The lid was lifted off the box. They struggled, stiff, through other boxes, filled with things, not people. Faris helped Jadda down.

The road stretched to nothing on either side.

The driver pointed. 'The refugee camp is that way. I do not know you,' he added. 'If you see me, do not nod or smile. Go with God.'

He drove away.

They walked. They found tents, the barbed wire. Food was given out from trucks, each day. They lined up to fill a bottle at the camp's only tap.

People waited.

Jadda didn't wait.

Jadda sold a gold bracelet in the refugee camp to a guard, to get them in the jeep to the small airport. Her mother's ruby earrings bought tickets on a plane to a larger airport, and the flight to Indonesia, and the tiny room there in which they lived, where the air tasted of bad soup. Strange bugs crawled over him while he slept and others buzzed around his head when it was light.

Her mother's ruby ring paid for their passage on the boat. There was no more jewellery now. There was just the boat, the passengers, the sky, the sea.

'Jadda?'

Jadda sat with her arms around her knees, her hair the colour of rain and spray against her head. 'What is it?' She spoke in English. They had spoken English together ever since his father reached Australia, ever since they had begun to dream they might join him there.

He wanted to say 'I'm scared'. Not just of the ocean, but what was ahead of them. There was nowhere to run to, after Australia. Somehow that was more frightening than the dangers of the sea. But a boy of thirteen couldn't say that to his grandmother. It would be cowardly to say he was scared at all.

Somehow she understood. She smiled. The grey figure beside him turned back into the Jadda he had known. 'Look,' she said softly. She pointed to the line where grey sea met the great sky. 'Australia is over there. Shut your eyes, Faris.'

When he was small and scared of night monsters Jadda had told him to shut his eyes, to dream of a gold light about his bed that shone all night and kept the monsters away. It worked.

'What should I dream of, Jadda?'

'Australia. A wonderful Australia. A home,' she said softly.

'It … it doesn't seem possible.'

'You must believe that everything is possible.'

'But some things aren't possible! It's not possible to fly like a bird, or … or to jump across an ocean.' If only he could jump across this grey sea, onto Australia.

'Impossible is a word for people who don't want to try,' said Jadda fiercely. 'If the people who invented aeroplanes thought "impossible" then we'd never have soared to the clouds. If enough people say "impossible" then no one will try to fight evil, to make the world good. How can you reach your dreams if you don't imagine them?'

Faris shut his eyes. The grey world vanished. The sky was blue, the beach was gold, the rocks were red, the fish swam in bright colours through the coral of the reef.

In Australia he would go to a school like the ones he had seen on the internet. He could see it: a big green lawn and a red-brick building with green plants growing on the walls, and laughing children sitting on the grass with their laptops and friends.

He felt himself begin to smile.

'What can you see?' whispered Jadda.

'Our house.' A house for him, and Jadda and his father, a big house just as the family of a doctor should have. A wardrobe filled with new jeans and T-shirts, instead of a spare shirt, a change of underwear and a mobile phone in a plastic bag.

'What is it like?'

'It's two storeys high.' He tried to think what Jadda would like too. 'There are walls with bookcases up to the ceiling. Every book Jane Austen ever wrote.' He heard Jadda laugh softly at that. Jadda loved the English writer Jane Austen, with her far-off world of women dancing in bonnets. 'You have a pet koala.'

'What's its name?'

Faris found himself grinning. How long had it been since he'd grinned? He opened his eyes. 'It's *your* koala. You have to name him.'

'Nosey,' said Jadda. 'Because of his short nose.'

Something was wrong. He felt his grin slide from his face as he looked around. The two crewmen huddled over the engine, their voices sharp as the wind grew in strength. Faris was good at languages, but theirs was one he didn't know.

The sky had grown a darker grey. The ocean was black.

Faris looked at the people next to him, huddled in their own family of misery: a man with his arms around a woman and a girl, three perhaps, another in the woman's arms. He wondered if they spoke English, hoped if they didn't they wouldn't find it hard to learn.

He tried to imagine them in Australian clothes, the sort he had seen on the internet. They would wear jeans, the man a flowered shirt perhaps as he walked along the golden beach, the children playing in the waves.

The rising waves smashed at the sides of the boat. He shut his eyes and tried to see the beach again. He had never seen a golden beach, only a rickety jetty that poked out of grey mud.

Thunder growled, not just above, but all around.

He and Jadda would live near the beach. All Australians lived near the beach, except those who were Aboriginal and had black skins and lived near a huge red rock at Uluru.

Someone shoved him. Faris looked up as one of the crew thrust an old tin can into his hand. The crewman gestured to the water in the boat. The meaning was clear. Faris began to bail the water out, can by can. Around them others were doing the same, with cans and hands, a bucket.

The rain hit so hard it stung. Foam flew through the air, dripping like shaving cream. The boat rose up, then crashed back down. Wet wave tops slashed their faces. A child screamed. Faris heard the words of prayers, a woman's sobs.

Not Jadda's. She moved closer, her arms around him now.

He lifted his voice above the wind. 'Is the boat going to turn back?' Indonesia was closer to them than Australia. He wasn't sure what he was scared of most: the storm or not reaching that land beyond the line of sea and sky.

Jadda shook her head. She spoke close to his ear, so others wouldn't hear. 'The owner of this boat makes too much money from each trip to turn back now.'

'But if ... if the boat sinks he won't have a boat.'

'I don't think the boat is worth much,' said Jadda. She hesitated then added, 'I think the boats are chosen so it doesn't matter if they sink.'

'And the people on it? His crew?'

'I don't think he values them either.'

Faris glanced at the crew as he scooped out water again. One was still bent over the engine, the other bailing. Faris had thought this was a fishing boat, that the owner would be on it. Instead the owner might be a rich man, far away.

Scoop and throw, scoop and throw ...

A wave slapped his face. He snorted to get the water out of his nose.

He looked at the other passengers, the children huddled with their mothers, the men and some of the women bailing. Jadda had paid fourteen thousand dollars so that the two of them could step into this grey boat.

The boat twisted so sharply he had to clutch the seat. On the other side of the boat a father clutched his child. Scoop and throw, scoop and throw ...

How had the other people in this boat found so much money? Were some of them rich, or did they have rich families? Were all of them desperate, like him and Jadda? Were some of them criminals, trying to sneak into Australia?

The boat lunged again. A wave rose high above them. For seven long seconds it seemed that it would crash on top of them. Somehow the boat managed to find its way up and along it, plunging down the other side.

Scoop and throw, scoop and throw. His arms ached. His throat was salt and bitter. A woman sobbed down the other end of the boat.

Faris tried to multiply seven thousand dollars by the number of people on the boat, to try to keep his mind away from the lurch and crash. But all his mind could hold were waves and water.

The boat would sink. The storm would break it into twigs and rust. The passengers would slide down, down, down, into the grey water. Were the depths of the ocean storm-tossed too? Or would the water feel calm as it sucked his life ...

Jadda moved closer. 'Faris?'

He nodded, trying not to show his fear. 'Will the boat break up?'

She looked at him, her gaze clear. Jadda never lied. That was why you couldn't ask her questions when the answers were too hard. 'Perhaps. But if it does ...' He didn't want to hear the words. This boat was all the safety in his world. But her voice was steady in his ear. 'Grab hold of anything that floats. A piece of wood. Anything to keep your head above the water. A rescue ship will come,' she hesitated and added, 'perhaps.'

She took a harsh, deep breath. 'Faris, will you promise me something? Please, will you promise?'

'Promise what?'

She spoke close to his ear, so he could hear. 'Promise that you will try to live. No matter what. Don't think of me. Think of your new life. Think of Australia. Never forget the Australia of your dreams. To get there you have to live! Please, promise.'

'I won't forget. I will think of Australia.' A wave reared up. They froze as somehow the boat shuddered up and past.

Jadda reached into their bag, and brought out the flask of water. She held it to him. 'Drink it. Drink it all.'

He thought: We should save some for later. And then: Perhaps there won't be a later. That is why I need to drink it now. For strength, to keep going, to get to Australia.

He said, 'You drink half. Then me.'

He thought she was going to refuse. But he was too old now to do his grandmother's bidding just because she said so. Instead she took a sip, and then another. He knew that was all she'd take.

He took the flask and drank the rest. If fresh water could make him stronger, he could help Jadda.

He put the flask in his plastic bag. He bailed again.

Scoop and throw, scoop and throw. A man vomited. The storm carried the muck away.

Waves. Wind. Air thick with water for so long that at last even the screams and sobbing stopped.

Faris tried to keep his eyes on the tin can as he scooped the water up and out. Think of Australia, whispered Jadda's voice in his mind. Don't think of the storm, the fragile rusty boat. He tried to think of a quiet bedroom, with clean sheets. But how could any dream help you survive when the world was ripped by storm?

The small grey boat still floated. And slowly the waves began to slacken.

At last Faris looked up. Grey sky again, not black. A sea like a rocky plain. He turned to Jadda, to try to smile at her, to tell her that dreaming of good things worked. He had ridden the storm without screaming. They had survived.

And then he saw the wave.

Had it waited till the storm had eased, the better to show its majesty? It reared like a sea beast from the ocean depths, high as a three-storey building. Foam danced about the top.

Jadda's hand gripped his. She yelled, 'I love you!'

The wave crashed down.

Pain. His body was crushed down, then up, then sideways, and down again. The water tried to tear him apart. Water that was green, not grey, and filled with bubbles. A sensation that was only down, down, down, but no knowledge of where 'up' might be. His arms and legs seemed lost. They didn't work. Nothing worked, except his eyes, no air to breathe, no ears to hear. More pain.

No, he thought. This is not happening. We will reach Australia! Keep thinking of Australia …

The green world of water began to turn black. I will open my eyes and I'll be safe, he thought. I will be in Australia, in my room. Safe in bed, a real bed.

And then darkness.

# Tails

*by Jack Heath*

The coin sparkled in the air, its faces polished by the endless worrying of the girl's fingers, before landing in her palm. She slapped it against the back of her other hand and took a peek. Tails.

'Stop that,' the boy said.

The girl balanced the coin on her thumb.

'They ain't going to give us nothing,' the boy said. 'Not if they see you got enough money to use it as toys.'

The girl watched a pair of stilettos, a leather handbag and a pair of polarised sunglasses move past without pausing. 'They didn't give nothing yesterday,' she said. 'And I wasn't playing then.'

'Well, we must have done *something* wrong.'

The girl flipped the coin again, watching it twirl. It came up tails again.

'Please stop.' The boy was tugging at his matted hair. 'I'm so hungry.'

'You're always hungry,' the girl said, although so was she.

She remembered saying almost the same thing to him, years ago. It was after an afternoon of rocketing down the hill in a billy cart, but before a big dinner of peas and condensed soup. He shouted *Mum! I'm starving!* Their mother had rolled her eyes, packed up her drawings and moved into the kitchen.

You're always starving, the girl had said.

But they didn't use that word any more.

'Can you help us?' the boy was saying. They had found this phrase more effective than *Spare change?* or *Excuse me.*

He held out the empty coffee cup she had fished out of the bin that morning. The cold liquid inside, when they guzzled it, had turned out to be chai tea — a rare treat, but not quite food-like enough to soothe their aching stomachs.

'You should be in school,' the man replied, peering over his glasses at their stained T-shirts. The girl wondered if he had astigmatism, like her. Perhaps he would offer his glasses rather than money.

'You're right,' the boy told him. 'Can you give a little towards our tuition?'

'I already do,' the man said.

It had taken only a few days of begging for the girl to realise that everyone who walked past did something to feel less guilty. Some of them did it with money. She called them *givers.* Others did it by ignoring them. She called them *power walkers.*

The power walkers were so common that the girl had once convinced herself that she was invisible. She had been hungry, even hungrier than she was now, and had started to hallucinate. She now knew why those old homeless women talked to themselves — they thought no one else could hear them.

The girl could already tell that this man wasn't going to give them anything. His shoes shone. His trousers were freshly dry-cleaned. His phone, clutched in one hand, was a new model. He had money, but was the sort to spend it on himself. He was the third type — a *lecturer.*

'My taxes pay for your school,' he said. 'Why aren't you at it?'

Because of the way he said *your school*, the girl knew which school he meant. A fort of battered bricks and barred windows where poor parents sent poor children to be taught by poor teachers, so the children could grow up to be poor parents themselves.

Fewer and fewer passers-by asked them about school. The last few months had aged them several years.

'Thank you,' the boy said. 'We're very grateful. If we had just a little money, we could afford something to eat, and then we could go to school instead of being here.'

'The church will give you something to eat.'

The last thing they had eaten had come from the church, but that was two days ago. Yesterday, by the time they had arrived, there had been no bread left. We should have run faster, the boy had said.

But other hungry children had crowded around the empty plates, which were already picked clean of crumbs. If we had all ran faster, the girl thought, would there have been enough to go around?

'Good idea,' the boy was saying. 'Perhaps you could spare some money for the bus? To take us to church?'

The man snorted. 'You know, I worked to get to where I am. I never asked for anything when I was growing up,' he said.

'Maybe you never had to, you pompous fat-head,' the girl said.

The man reared back as if struck. 'How dare you!'

The boy looked even more horrified. 'Shut up!' he hissed.

'Oh, I'm sorry,' the girl told the man. 'Did I interrupt? You got more excuses not to give us no money?'

'I don't have to —'

'Ain't you got somewhere to be? Like a job? A home? Get lost.'

The man stumbled away, sputtering like an old car.

'Why would you do that?' the boy demanded.

'He wasn't a giver,' the girl said. 'Every second he stood here, he was taking the pressure off someone else.'

'I nearly had him.'

'You didn't.'

'I'm so hungry,' the boy moaned.

'We could have eaten him,' the girl said. 'His head *was* nice and fat.'

They glared at one another for a moment before lurching into sudden laughter. The girl's cracked lips split, and she tasted blood. It had been so long since she smiled that her lips had fossilised into a stern pout.

She flipped the coin again. Tails.

'You know what the chances are of us getting out of here?'

The girl looked around at the concrete, the dust, the overflowing litter bin. 'I don't think anyone will stop us.'

'You know what I mean,' the boy said. 'The chances of us not being poor any more, someday.'

'Oh. One in ten?'

'Nope. It's about seven per cent.'

'Where'd you hear that?'

'I just remembered it,' the boy said.

'Where did you hear it before you remembered it?'

'Does it even matter?'

The girl frowned. 'Tell me.'

'I heard it from an architect.'

'When did you meet — oh.'

The girl stopped talking. Looked away.

'I'm sorry,' the boy said.

She didn't reply.

'I miss her too,' he said.

Still she said nothing. She sniffed and pressed her palms into her eyes.

When she looked back at the boy, he was staring at the cup, the rags, his filthy hands.

'We must have done something wrong,' he said again.

She leaned over, pressing her head against his shoulder. He smelled like sweat and earth, but she no longer cared.

'Seven per cent,' she said. 'That ain't bad. It's just like getting tails four times in a row.'

She balanced the coin on her thumb, flicked, and watched it shine as it spun.

# I make peace

*by Danielle Gram*

I make peace,
Because wars continue far too long;
A decade trapped inside a home,
Hearing walls crumble and sirens moan.

I make peace,
Because genocide rolls through the hills,
Neighbours turning on each other,
Willing to kill their best friend's mother.

I make peace,
Because armies train children to kill;
Taken from home and given a gun,
Ordered to slay a neighbour's son.

I make peace,
Because a bomb is worn as a belt;
Crowds in a market feel the blast,
For victims, paradise comes too fast.

I make peace,
Because for years we've abused our earth,
Like pirates pillaging our land,
Turning fertile dirt to useless sand.

I make peace,
Because there are gangs in the cities,
Boys and girls looking to belong,
Avenging hurt with another wrong.

I make peace,
Because I've know the pain of violence,
Wept at the grave of my brother,
The senseless death of yet another.

I make peace,
Because in a world that is suffering,
It takes hard work to keep the hope,
Restore beauty and help children cope.

# On the Somme

*Libby Hathorn*

After an offensive by the Allies against the German Front
Line on the Somme in July 1916, Private Maurice Roache
has lost his way ...

Maurice became aware of his body spread-eagled on the
uneven, cindery ground. His mud-caked boots were the first
things he saw when his eyes opened, then, beyond them,
the rise and fall of an unfamiliar landscape. Something
told him not to stand. Just wait a moment and it would all
come back.

It was as if time had gone missing; as if he were
awakening from something deep and dark and of
unbearable significance but which he could not yet quite
remember.

He raised his head to see more of the blackened
landscape, turning it to take in other directions. So put
upon, this chewed-up, spewed-out place. A rush of pain at

his temple and a rush of understanding. A terror that made him want to run wildly, screaming. This was *war*, wasn't it, still the bloody war. He wasn't waking from a drunken trawl through darkened paddocks to his Casino farm home after a late one at the pub.

He groaned but still didn't attempt to sit. He had to think, to work out where he was. He breathed deeply and felt a twinge of pain in his lungs. A noxious odour, familiar and rancid, filled his nostrils. Not the smell of the eucalypts of home and the reassuring familiarity of cow dung but the stench of war. He looked up at the ominous sky above him with its great fists of cloud. The enemy might be anywhere in their dark threat.

He watched a lone bird arc across the sky. Not a crow, or a kookaburra, or a brilliant lorikeet, the reassuring sights of home. Was it a kestrel, heading back to its supposedly safe nest? But the only nests around here were machine gun nests, weren't they? And, with a jolt, he realised he should be in one. He was a gunner. A machine gunner.

He felt relief that he was regaining some memory, yet that was all that came. The rest of his mind remained blank, hopelessness hanging over him like the ominous clouds above.

Where am I? Where the bloody hell am I?

He remembered how many times he'd seen the hero of a cowboy film — black and white, shown in the community hall in Casino — coming to after a resounding blow to the head and asking the air, 'Where am I?' The country lads watching had thought it a ridiculous line and always laughed uproariously. How he'd laughed too. But not now. Not bloody now. What in the hell had happened? And which was the way back to where he was supposed to be?

He'd gone up and over, out of the trenches as commanded — must have! And then what? He tried but couldn't recall hearing the dreaded whistle that always signalled the commencement of an advance and the very English, 'Come on, lads!' Or who'd been beside him as they ran towards the wire, bayonets thrust forward. He realised he didn't even know where the enemy was in this godforsaken place; in front of him or behind him?

His head was pounding. Had he been hit? First things first: if he couldn't remember anything, he could at least see if he was wounded. He ran his hands over his face and his head. No thick wetness of blood, and no taste of it in his mouth either, though his throat felt charred and sore. But the pain in his head was incessant. Was he wounded somewhere else?

He rolled over and raised himself onto all fours, moving easily on the gritty earth. He was sound, whole in body, except for the pounding in his head. He needed to get out of here and rejoin his company. Only thing was, he had no idea which direction to go in or who the hell they were!

A rumble of thunder overhead made him pause. He sat back a minute to think. He didn't want to end up crawling towards the enemy lines. The thunder sounded again and he thought it would be good if it rained. He was very thirsty.

Just go quietly, Private Roche, he told himself, then smiled. Well, at least he remembered his name and rank. Go quietly, Private Roche, and it'll all come back.

And then up ahead, in a small depression, he saw the body of a soldier, face down. He could tell from his kit that he was one of theirs. A sob rose in his throat and he knew he didn't want to recall what had happened out here today. At the same time, he knew he must. If he didn't, he might become one of those husks of men, pitiful and finished, who sobbed and yabbered aloud, inconsolable. He'd seen such men borne away somewhere, who knew where? Was there anywhere left on this earth that wasn't pulverised, blackened and bare?

He looked around. So what in the name of God had happened here? And why was it so quiet now? The silence was eerie.

He could see a hillock ahead. Behind it, he thought he'd find the trenches. And then it came to him. He was on the Western Front, God yes, at the Somme, in the first line of attack. The flood of relief at remembering was short-lived. What in the hell am I doing out here alone? He had to quell the cry of alarm, the panic at not knowing. Had he lost his mind?

He looked around wildly, and saw in the far distance a church spire, just a pencil of a thing, and a stand of birch trees. Both were familiar, though God knows why. Still, they reassured him that he would be heading in the right direction, back to where he'd come from.

He crawled towards the dead soldier to check his pulse, hoping there'd be the smallest sign of life. The bloke was whole, at least, or that's how it looked. He grasped the man's shoulder and turned him over. He didn't recognise the dirty face. When he held his own grimy paw to the smooth neck, he felt the clammy coldness of death.

Further back, all around, he saw other bodies, many contorted grotesquely in death. Was he the last man alive in this hellhole? How long had he been out here in no-man's-land, for he knew now that's where he was. But why the absence of gunshots, whistling shells and whining explosives? And where were the stretcher-bearers to pick up the wounded, the dead and dying?

He'd seen corpses before, plenty of them. That was what this place was all about. They had to drive the mules right over the top of them sometimes, Fritz and Allies alike, as they dragged the gun carriage to a new position. The noise, the disgusting crunch of bones under the wheels, would haunt him forever.

He should move on. But then the pain in his temple came again, and with it a thread of something. He was holding someone in his arms, a bloke, his eyes were rolled back and he was bleeding badly. His body was limp but he was still breathing. It was someone Maurice knew well because he was screaming for help in the way you do for a mate, when you just let go and scream over the cacophony at the insanity and uselessness and despair of it all. He realised that was why his throat was sore now. Had the bloke died there, in his arms, with Maurice bellowing for mercy or help or whatever he'd been hoping for? Had they all died out here except for him? It seemed as if days had been swept away. How many?

He sank down onto the cindery earth. All he had was that thread of memory and not a bloody thing before. C'mon, he told himself. Remember the date you joined up. C'mon, Private Roche, you can do it.

A picture came: his father gravely and reluctantly dipping his pen into the ink bottle and labouring over the paper Maurice was waiting eagerly to take to Lismore Town Hall. *I, Michael Maurice Roche, do hereby give permission for my son …* Yes, it was well into 1915; at last he'd turned eighteen and had got the old man to sign his papers. He could remember the day crystal clear. The fight that had raged between his parents; his mother imploring, 'Will's already gone, Michael. Isn't one son enough?' Then turning to Maurice himself with a look of fury: 'You're only eighteen! If it were up to me and not your father here, you'd wait another year at least. Don't you realise how we need you on the farm?'

The awkward silence that followed, interrupted by the buzz of a blowfly blundering against the window behind his father's dark head. Then the further awkwardness of his father's uncharacteristic opposition to his wife: 'Leave the boy, Margaret. I've agreed and there's no going back now.'

The swish of her dress and the indignant crackle of her starched apron — it was a baking day — as she swept from the room. He could remember that, so why the bloody hell couldn't he remember the here and now? A gaping hole loomed before him: lost time, lost dates, events and action. Okay then, what next?

He pulled himself to his feet and started walking towards the stand of birches, the church spire. But his head was throbbing and flashes of memory came: strafing fire, tanks toppling forward, machine guns stuttering, firebombs and guns and battle gear and men crowded into the trenches, jostling for position, waiting for the order to climb up and over to meet their fate, ready or not. He was shivering now, his teeth chattering. Up ahead he saw a crater and thought he'd rest there, take stock, wait till he was more certain of which way to go.

He lay face down in the dirt, his arms cradling his aching head, and closed his eyes. Saw Brisbane, the HMAT *Karoola*, his mother refusing to cry when she said goodbye, his father's anxious face and firm handshake, then his tears as he hugged his second son to him. On board, they were all of them cocky with the hope of easy victory. 'Home by Christmas,' some of them chanted as they left port.

Brisbane had seemed a big city to him until he found himself in Alexandria in Egypt. The place was a living history book, of course. The wonder of the pyramids, real and vast, built of great rough slabs of stone that were unimaginably heavy. The training was heavy too, but the heat didn't worry him like it did some of the southern boys. And it was exhilarating, because it meant they'd soon see action and they all wanted that. During their time off, they wandered the bazaars at all hours in a city that never seemed to sleep. The nightlife, the strange music, the long water pipes, the coffee and the coffee houses — it was all an eye-opener; so much to tell the folks back home.

The training ended and at long last he got his first taste of war: 9th Battalion at Gallipoli, where boys became men. But Gallipoli was over. What was his battalion now?

His inability to remember sent him into another panic, and to calm himself he went back to what he could recall. Gallipoli, the horror of the first month, the gradual acceptance of death on such a scale; it was hardly credible except that he was there, watching it. They'd dug in on the beach front, which pretty much made them sitting ducks. A hard, beating madness had grown up inside him; it was the only way to take it, day after day, as mate after mate went down. And in between, the boredom and the mounting fear as they waited for further orders.

He'd been wounded by shrapnel there; had been taken to Heliopolis with the other wounded, remembered the painful voyage on the ship ... the *Ascanius*. It was August 1915, and he stayed there two months until his ankle was working again and he was sent back to Anzac Cove and the 9th. So many new faces. The slow months grinding by ...

That ship where they disembarked again at Alexandria ... his head was pounding but he'd get the name for sure. *Grampion*, that was it. 'Champions on the *Grampion*,' they'd joked. And then Serapum and Habieta and Tel-el-Kebir until March 1916, after which he'd ended up at the school of instruction at Zeitoun — 'taken on strength into 13th Machine Gunners'.

Ah, that was it — he was in the 13th Machine Gunners. Relief swept over him. So he hadn't lost his mind despite the fire raging in his head and the raggedness of the immediate past.

They'd left Alexandria aboard the *Arcadian*, June it was, and had disembarked at Marseilles on the twelfth. Clear as clear that was: off to the Western Front, Private Roche, 13th Machine Gunners.

Details of troop movements, of battles, of training and supply lines, rotations to the front line, flooded back, but the events of today refused to come. The emptiness terrified him. But at least he knew for sure that he was at the Western Front, the Somme. He had to get back to the trenches and then it'd all come back.

Rain began to fall as he clambered to his feet. A war-weary tree leaned over him, as if in apology for what it had seen. And then another tree filled his mind: the orange tree that stood outside the dining room window at home, amid the green rolling countryside of Casino, its branches heavy with bright globules that scented the air. He'd sketched that tree over and over, and a girl sitting under it. For long minutes, the rain falling around him, he drenched himself in her memory. Rosie. Shy, trembling, beautiful Rosie. Remembered her face, their first kiss.

He knew she was safe and sound at home in Kyogle. He knew it. But he made a strangled sound in his throat as he pictured her body in his arms today, saw himself holding her instead of the dying soldier, screaming and screaming for help that had not come. Ridiculous as it was, the horror of the image left him quivering, robbed him of a slab of his mind.

'Rosie … ' He whispered her name to the tree, invoking her memory as he had so many times before. He wanted to yell it at the church spire against the grey sky, yell it over the trenches, which were probably just a hundred yards away. It was dangerous to call out in this strange quiet, but Maurice knew the risk was worth it, because Rosie's name brought him a courage of sorts, roused in him the hope that he'd make it.

'ROSIE,' he shouted at the dark sky, towards the eroded hillocks and the bent, lifeless trees. 'ROSIE!'

And then he was running — back to the war, his war, and the hellish shelter of the trenches; back to his comrades, what was left of them, and their unerring humour that helped carry them, and him, through the worst of it. He was running because the thought of Rosie made him want to live. It didn't matter that he couldn't remember what he'd done out here today, or who he'd held in his arms, or who he'd left to die. Maurice Roche was running for his life because he knew there was no place for him in no-man's-land.

*Author's note*

This is a piece from a novel in progress called *Eventual Poppy Day*. It tells the story of an Australian farm boy from Casino, New South Wales, Australia, who joins up in 1915, eager to see action in World War I. He experiences one horror after another, from the battle at Gallipoli to the Western Front, specifically the Battle of the Somme, which took place along the Somme River in northern France. It was one of the longest battles of the war with over one million deaths.

Though this is a work of fiction much of it is based on the war records of my mother's brother, Private Maurice John Roache, who was an Anzac who served first in Gallipoli and then at the Somme for two years. Maurice died in action on Messines Ridge near Ypres, a town I recently visited. I am only the third Australian, as far as I know, who has visited Ploegsteert Wood where he died and the small but beautifully kept cemetery nearby where he now lies.

This extract is based on notes I made in Ypres, on the Belgian–French border, in September 2012.

# I am alone

*by James Phelan*

The last fire went out today. It was early morning and I was
looking at the city through binoculars. Central Park was
shrouded with mist or fog. The tops of tall buildings sparkled
with the first rays of sunlight that caught on shiny surfaces
down below. The streets were still clear of movement. Slushy
snow remained in situ until the sun would come or the heat
of humanity might return. I was sixty-five storeys up in 30
Rockefeller Plaza. The whole building is mine but things like
ownership are now vague notions. I sat and I watched the
morning arrive and I wondered if I'd ever see fire like that
again. Smoke remained, rising from the crumbled ruins of
a thirty-storey apartment block that had come down in the
first week. This place needed saving, and after three weeks
of being alone, I knew I couldn't do it all by myself.

'Don't go there alone,' I said.

There was a person alone down there in the street and
I'm not sure if they were infected or not, but they were alone

and walking and it seemed like they had no idea about the chase that was about to go down.

It was a woman, I think. She was chased and they disappeared out of sight and whether she was infected or not, it was too late for her either way.

That was this morning.

Now, I'm sitting in the driver's seat of a New York City police car.

I've got the engine switched off. I'm hiding. There are at least six people after me. Chasing me. If you could call 'chasers' people — but why not, they were, once, and there's every possibility that they will be again. The windows are fogged over and not for the first time I'm wondering if that's a dead giveaway, like surely the empty cars don't look like this. I try to breathe less.

There's a loud bang on the car next to mine, like a cricket ball's hit the metal sheeting. There's a scream, close by, then gunfire.

The long, staccato, machine-gun fire of an assault rifle.

I watch the passenger windows to my right then something bumps against my car, slides down to the ground, wiping part of the frost and snow cover from the glass and replacing it with two even streaks of blood. They're almost perfectly mirrored forms, like a Rorschach ink blot. I see a beautiful face there in that pattern, talking to me.

There's silence. Four minutes later there's a single gunshot, a block away at least, this time the hollow sound of a pistol instead of the sharper crack-crack of an assault rifle. Twelve minutes later I wonder when I figured out the different sounds of firearms. Not the type of information that a sixteen-year-old from Melbourne is especially savvy with. I will wait until it's been dead quiet for an hour before I make my move.

I sink lower in the seat, my hand on the key in the ignition. The car's in gear and the handbrake is off, so all I have to do is turn the key and floor the accelerator and I'll be out of here. Not that driving away in the snow will particularly help against someone firing an assault rifle at me. Pity cop cars aren't bullet proof, but things like that don't worry me; if I could change anything — and believe me there's a long list — something like the defensive capabilities of a place or vehicle are right at the bottom.

I hear voices outside the car. I'm still, hardly breathing. I listen to my heart, its rapid beat familiar to me now, and I can't convince it to settle. I close my eyes and when I open them snow is falling hard. More time passes before I rub my index finger on my side window to make a little circle of clear glass to see through. I can't see anyone. I can't hear anyone. I give it five minutes before I get out of the car and run north up Fifth Avenue.

I turn right onto East 54th Street and go into a grocery store — dark, lit only by my torchlight. There are a dozen or so cell phones on the counter and floor, their boxes and packaging ripped open and scattered around, like someone has been here searching for some measure of salvation. All the batteries are dead.

I begin to fill two large canvas bags with a mix of canned goods. There's a noise from the back of the shop and I stay still, my torch beam steady on the ground at my feet. I hear a shuffling noise, coming towards me. I want to run.

It's a dog. His big eyes shine back at me and his face looks friendly. I reach out to him but he growls, shows his teeth. He's lean but not skeletal — he's been scavenging something. I look through the aisle of tinned food, take a couple of cans of frankfurts, pop them near him and tip them on the floor. He edges closer, sniffing the air, his eyes never leaving mine as I back away and get out of the store.

The fire may be out but I carry something just as significant: radio handsets. Not just any — these operate on some special band that, unlike all other radio frequencies, does not have that woodpecker sound. For three weeks I've heard nothing but static and interference and silence on every radio and telephone that I've tried, and now these are … they're a salvation of sorts. I found the two of them in the NBC security offices in 30 Rock. I wish I had three but it's a start and I know better than anyone that wishes don't come true in a hurry. I imagine what it would be like to hear another person's voice over that radio.

It's time to go.

I stand at the door of the bookstore at the corner of Park Avenue and East 57th Street. I've stashed the canvas bags of food behind a car around the corner. I bang again on the glass door, sit on the curb, take off my backpack and watch the street. The sun is shining now. There's a sound behind me: Caleb. He unlocks the door, all smiles, and gives me a big bear hug as I pass through into his home.

'Hot chocolate?' he asks.

'Sure, thanks,' I reply, following him up the stairs.

Caleb is a great guy, an older brother I never had. I met him three days ago after he practically crashed an ambulance into my cop car. We were both going slow and out of control in heavy snow and he pushed my car off the road. Our bumpers were hooked together and in the half hour it took to free them and get back on the road, we knew we'd be friends.

He lights up a little gas burner stove and puts long-life milk into a saucepan. There's stacks of food and drinks that line a wall. Games of every kind cover a conference table. He's got a petrol generator set up in a storeroom, bigger capacity than the one I've got back at 30 Rock, and he runs it all day long, charging things like laptop computers and iPods and running a fridge. There are a few television screens set up for different consoles, and he has a massive LCD screen hooked up to a PS3 on pause. That first day I was here we had races on book trolleys, then he showed me some tricks on his skateboard, but he soon crashed and skinned his elbows and wouldn't let me help him with the bandages. I hadn't seen him for a couple of days. Today as I came in downstairs I noticed the skateboard was broken in half. The milk in the pan steams and he heaps in a couple of spoons of chocolate powder. We take our drinks into his lounge area.

'Think the power will ever come back on?'

'Maybe,' he replies, talking though the steam of his drink. 'Depends if it's just that the lines are cut, or if the power plants have been attacked too.'

'I saw street lights on in New Jersey.'

'When?'

'Last week. Stayed on for two nights, several blocks, all lit up. Gone now.'

He nods at this new info, fleeting optimism.

He's made a stack of comic books and graphic novels for me to read since I was here last. Big collection, arranged in the order that I should read them, he says. Says it's a crime I've only ever read a couple of Spiderman and X-Men comics back home. We talk about how neither of us really understands why no one has yet been a superhero. Maybe we've had leaders like Gandhi or Mandela or whoever who've made a massive difference, but that's not what we talk about.

'I'm talking about an average guy or girl, driven to get organised and skilled up enough to put on a costume and get out there and make a difference,' he says. 'Kinda like Batman or most of the Watchmen, some ordinary guy or girl who decides to tool up and kick some criminal butt. A guy like me.'

I laugh and take my jacket off as he sets up a little gas heater.

'Dude, that's awesome,' he says.

'Thanks.' I'm wearing a Spiderman outfit that I tried to dye black but it's streaky, several shades of grey in places, and there are even a few tiger-stripes of red where the dye hasn't taken at all. It's a wreck of a job, but at least the food stains are covered. I've worn it on and off for over three weeks — I like it, it's easy and comfortable to wear, mostly.

We play a couple of sports games on the 70-inch screen, then shut the generator down and eat some hot bread he's made with a bread-maker, thick slices topped with some canned bolognaise sauce. I wash it down with juice and he has two beers. He talks about his family and his job and his tiny apartment down in the East Village and how at least he doesn't have to worry about paying rent and bills any more.

'I just don't know who to blame.'

'Like who did this?'

'You're a little bit different, aren't you?'

'Little bit,' I reply, realising I'd zoned out before.

'It was a country though, no doubt,' he said. 'Russia maybe, China, North Korea.'

'France.'

'Yeah, bloody French. Maybe even the Brits, who knows?'

'What could cause a sickness like that?'

'I've been through every book here I could find on chemical and biological warfare. There are a few things that make people thirsty, like what we see here, but that doesn't explain how they're … you know, how they don't talk or anything.'

'Regressed.'

'Yeah. In the first week, I spoke to a few people I saw around, including an army guy. He said it was an attack by either China, Russia or North Korea. I haven't seen him since.'

'Well, that narrows it down.'

'Yeah, I got the sense he was just rounding up the usual suspects. But what he was saying was, this was a coordinated, large-scale attack on this city, and probably a nation-wide thing.'

'What about the sickness that makes them chasers?'

'That's funny how you call them that,' he says. 'You know only a few, like maybe one or two per cent of the total affected population, actually chase. Rest are smart enough just to stand around and drink water or eat snow.'

'Yeah, the name "chaser" just kind of stuck after … when I saw them on the first day,' I say. 'Have you thought … like, maybe it was better for those who died during the attack?'

He looks off to the doors and after a while he nods.

'Wanna go crash cars, see if the airbags go off?'

'Maybe next time,' I reply.

'Golf?'

'Nah.' I smile, thinking of when we spent all afternoon playing golf, having putting competitions through the self-help and crime isles, and driving off the roof, aiming for a large window in the building opposite. 'I wish I could find a cricket bat.'

'That game seems pretty gay to me.'

'And baseball's what?'

'A real man's sport.'

'Right.'

'More PlayStation?'

'Nah,' I say. 'I might have a sleep for a bit, if that's cool?'

'Sure.' He looks at me, concerned. 'You right?'

'Yeah. Couldn't sleep last night.'

'Wake you for dinner.'

He leaves me. I take a heavy feather duvet and pillow, take off my boots and lie on one of the couches. It's so warm and comfortable that I sleep then and there.

I dream of an apartment at 30 Rock. In my dream I see it as clearly as when I'm awake, but I know it's different. There's a room in there that was locked once, locked from the inside. I'd smashed it down, with the old typewriter from the study. In my dream I stand there at the door, which is all busted up around the handle, and I push it open with my foot, and the room is not how I remember it in reality. In my dream it's a basement, a brick wall with a bare concrete floor. I take a step inside and it feels like it's carpeted.

There's a wooden chair with a telephone on it. It's one of those phones that were around before I was born, with a circular thing to choose the numbers rather than the buttons of today. It has a long lead that runs into the shadows, a place so dark there's no telling where it goes. I've seen darkness like that before, in a subway tunnel, the cavernous holes of what remains of Rockefeller Plaza, road tunnels that lead off Manhattan —

The phone rings.

It's the first phone I've heard ring in over three weeks. It's louder than I remembered a phone's ringing could be. I don't want it to end. I listen to it like it's music, think of the possibilities of the conversation that could ensue if I pick up the handset. I'm too scared to do anything about it. I forget it's a dream and I stand there until I'm making the ringing sound in my head. It's implanted in there now like, no matter what happens, I can make the noise in my mind and hear it, no matter where I go or what's going on around me. I take three steps and pick it up.

I listen.

Silence.

No one's there, and the ringing has stopped.

Was it for me? I will never know.

I wake up.

I'm in 30 Rock. Looking out at night sky. I want to pack the stars away. Most of them are dead, long gone, their light travelling though the cosmos for thousands and millions of years after their demise. I'm surrounded by death, and I know that there's so much that I will never know. I leave the observation deck. I head downstairs. I want to sleep and wake up in a different place and time, where the ground isn't frozen and the people are warm.

'Jesse?'

I wake up, for real this time. Caleb is there, looking down at me.

'You were talking in your sleep,' he says. He hands me a steaming cup of hot chocolate. Our fingers touch and it's a moment of electricity. I'd forgotten what it's like to touch another person.

'Sorry. Thanks.'

He sits on the edge of the couch. I'm in his place. In my dream I had woken up but really I hadn't. I'm sweaty.

'Hell,' he says, 'you're lucky. The only people we dream about now are dead, right?'

I don't answer him and he sits there in silence next to me as a storm cracks outside and snow falls.

'I'm going to watch the street,' he says, getting up and putting on a big snow-suit. He picks up a set of night-vision goggles and a high-powered rifle. He puts a little short-range walkie-talkie next to my couch. 'You sleep. I'll call you on that if there's trouble.'

He leaves the room and I roll on my side and put the empty cup down beside the walkie-talkie. I wish I could call my family on it. I watch it and feel my eyes closing, heavy. Sleep comes easy here, easier than back at 30 Rock, and not the least, I suppose, because of the …

Over three weeks have passed since I took a subway ride from the UN Secretariat Building towards lower Manhattan. There was a bang and it was hot and then black, and an hour or so later I came to. By dim torchlight I found my way to street level.

The power was already out and the phone dead. I wish I'd had a phone call, even just one. A ringing in the night or a dial tone as I placed the call. On the other end of the line would be home, back in Australia, and they'd tell me how everything was okay there and that help was on its way and that they missed me. The phone would ring, I'd pick it up and it would crackle to life.

I can hear my father's voice, and I know I'm asleep because that's something that I can't do otherwise. I think I hear gunfire in the distance, but maybe it's close by and I'm so deeply asleep that I can't move, despite my desire.

I don't think you can ever really choose the sound of the voice in your head. Not with any clarity, nothing beyond a static of background chatter. You can pretend to hear it clearly. You can mimic someone, you can dream, but it's never like the real thing. I can hear his voice now, full of urgency and warning. Maybe this is it; my last, long sleep. I'd closed my eyes and listened to the wind and wished for the day when my call would come, and now I sense it's come and there's nothing I can do about it.

Before sunrise I am dressed and packed and I put the long-range radio handset on Caleb's bedside table and scribble a note: 'This is for you. A real radio. See you soon.'

He looks like a child as he sleeps.

I put my jacket on and I quietly slip through his barricade.

Outside, it's still dark.

I travel at or before sunrise because the streets are quiet. I've not seen chasers active until mid-morning. Maybe they like it when the sun is hitting the streets. Maybe they move around late at night and need to sleep in. Maybe they really are just like me. I walk north along Park Avenue, dragging the canvas bags behind me.

This morning I am to meet my other friend, Rachel. She lives in Central Park Zoo. The way is clear. I walk north, my booted feet quiet in the silence of the post-apocalyptic streetscape.

I go around and over rubble when I have to. I recognise things I've seen pre and post the events of that first day. Little has changed, although some more buildings have come down and there are no fires any more and the ash has stopped falling.

There are more sounds. I hear two cars, or maybe it's the same vehicle that I hear twice within the hour. I hear a gunshot, far off in the still, clear morning. More an act of culling than an exchange of hostilities.

I go out wide to avoid the southern end of Central Park and I approach from the east, from 64th Street and across Madison Avenue into the zoo.

The entrance is through trees, with bare branches holding up the sky, and everything here hides under shadows.

I've been here twice this week and I know how to find her.

I knock on the glass doors, wait for five minutes, knock again. Rachel emerges, wide-eyed at first, looking around me, then she comes and lets me through the heavy doors and locks them behind me. She is slim under her khaki zoo-keeper's uniform and her face is pale, her eyes always wet and searching. I present her with the two big canvas bags that I half-dragged here. I told her I'd look for a clear road so I could drive here next time and bring a bigger load of food and she nods. She doesn't take the bags from me, just points to a spot to put them down, as if this is like selling herself and if she did then she'd never get up on her own again.

Inside, everything is covered with dust and ash. I follow her down dark hallways, beyond rooms with dappled light and quiet groans.

It's warm in here. There's occasional movement in the near-darkness and the hum of a petrol generator lighting some greasy old lamps. We stop by a sheet of glass. She crouches down and I do too, and she shines a small torch into the gloom that's eating up the light. There's a big hairy mass and I can't imagine what it is, but then a face looks at me, big and expectant and familiar in some way.

A brown bear, and a little cub nestled into its side. Here is life and it's new and innocent in every way.

We stand in silence and the mother bear watches us, then goes back to her cub, and I don't know what to say to Rachel. But her eyes seem to soften and after a while her face falls and I follow her out into the cafeteria.

'Hungry?'

I shake my head. She shrugs, eats tinned fruit, which could be what I gave her two days ago. I don't think she will leave her animals, even to go and get food for them or herself, although she won't say as much and she certainly won't ask me for help. I wish it was otherwise, but then why would she need to ask anyway — I'd give whatever I could, whenever I could.

I watch Rachel eat her fruit and then she gets a drink from a vending machine that looks like it was smashed open by a truck, and she stands there, drinking, maybe waiting for me to say something. But she never really looks at me, and after a minute she leaves, going back to her work. She does so much and what am I doing? I don't even know who I am any more.

Four hours later I finish collecting water from the neighbouring pond, hauling drums through the southwest gate as I've seen Rachel do once. I've stacked them up four high and three deep and twelve across. They're not drums, they're empty water-cooler bottles. I assume she uses them to move water around for the animals to drink. Now I can hardly lift my arms and I turn back to the zoo's entry building and she's there, some hay in her hair and her face flushed — she hasn't stopped working either. For the first time she looks me in the eyes for more than a couple of seconds and, as I go to walk past her, I think she whispers: 'Thanks.'

I have a can of cola from the vending machine and she comes into the cafeteria and I felt guilty but she smiles, and maybe I should have taken something from her at the start.

I show her the radio handset.

'What's this?'

'Radio. Works.' I hand it to her, the charger too.

'You have one?'

I shake my head. 'My other friend, Caleb, who I told you about?'

She looks at me weird, different. She tries to hand it back but I don't take it. I know I'll be okay. I know I can avoid the chase, hide out. I've nothing other than myself to protect. She puts the charger on her desk and clips the radio on her belt.

'You can call him.'

She says she will but her eyes say otherwise. She has a PhD and I have two years of high school still to do. I can't bring myself to tell her that it'll be okay, that things can only get better. I am capable of the darkest things.

'I had an idea,' she says, not looking at me. 'I thought maybe, you could, like, you could stay here with me.'

I look out the doors to the empty street. The day is getting dark. I imagine seeing my friends standing across the street, waiting for me to join them for the walk back to 30 Rock. They'd make everything easier and harder at the same time.

'I'll come back tomorrow,' I say, attempting to meet her eyes. 'With petrol for your generators.'

Her eyes meet mine, just for a moment. She then looks across the street, to exactly where I imagined my friends had been.

I put on my pack and leave, following the departing sun, hoping that I have not left it too late. About ten blocks south I hear a scream and I know I've been seen.

Chasers are after me.

I run around the first corner, disappear into a restaurant.

Wait in the darkness, pressed up against a wall. They pass the window, a dozen of them, in a half-run. They're out there and they might come back. I head down into the basement, barricading the door shut behind me. A smell like rotten food. I shine my little wind-up torch around in the darkness, walking past the walk-in refrigerators and shelves stacked with Italian foodstuffs. There's a camp-stretcher set up as a bed, like maybe someone had been here for the first little while, but they're long gone, dust or ash coating the pillow.

I take a blanket, shake it clear, cough from the dust. I roll it and tuck it under my arm.

I will wait here until sunrise. I look around. There's a metal staircase that leads up to metal doors that must open onto a side street. The smell gets worse in a far corner, like the worst kind of garbage. I stand at the doors to a room-size fridge and there's slimy red-brown sludge oozing from under the door. In one corner of the brick room is a small office. It's bare, just a timber chair like the ones in the restaurant upstairs. I walk towards it, shining my light, which is getting dim, and I wind the handle to make it shine bright again. Everything is illuminated. On the chair there's a telephone. The line travels off into the darkness.

I close my eyes. I see the radio. I see that telephone on the seat in that concrete room. I have dreamed of this place. I open my eyes and the phone's still there. I set the torch on the ground and close the office door. I break out some biscuits from my pack, sit on the blanket, stare at the phone. There are so many calls I want to make, so many calls I want to take.

Part of me is always afraid that I'll wake up and not remember how to get to my friends, Caleb and Rachel. Worse still, that they've moved on, or that they've forgotten about me. Or that I've forgotten about them, and I sit there in 30 Rock and watch the streets from up high and never come down to street level again. How could I forget them? They're the only people I know.

I think of that woman I saw running in the streets.
Alone.

I am alone.

Don't go there alone.

In my thoughts I hear a reply:

'Why?'

War
*by Alison Lester*

Peace
*by Alison Lester*

# Mahtab's story

*by Libby Gleeson*

A bell woke them. A shrill, raucous sound, drilling its way into their heads.

'What do we do?' Farhad stood in the middle of the room, his clothes rumpled, his hair sticking up like grass after a windstorm.

'We get dressed neatly and then we go to wash and we find out what we are to do.' Their mother's voice was firm but there were dark bags under her eyes.

They came out of their room and saw those who had arrived on the coaches with them walking towards a separate green building. They fell in behind Hamida, carrying her baby, Ahmad grabbing at her legs.

Beyond the fences they could see more buildings and people.

'Why are we here and they there?' said Mahtab.

'I don't know.' Her mother led them to the queue, waiting to enter the green building. They were served a plate of chicken and rice and sat down at a long table. Mum and Hamida talked in soft voices. Mahtab stirred her food and looked around to see if there were any other girls her age. How long since she had thought of Leila. Where was she now? Was she in prison too?

Table after table was filled by men with occasionally one or two women and their children. Some men were like her dad with dark hair and beard. Some men were black. One or two had their young children with them but most were alone.

After breakfast, they went back to the room to wash, and their mother told them that she had some news of what would happen.

'We will be interviewed,' she said. 'Hamida spoke with a nurse who came to check the baby. She says they will ask us about why we came here to Australia and why we have no papers. I will ask them to help us to find your father. I will tell them of the things that were happening to our family, what happened to your grandfather, and then I know they will tell us that we can stay.'

'Here? In this prison?'

'No. No, this is just while they check us to find out who we are exactly and to make sure that we are not some dangerous person who wishes to bring harm to this country. Then we move next door, to the bigger camp, where we saw those people this morning and then, when they find your father, we can join him.'

Then what happens? Where will we go?'

'I'm not sure. Your father told me about big cities where he would be able to work and you children would go to school and you would grow up free.'

Free? Free was how she felt when the boat came into the harbour and she touched land again. Would that feeling ever return? Mahtab dropped her veil and began to brush her hair. It was long now, way past her shoulders, and it was hard to pull the brush through the thickness of it. The scratches and sunburn on her fingers ached. Mahtab looked out through the doorway, across the bare brown earth, through the wire fence and then over more flat, brown land. She closed her eyes and tried to remember what they had seen in the city, Darwin, such a short time ago. Green gardens and green beside the road, trees along the edge of the streets and buildings that looked so new, so shiny, some as tall as any in Herat. The shops, the cars, the naked arms. Would they live in a place like that? Would they too have a garden again, fruit trees, a swing, a paddling pool for Soraya, a room of her own?

On that first day Mahtab's mother washed and washed her hands and face. The dust of the road and the salt from the sea had worked their way into every scratch and tear in her skin. Her burqa was sun-bleached but clean, her feet brown from sun and dust. She didn't know when she would be called.

Mahtab sat with Soraya, on the step closest to their door.

Men squatted in groups, talking quietly. Guards lounged on white plastic chairs, soaking up the sun. A young woman, her head covered in a short black veil, walked the length of the perimeter fence and when she reached one end she turned and walked back again. Sometimes she stopped and held her arms high and wide, making a strange shape against the sunlight. She carried a stick that clicked softly as she ran it against the wire. Up and back. And again. And again.

Farhad and Ahmad found a friend, Hussein, from Iraq. They couldn't speak the same language but they too found sticks and started drawing in the dust. First they drew a big ship and all three stood on it and rocked and swayed but they tired of that and with their sticks behind them they rushed in wide circles, creating swirling, crazy patterns that sometimes overlapped and sometimes went off in wild designs.

And they laughed. Mahtab hadn't heard such a sound for a long time, and she found herself smiling. She knew her mother felt better for it too because she came and stood on the step and she smiled and clapped her hands at their antics. Mahtab looked again to see if there might be a friend for her, but she saw no one her age.

The interview didn't happen that day. They waited and waited and when Mahtab asked why no one came to talk to her or to send for her, her mother shrugged. 'Many people arrived yesterday, Mahtab. Why should we be the first? It may take days.'

It did.

Each morning they had their breakfast, washed and readied themselves to be called and to answer why they had left their country. For a whole week, they waited. They listened to the stories of others who had come the way they had. Some would not speak when Mahtab's mother asked them about the meeting. Others said there were too many questions and there was no way they could answer them all. One woman said that the man who translated her answers did so wrongly, she knew it from the look on his face but she didn't know the words to say it so the man in uniform would know the truth. The Iraqi woman, the one who had wanted to save the water for her children, cried.

Mahtab sat, shielding her eyes from the sun, watching the girl at the wire.

One morning, a young woman approached Mahtab's mother. She was the nurse who had spoken with Hamida and she did not wear the same uniform as the guards. She smiled and held out some brightly coloured books, saying words that none of them could understand.

Then she turned and said slowly, 'Cath-er-ine.'

Mahtab didn't know what to say. She looked down at her dusty feet.

The woman reached forward and took her hand. She pointed to herself. 'Cath-er-ine,' she said again. She pointed to Mahtab and raised her eyebrows.

Mahtab didn't answer.

'Cath-er-ine,' the woman said again.

'Mah-tab,' Mahtab whispered.

'Mah-tab. My name is Mahtab,' said Catherine, each word coming from her as a slow, distinct and rounded sound.

'My — name — is — Mah-tab.' Slowly the sounds came, louder now.

Catherine smiled and said something that Mahtab didn't understand. She pushed the books into Mahtab's mother's hand.

'My — name — is — Mah-tab,' said Mahtab to her mother. 'My — name — is — Mah-tab,' as she stood beneath the shower, as she brushed her hair at night, as she lay in her bed, waiting for sleep to come.

Catherine came a second time. She sat, repeating the phrases, smiling at Mahtab.

My name is Mahtab.

I am from Afghanistan.

I am twelve years old.

How are you?

I am well, thank you.

Gradually the writing in the book began to make sense. Sometimes Catherine came to where Mahtab and her mother sat on the steps of their building and she would point to the words beneath the pictures on the page. 'Bus. Tram. Train. Ship.' They repeated the words slowly. 'Bread. Rice. Carrot. Potato.' Sometimes it seemed to Mahtab that the words came out like the strangled sounds of a fighting cat. Catherine laughed and they laughed with her.

During that time, the interview happened. Mahtab wanted to go with her mother, to ask why they were in prison like this, like common criminals, when they had done nothing wrong. But when she went with her mother to the main building, the pink-and-ginger man told her to go back to their section.

She sat in the doorway watching Farhad, Ahmad and Hussein. They had some words now, or at least they spoke to each other in their own languages, but whether they understood, she couldn't tell. Soraya climbed on her lap. 'Tell me the kangaroo story.' She pushed her head into Mahtab's shoulder.

'No.'

'Please.'

'I don't feel like it.'

'Please, please.'

'Oh, all right.' Mahtab told her again the story of the father who buys the pet kangaroo for his little girl. She wondered, as she spoke, if their own father was alive or dead, if such a creature did exist, or if it was all a fantasy from the storybook he had read. Maybe nothing he had told her then was true. Or had he arrived like they had? Was he too locked up behind some barbed and cruel wire?

Their mother came back. Mahtab couldn't tell from her face what the meeting had been like. She went straight into the room and she sat on the bed and Mahtab followed to sit at her feet.

'What did they say?'

She shook her head.

'Tell me, Mum. What did they say? Why are we here? Can we leave now?'

She reached down and stroked Mahtab's hair. 'Sshh, little one. They say we are illegal. Queue-jumpers.' She laughed, bitterly. 'As if there was a queue for us. We have broken the law by coming the way we did. We must wait while all our documents are checked and our situation is examined, and they said that can take a long time, maybe years.' Mahtab heard the tremble in her voice.

'It could take years, and sometimes ...' She stopped whatever it was she was going to say.

'Sometimes what?'

'You don't want to know, darling. You don't want to know.'

'I do. I am old enough to be told. I am old enough to hide silent in a truck as it goes through the mountains, as it was crawled over by Taliban, to stand with you in airports and on the deck of a ship. I haven't cried out or betrayed us. I am old enough to know.'

'Sometimes people are sent back to the country they came from.'

Her words were a kick in Mahtab's stomach. A heavy boot that sent the air gasping from her throat. Go back! Back to the black turbans and the whips and the cries of the women and fear, the cold, cold fear that one day there would be that knock on the door.

*No*, Mahtab wanted to scream, *No No No*, but the trapdoor had dropped, shutting her throat, and she flung herself on the bed in silence.

The two young children were already asleep when Mahtab and her mother prepared for bed. 'You sleep with Soraya,' said Mum and she took Mahtab's mattress and pushed it on the floor across the doorway.

'To protect you all,' she said simply. 'To make sure no one comes in here at night, to get at any of you.'

'But who would want to come in here?' Mahtab said.

'It has happened. One of the women told me. You're too young to worry about things like this. Let me do that.'

But Mahtab did worry. She lay still in the dark listening to her little sister's breathing. She tried to understand what her mother meant. Was it the guards with their torches? She had grown used to that. It happened at the same time every night, the boots, the turning of the door handle, the light flicking from Mum's face to hers, Soraya's and Farhad's. Sometimes she didn't even wake. Or was it someone else, someone who might mean harm to them? And in what way?

The nightmares began that night. She was on a mountain in a village that she didn't know and she was alone but she could see a small child, a girl on the other side of the road calling for her. Whenever Mahtab tried to cross the road, the child moved beyond her reach, still calling and calling her, begging Mahtab to reach her. The child had a face that Mahtab didn't recognise but she knew it was Soraya. Then the child had gone and Mahtab was running as if she was escaping from someone, but when she turned to see who was following her, there was no one. Still she ran. She knew she had to, even when her feet were cut and bloody. She ran so fast that she could not breathe. She called out for her mother or her father but no one came, and she was falling, falling.

She woke then.

The dream came every night. Sometimes it was Soraya who called her. Sometimes it was a boy with the face of a stranger, but she knew it was Farhad. Sometimes they were in the streets of Herat, sometimes in villages she didn't recognise. Always she ended up running and falling and always she woke before she landed.

Sometimes when she opened her eyes she found her mother kneeling on the floor, her face close, whispering soft words of consolation. 'It's all right, my little one, it's all right. You are safe now. Mumma's here. It's just a bad dream.'

Then Mahtab would say that it was nothing, she was fine, her mother should go back to bed, and she would roll over and push her face into the hard pillow and sleep again. One night, by chance, she felt in her pocket and her fingers closed over the tiny shell from the sand the night they took the boat. She rubbed the rough edges as she had that night, and remembered salt air filling her lungs, and the shimmering, beckoning water.

She slept later and later.

In the first few weeks, they had all got up and joined the breakfast queue soon after the meal began. As time went on, they were moved into the open camp and there they became part of the later meal group, the stragglers, and there were times when Mahtab told her mother that she wasn't hungry, that she didn't want to eat and she wasn't coming to the dining room. At first, her mother thought she was ill and let her stay in bed. She brought back bread from the kitchen, thin slices of soft white bread that Mahtab couldn't eat. After a few days of this, when Mahtab refused to see Catherine, her mother insisted that she get up when the others did, that she come to the dining room with them to eat.

'You must set an example to the others,' said her mother. 'If you give up, then how can I keep Farhad and Soraya well and happy?'

'How can anyone be well and happy here?'

'We must try, Mahtab. We must try.'

'Why? Why should we try? They do not want us here. Our father is gone. He should never have left us because now he's dead. You keep pretending, keep hoping. We have no hope, no life here.'

Her mother slapped her hard across the face. 'Do not say those words.'

Mahtab fell back against the bed, her cheek burning.

'Why not? You must think so too.'

'I do not know what to think. I just know who I am and that I am to look after you all and protect you.'

Mahtab dropped to the floor and drew her knees to her chest. She wrapped her arms around them and hid her face, rocking, silent.

Mahtab watched her little brother and sister. Farhad still spent most days with Ahmad and Hussein, but their wild, joyful games grew fewer and fewer. One day they fought, wrestling in the dust, pushing and shoving, each grabbing the others by the hips, the shoulders, the neck, rolling over and over while other, bigger boys cheered them on. A guard, the woman who had shown them to the room the first day, laughed too. She threw her head back and the sun gleamed off her bright red lips and the flashes of gold in her teeth. The pink-and-ginger guard came then and spoke angrily to Hamida and to Mahtab's mother. He brought with him the translator, who said that they must control their sons or the boys would be put in special rooms by themselves where those who broke the rules were sent.

They had heard of these rooms. The prison within the prison. One of the Iraqi men from the boat, the one who had struck his wife, was there. He had attacked a guard, cursing him and his country, using language that Mahtab's father had once said belonged only with sailors and common criminals. For ten days he was alone there while his wife and his children begged the guards to let him out.

'They wouldn't do that to a child, would they?' Mahtab's mother wept as she spoke to the translator.

He just rolled his eyes. 'It's a warning,' he said. 'Tell them.'

So the boys were made to listen as their mothers told them in great detail of the risks they were taking.

'You will be alone with no one to talk to or to play with,' said Hamida. 'They will feed you only bread and water — the bread they have here which you don't like. You must be friends. You must support each other. We will not be here for ever.'

After that, Hamida and Mahtab's mother made sure that every day one of them was watching. If it seemed a fight was coming between the boys they broke them apart. When they felt that older boys, bored in the long, hot day, goaded the younger ones to brawl they spoke harshly to them and brought Farhad and Ahmad inside. Sometimes they felt nervous when they saw the older men watching their boys.

'They are just missing their own children,' said Hamida. 'Our husbands would be the same.'

'Maybe. But I trust no one,' said Mahtab's mother and she watched all the more closely.

# Francesca

*by Melina Marchetta*

It's Thursday afternoon, and we have sport. These are the choices for the girls: watching an invitation cricket game; study in one of the classrooms; or watching the senior Rugby League. As you can imagine, I'm torn.

William Trombal is standing on the platform of the bus in his League shorts and jersey as I step on.

'What are you doing?'

He's speaking to me. There is something on his face I can't recognise. It looks a bit like panic and I'm confused.

'Going to the football,' I explain politely.

'I think you'll enjoy the cricket.'

'Based on the match fixing and controversial rotating roster, I'm ideologically opposed to cricket.'

I try to step past him but he goes as far as putting his arm across to block me. A you're-not-going-anywhere arm.

'Is there a problem here?' Tara Finke asks, pushing forward. He has no choice but to let us on.

I get a glare the whole way there. I don't know what it is with this guy. One minute he's totally up himself, next minute there's a bit of sympathy, then there's the hostility and today there's everything including a bit of anxiousness.

I've got to give the Sebastian boys this. They've got heart. But skill? After watching them play, I feel a whole lot better about the basketball game. They get so thrashed that even Tara Finke is yelling, 'This is an outrage!'

But they never give in, not once, and half the time I think they're bloody idiots and the other half I can't help cheering if they even touch the ball. The score is too pitiful to divulge. The other side are kind of bastards and our guys are bleeding and, strangely enough, every single time William Trombal gets thumped by those Neanderthals, my heart beats into a panic.

On the way back to school, I sit facing him and he's in his own miserable world. I actually think he wants to cry, but that revolting male protocol of not crying when you feel like shit just kicks in. He looks at me for a moment and I feel as if I should be nice and look away, but I don't.

'Why don't you just stick to what you're good at?' I find myself asking.

'I warned you,' he says, gruffly.

'You didn't say there was going to be blood.'

'You should have gone to the cricket.'

'Do they win?' I ask.

'Every time.'

'Then why don't you join the cricket team?'

He's horrified. 'It's not about winning!'

We approach the school and the first of the guys shuffles past and pats William Trombal on the back. He's their leader, although half their size.

'Maybe next week we'll be able to score, Will.'

'You played a great game,' one says.

'No, mate, you did.'

'No. *You* did, mate.'

They go on forever. It's nauseating stuff, but there's no blaming. They get off the bus smiling tiredly.

*Oh God, don't let me like these guys.*


In Legal Studies, we debate refugees, because Mr Brolin hasn't prepared a lesson and he wants us to do the work. Based on our detention relationship he always calls on me, and on principle I always refuse to give in.

'What's your opinion, Miss Spinelli?' he asks (he pronounces is spin-a-lee). He does the stare that doesn't intimidate any of us. It almost makes me want to laugh out loud.

'What's *your* opinion, Mr Brolin?' Tara Finke asks.

She gets into trouble for speaking without putting up her hand.

'What *I* think isn't the issue, Miss Finke.'

'Why?' she persists.

I can guarantee he won't give his opinion. He sits on the fence in the name of professionalism and gets someone else to voice his fascist views (I've got to stop sitting next to Tara Finke) and around here, there's always a candidate.

'Why should we let people in who jump the queue?' Brian Turner asks. He's unimportant in the scheme of things, but he would be so shocked if someone pointed his unimportance out to him.

'Because in their country there mightn't be a queue,' Tara Finke says.

'They just want to come here because we're the land of plenty,' this girl who always states the obvious says, stating the obvious.

'Yeah, plenty of bullshit,' Thomas Mackee mutters under his breath. Tara Finke and I look at him, surprised, while Brolin comes stalking down the aisle to write in Thomas Mackee's diary for language.

'I agree with Thomas,' Tara Finke says.

Thomas Mackee looks horrified. 'Don't.'

'Don't what?'

'Don't agree with me.' He looks around at his friends and with his finger twirling around his head, he makes the 'she's cuckoo' sign. They snigger with him.

'We have a responsibility,' she continues.

'What? To let terrorists into the country?' Brian Turner asks.

'I thought we were talking refos, not terrorists,' Thomas Mackee says.

'See, you agree with me,' Tara Finke argues.

'I *do not* agree with you. I just don't agree with them,' he says, rolling his eyes.

'In what way don't you agree with me?' she snaps. 'We're saying the same thing. That there's plenty of bullshit here and that refugees aren't terrorists.'

Brolin grabs Tara's diary to record the 'bullshit' because it gives him a purpose.

'We're the only democratic country in the world that puts children in gaol,' she says, looking around at everyone.

'It's very easy to express outrage from your comfortable middle-class world, Miss Finke,' Mr Brolin says, pleased with himself.

'Well, that's pretty convenient,' she says sarcastically. 'Shut the comfortable middle class up and rely on the fact that the uncomfortable lower classes in the world aren't able to express outrage and offer solutions. They're too busy trying not to get killed.'

'I don't like your tone,' he says.

'My tone's not going to change, Mr Brolin.'

'You have to question where you get your facts from,' Brian Turner says.

'Where do you get yours? *The Telegraph*? *Today Tonight*? Your parents? Well my mum works for the Red Cross Tracing and Refugee Agency and she goes and visits the people in

Villawood every fortnight. We don't put on our uniforms just when it suits us and I resent someone stopping me from saying what I believe just because I live happily in the suburbs.'

Mr Brolin looks uncomfortable. He's saved by the bell and he's out of there before we can even pick up our books.

Ryan Burke, a guy from my English Preliminary Extension class approaches us, smiling.

'We're trying to get a Social Justice group thing happening around here,' he tells us. 'You interested?'

'Sounds cool,' she says.

'Oh shucks. Wish I belonged,' Thomas Mackee snickers as he passes by with his posse.

'Ignore him,' Ryan Burke says, walking alongside us. 'He's just trying to rebel. His mother's high up in Anti-Discrimination.'

'That should come in handy when he gets discriminated against for not having a brain,' Tara says, before leaving us for her Design and Technology class.

We're outside our English Preliminary Extension room and end up sitting together.

I like Ryan Burke and his group. They can be cool, and take their work seriously at the same time. Even the slackers like them, although once or twice there'll be a dig about their dedication. These guys feel just as comfortable surfing as they do going to the theatre. They like girls, but don't feel the need to date them and at first they were the hardest to get to know because they had so many female friends from outside the school. More than anything, they enjoy each other's company and although there is a lot of tension between them because of their competitiveness, they're the type of guys you like to see around the place.

Ryan Burke is good-looking. He has that golden-haired look, with a gorgeous smile. I think he hates the perception that he's the good old boy and once in a while he rebels against the image. But deep down he has a decency that I think will stay with him.

He becomes my English Extension companion. Like Shaheen from Biology and Eva from Economics, our relationship is confined to sitting next to each other in class and whispering. In the playground we acknowledge each other, but there is no need for in-depth chatting. The bonding takes place in class.

In English Extension, we're doing an Austen unit and Ryan and I analyse who we are in *Pride and Prejudice.*

'I'd like to think I'm Darcy,' he says, 'but I think I'm a bit of a Bingley. I can be talked out of things sometimes. You?'

'I'd like to think I'm Elizabeth, but deep down I think I'm the one whose name no one can remember. Not Lydia the slut or Mary the nerd or Jane the beauty or Elizabeth the opinionated. I'm the second youngest. The forgotten one.'

'Yeah, I know which one you're talking about. Whatshername.'

'Yeah.'

Later, I walk down the senior corridor and William

Trombal is coming from the opposite direction, speaking to his friends. They're having one of those Treckie versus Trecker discussions. There's just something about William Trombal that screams out 'Star Trek' fan. I personally can't do the Vulcan salute with my fingers and have felt inferior because of it, so disliking William Trombal more than ever suits me just fine. He's laughing at something one of them says and it transforms him completely. It's the first time I have ever seen him smile and it's kind of devastating. They walk by me, completely oblivious. Until the very last moment when he looks over at me and our eyes hold for a moment or two.

And I get this twitch in my stomach.

I walk through Grace Bros to get through to George Street to catch my bus and I find myself going straight to the counter that sells my mother Mia's favourite perfume. I spray it in the air and it's as if the scent's a genie and it triggers everything off inside me and I can't get over what comes up with that one spray. Memories and photos and sayings and advice and music and lectures and shouting and security and love and nagging and hope and despair … despair … why has despair come up? I don't remember despair in her life, but it is evoked by this magical spray. But more than anything, I remember passion.

I look around for the counter that sells my scent, but I'm so petrified that if I spray it in the air, nothing will come out. And then Mia's scent seems to fade away and everything else fades away with it and I know that all I have to do to recapture it is press the spray button again.

But I don't.

Later, my dad picks us up from Nonna's and Zia Teresa's and takes us home for the afternoon. We lie on their bed and my mum is holding on to us so tight that I can't breathe. She holds us and she's crying and she says, 'I'm sorry, I'm sorry, I'm sorry,' over and over again until I can't bear the sound of those words.

And I want to tell her everything. About Thomas Mackee the slob and Tara Finke the fanatic and Justine Kalinsky the loser and Siobhan Sullivan the slut. And I want to tell her about William Trombal and how my heart beat fast when he looked at me, but more than anything, I want to say to her that I've forgotten my name and the sound of my voice and that she can't spend our whole lives being so vocal and then shut down this way. If I had to work out the person I speak to most in a day, it's Mia, and that's what I'm missing.

My nonna comes in and I feel her gently pull the skirt of my school uniform down over my thighs because my underpants are showing. I bury my face in my mum's neck and I inhale her scent as they pull me gently away from her. I inhale it with all my might so I can implant it in my mind.

Because I need it to be my badge.

Poverty equals hunger
*by Bruce Whatley*

# The siren

*by Anna Snoekstra*

Really, our friendship started in the worst way. Azzie and I were thirteen; the unlucky age. It was our first term of year seven and suddenly there were no uniforms. A group of girls traded their backpacks for handbags and pulled the straps of their G-strings up above their white hipster jeans. It was the year 2000, it was high school and now all bets were off.

During primary school my sister and I were banned from using the word 'cool'. First we'd be saying cool, my mother said, and next she'd catch us down at the local shops smoking cigarettes. This may be part of the reason, perhaps, that I left year six with my idea of cool being matching my apple-green overalls with my apple-green T-shirt underneath. I started year seven wearing this ensemble and realised very quickly I was completely wrong about what I had guessed cool meant. The G-strings and the handbags were what were cool and I just looked like a big green apple. I knew for sure what cool was and now, and I also knew that I would never be it.

My first friend in high school was Tegan. We'd made the transition from primary school together, when most of our other friends had decided to go to private schools. Tegan had science class with a Pakistani girl whose father was a diplomat and had a three-year posting in Canberra. This was Azzie. I wasn't sure about her at first. Tegan was my friend, the only friend I had so far, and I wasn't sure if I wanted to share her. But Azzie was someone you just had to like. She was filled with so many stories; about Berlin, Canada, Jakarta. She'd lived everywhere. I'd never really been anywhere, except for a week away to Noosa which was ruined by a chronic case of head lice.

We were a happy little trio for a whole month, until Tegan realised she could be one of the popular girls. She started lending them money, finding any excuse to talk to them, while we just watched. After school one day the three of us went down to the local shops and Sam Fernson was waiting there to meet her. Sam Fernson: a girl more legend than reality; whose reputation preceded her so greatly that she was always called by both her first and last name. But there she was, waiting for Tegan on the steps. She had news too, which she displayed by pulling a ribbon of condoms out of her tiny handbag like a magician. She'd had sex. With a man with a moustache, she exclaimed, while puffing away on a cigarette butt. It was then I understood: my mother was right! If this was what cool was I didn't want to be it. Though really, I was just completely terrified. Me and

Azzie made our excuses and ran for it.

The two of us went to the bush reserve behind her house. We sat on a giant orange boulder and discussed it. As the sun slipped down behind us we became black imprints against the sky. Our plan was made.

That night, I slept over. We watched the first scene of *Bride of Chucky*, then turned it off to dance to the Backstreet Boys instead. Again, we were just scared. I sang my best rendition of 'To the Moon and Back' by Savage Garden and Azzie confirmed that I should definitely become a famous singer. We slept in her pull-out sofa bed together and by the morning it was decided: we were best friends now. If Tegan thought she was better than us, that was just fine: we didn't want to be her friends any more, either.

Together we ignored her, together we ran away giggling when she came up to talk to us at lunchtime, and together we got a call from her father after school yelling at us for bullying his daughter. From then we really were locked together — in guilt.

We apologised, but it was too late; the damage was done. Tegan was lost to the handbag-toting G-string wearers, who apparently were nicer than us. And so, for the next two and a half years, it was just the two of us.

I managed to hold back my tears during the drive to Azzie's house. Staring blankly out the window, I thought about how terrifyingly alone I would be once semester two of year nine started. Why did she have to leave mid-year? When my mum pulled into the driveway Azzie and I held each other and cried. I cried because my best friend was leaving, I cried at the prospect of sitting alone at lunchtime and we both cried because Azzie was going to Afghanistan and we had no idea what that would mean.

Guess who?

**FROM:** azraishere88@hotmail.com

**TO:** krisskross@gmail.com

**SENT:** 15 JUNE 2002

Dear Kris,

This is your secret admirer. Can you guess who?

Ha ha, no it's not Daniel (I knew you would think it was him!!) it's me, Azzie! I've arrived! See, I told you I would email you as soon as I got here. It's 9 in the morning here which is 2pm Australian time I think (actually I know it is, I just looked it up on the internet). I wonder what you are doing; I hope you are singing right now, that would be nice. Or writing lyrics in your secret notebook (*why* couldn't I read it?). Okay, okay. I know I'm avoiding telling you anything about what it's like here. If we were having a real conversation you would tell me to get to the point in that gruff way you do when you are annoyed. But the truth is I don't even know where to start. Things here are so so different. I think I was expecting it would be more like Pakistan but really it's nothing like it at all.

Okay, I'll start from the start. We got out of the airport and

169

the heat smacked us almost off our feet (no, really!). The air felt and smelled totally different from anywhere I've ever been before. We got into a car that was waiting for us and the driver had his air conditioning on soooo intensely. It was nice at first but after a while it got so cold I felt like all my snot was freezing inside my nose.

Kris, the main city here is just amazing. Really. There's this yellow dust everywhere and all the buildings look like they are made out of clay. And there are so many people. And soldiers! I thought the soldiers would be hiding in compounds somewhere, but they walk around the streets just like everyone else. I think it's going to be a really strange place to live, but I also think it's going to be a great thing to put in my memoir.

The other thing is … I miss you. I thought I was used to all this coming and going. But I'm not. I miss you so so much.

So write to me.

Love Azzie

**RE:** Guess Who?

**FROM:** krisskross@gmail.com

**TO:** azraishere88@hotmail.com

**SENT:** 16 JUNE 2002

AZZIE!

I'm so glad you wrote! I think I was afraid you'd disappear and I'd never ever hear from you again. I miss you too! And I do NOT have a mean gruff voice when I get angry, that's horrible!!

But I forgive you.

I don't have much to tell you about here. It's gotten colder. My front steps are so frosty I keep slipping over when I leave the house. So I've just been hanging out at home a lot and I have been doing some singing actually. In fact it's possible that that is exactly what I was doing yesterday at 2pm. Really, things here have been pretty boring. My dad has figured out that the best way to clean the dog is to vacuum him and he spent Monday chasing him around the house with it. Now when we vacuum the whole house smells like smelly wet dog.

Tell me more about you! I miss you. I'm really worried about next semester. I start in one week and I just want to hide.

Reply quickly.

Kris

Ps. I DO NOT have a thing for Daniel. That is soooo disgusting.

Rockets!!!

**FROM:**  azraishere88@hotmail.com

**TO:**  krisskross@gmail.com

**SENT:**  19 JUNE 2002

Kris.

Guess what? Someone shot off rockets in Kabul yesterday and the place went crazy! There were troops running around and all these little explosions. It was mad. Also, I start school tomorrow. We'll have to compare notes. It'll be the first time I get to leave this one block of land since I got here. Which hasn't been too bad because … guess what again? Our embassy is right next to the British embassy! I'm just waiting to meet all those British men and hear their beautiful accents. It's going to be fantastic.

Got to go. Only allowed ten minutes on the computer. You'll be fine at school, just chat to everyone. Trust me, making friends is easy.

Love ya! Azzie

Rockets????

**FROM:** krisskross@gmail.com

**TO:** azraishere88@hotmail.com

**SENT:** 23 JUNE 2002

Azzie-What do you mean Rockets? That sounds terrifying. Are you sure you're okay? Also, you should definitely try and make one of the British men your boyfriend. Just think how good it would be for your memoirs!

Kris

Black Windows

**FROM:** azraishere88@hotmail.com

**TO:** kriskross@gmail.com

**SENT:** 01 JULY 2002

Dear Kris,

I haven't replied for a whole week as punishment because in your last email you didn't say one word about what school was like. I know you think I wouldn't notice but I DID. Also, I'm barely allowed to use the computer here any more and our family doesn't have one in our apartment (that's the real reason I haven't written). It's SO annoying!

I started this week. It's okay, I don't mind it. The school is mostly diplomats' kids which is interesting because there are a lot of people from different places. Also it's an all girls' school which I don't like. But there are NO libraries here and so I can't borrow any books and I'm going crazy. What am I going to do without reading? Also I have to wear the burqa now which is uncomfortable with it being so hot.

The really scary thing is the drive to school. A whole group of us kids from the embassy drive in the back of this big van through Kabul (our school is in the south). I noticed that all these windows were blacked out. When I got home I asked my mum why and she said it was because when the Taliban was ruling (until just last year!) women who had no husband weren't even allowed to go outside. They had to black out their windows so know one could even see in. Can you imagine it? I had a nightmare about it last night. Living in darkness all alone. I think I would go crazy.

Anyway please please tell me about Canberra I want to hear everything!

Azzie

Guys n Dolls

**FROM:**   kriskross@gmail.com

**TO:**   azraishere88@hotmail.com

**SENT:**   10 JULY 2002

Hey Azzie,

I'm worried about you. It sounds really scary. I feel stupid telling you about life here when it's so boring in comparison. But you asked me so I'll tell you. Be prepared to fall asleep though. It's been raining everyday. Big sad heavy raindrops. So I've been hiding in the library. I know it's easy for *you* to make friends but I've never been good at it. The only girl I even talk to at school is Jess in Science — do you remember Jess Tenson? Apart from that I'm all by myself. I like her but I feel so pathetic if I make too much of an effort. The problem is that everyone already has proper groups of friends now, it's all sorted out and there isn't room for extra members. I know everyone thinks I'm a loser and it's so embarrassing. I think I'm going to have to wait until year 11 and start again at College. That's a whole year and a half though. I hate feeling this pathetic.

The only thing that is exciting is that I am going to audition for this year's play! It's a musical so I really think I've got a chance. What do you think? I've been practising every single day.

Email me very soon so I don't worry about you!
Kris

**RE:** Guys n Dolls

**FROM:** azraishere88@hotmail.com

**TO:** kriskross@gmail.com

**SENT:** 20 JULY 2002

Hey Kris,

I've only got two minutes left on the computer but I just

wanted to say good luck! You are going to blow their socks off! Seriously, no one will have any socks by the time you finish singing! This is just the beginning; you are going to be a celebrity soon.

Love Azzie

PS. When you're famous can I write your biography? I really think I'm the most qualified.

PPS. You don't have to answer right away, think about it. I promise I'll make you sound really cool and interesting.


Where are you??

**FROM:** azraishere88@hotmail.com

**TO:** kriskross@gmail.com

**SENT:** 06 SEPTEMBER 2002

Where are you Kris?

It's been ages and I haven't heard from you. I'm worried. If you didn't get the part in the play don't worry I won't be disappointed. I just want to see how things are going for you.

Things here have changed. Or maybe it's me that's changed. I think I didn't realise how dangerous it is here. It's actually really really scary. Yesterday I was on my way to school when suddenly the whole world shook. The explosion was so loud I felt it vibrate right through my chest. Then everyone started running, soldiers appeared from everywhere. It was chaos. Turns out there was a car bomb that exploded. Thirty people died; not soldiers or anything just people walking past going about their day. If we had left ten minutes earlier it could have been us.

I started thinking about it though and I realised something. I thought I was safe because I was protected by our embassy and the big UK one next door. But then I realised really it just makes us even more of a target.

Please write.

Azzie

**RE:** Where are you?

**FROM:**    kriskross@gmail.com

**TO:**       azraishere88@hotmail.com

**SENT:**    07 SEPTEMBER 2002

Dear Azzie

I'm so so sorry I took so long to write. I feel awful. I didn't realise how scary it was there. I hear about it on the news but I always thought you were protected too. Don't think about being a target. There is no point in thinking that way, you'll just freak yourself out. Also, I really think that the embassies would know that and have heaps of guards and safety measures wouldn't they? I don't think your parents would let you be there if it wasn't safe.

The reason I didn't write was because I didn't want to tell you that I didn't audition for the play. There was so many people sitting around watching and I knew they would laugh at me.

Please write back and tell me how you are.

Kris

(No Subject)

**FROM:** azraishere88@hotmail.com

**TO:** kriskross@gmail.com

**SENT:** 20 OCTOBER 2002

Kris,

My school got blown up. I'm so upset. You don't know what it's like here. I'm scared all the time now. I really want to have an education and get a scholarship somewhere. But now my parents think it might be too dangerous to go to school at all because people are targeting girls' schools. I don't know what I'm going to do now. I feel so awful for the girls here, it's like they don't even get a chance. I wish I could do something.

Azzie

PLAN!

**FROM:** kriskross@gmail.com

**TO:** azraishere88@hotmail.com

**SENT:** 21 OCTOBER 2002

Azzie!

That sounds absolutely awful I'm so so sorry. I have a plan though and I'm super excited. Why don't you come back and live here with me? I already asked my parents and they said it's okay! It's too scary there, I'm sure your parents wouldn't want you to be somewhere that wasn't safe.

What do you think?

Kris

PS. Me and Jess are friends now. I've been hanging out heaps with her and her brother. It will be so perfect when you come back!

RE: PLAN!

FROM: azraishere88@hotmail.com

TO: kriskross@gmail.com

SENT: 22 OCTOBER 2002

You don't understand it at all do you?

It's not just me I'm sad for. It's the fact this is happening at all. I can't just leave my family here because I'm scared. Plus they would never agree in a million years. Plus what about everyone else that lives here? This is their home and it's being destroyed by everyone. I can't just pretend its not happening

Also I cannot BELIEVE you didn't audition for that play.

Azzie

Happy Birthday

FROM: azraishere88@hotmail.com

TO: kriskross@gmail.com

SENT: 10 DECEMBER 2002

Kris,

Happy Birthday! It's been two months and I've been thinking about you. Please let me know how you are.

Azzie

Sorry

**FROM:** azraishere88@hotmail.com

**TO:** kriskross@gmail.com

**SENT:** 1 JANUARY 2003

Dear Kris,

I am so so sorry for my angry email. I've been thinking about it a lot these past few months and I realised I wasn't fair. It was a nice plan it just would never work. I really hope you've had a great summer! And a great birthday and a happy New Year! Please write sometime. I still miss you and I really hope things are going well.

Love Azzie

Yesterday

**FROM:** kriskross@gmail.com

**TO:** azraishere88@hotmail.com

**SENT:** 19 JANUARY 2003

Azzie,

I wasn't going to write. I was angry with you and I was going to be so stupid and resentful that I just would never write back so that you would feel bad. But I realise now that you were absolutely right about everything. Something awful happened yesterday. It's like it was a dream. But I know it wasn't because all the power is still off in my house. I'm sitting in my Dad's study right now using his work laptop that I'm usually never allowed to touch.

It's been hot here these last few days. Like 47 degrees. This strange dry searing heat with wind that actually hurts your skin. My mum had been acting all worried and strange and I didn't know why. She took us to the shopping centre to take advantage of the air conditioning. As we drove up the exit ramp from the underground car park we were all so shocked: the sky was bright blood-red. It was only midday but the sky was crimson and it was already getting dark. We drove home quickly, I wasn't sure what was happening but I didn't want to ask. When we got out of the car at home these little bits of black ash started drifting down from the sky. My mum turned the radio on as soon as we got in. There were fires coming. A firestorm that was jumping highways and burning through the suburbs. She told us to pack our bags while she called her sister. I knew why she wanted to call her sister and I didn't want to listen. I was afraid she might cry. My grandparents died in a bushfire in Victoria, did I ever tell you that? Anyway, me and my sister packed overnight bags. The radio wasn't telling us to evacuate but I didn't want to argue with my mum.

My dad refused to leave. He said he wanted to stay to look after the dog, but I guess it was the house he was worried about. He stood in the driveway as our car pulled out and watched us go. Next to him was a pile of woodchips even taller than him. We were meant to be mulching our garden but the woodchips had just been sitting there for weeks. As we pulled out I suddenly got the feeling that I wouldn't see him again.

It was only two o'clock but it was almost dark as we drove

through the streets. The air was thick with this foul, acrid-smelling smoke. All the traffic lights were just flashing red but it didn't matter because there wasn't even one car on the road. The radio said the evacuation centre was full up already so we drove to my mum's friend's house. She made us tea, which seemed so stupid since it was so hot, and we all sat around listening to the radio. Every fifteen minutes or so, the ABC announcer would read out a list of suburbs that were in high danger. My suburb was on it already. I thought my mum was being too careful, but it seemed we'd only just left in time. I wanted to call my dad but I didn't. I didn't want to even think about it any more. My sister went and sat up on the roof; she said she could actually see the fire from there. She wanted me to come up but I was too scared. I'm not sure if it was because I was scared to climb onto the roof or if I just didn't want to see it.

Then they started playing the siren on the radio. That same siren you hear in movies when there's a tornado or an air raid. Well they were playing it for real and it made my whole body turn cold. I realised suddenly that I wasn't safe. That just because nothing bad had ever happened to me before didn't mean it wouldn't. Anything could happen and I had no power to stop it. Every time they read out the list of suburbs it was getting longer and longer. And closer.

Azzie it was so awful. I really didn't know what was going to happen. We came home today and my dad was okay. The fire got to the end of my street though, just seven houses up. Apparently one of my neighbours had this water tanker thing he used for work and some of the people on my street used it to fight the fire themselves, can you believe that? I can't believe people could be that brave. Or maybe it was stupidity. I'm really angry at my dad for not coming with us. I wouldn't care if something happened to the house, or the dog really. Dad's life wasn't worth risking.

Anyway the real reason I'm writing this is to say how sorry I am. You were right, I didn't get it. I still probably don't. It was just one day for me and that's what things are probably like for you every single day but worse. But I'm sorry, and I care about you so so much. And I want to help somehow but I haven't figured what I can do yet. I'm going to do something though.

Kris.

RE: Yesterday

FROM:    azraishere88@hotmail.com

TO:       kriskross@gmail.com

SENT:    20 JANUARY 2003

Kris, Your email was terrifying. I can't believe that happened in Canberra. Is everyone okay? Did anyone from school get hurt?

I'm so glad you wrote back and please don't say you feel bad because that just makes me feel bad. I'm getting used to things here now. The only bad thing is that they don't have the resources to rebuild the schools so I've been trying to learn from home for the last few months. But it's not easy without any books and I feel like my brain is turning to moosh.

Please tell me what's going on in Canberra; it's not on the news here.

Love Azzie

NEW PLAN

**FROM:**   kriskross@gmail.com

**TO:**   azraishere88@hotmail.com

**SENT:**   03 FEBRUARY 2003

Okay! I have a new plan! And don't worry it's not anything like the other one. I went back to school today. A lot of people lost their houses but no one we know was hurt. Everything is already rebuilding too. It's crazy how quickly things are going back to normal.

So about my plan. I'm going to sing for you Azzie. I know that's what you want me to do. I've already talked to some teachers and it's all set in motion. We are going to do a musical benefit. And I'm head of organising it. Anyone that wants to can perform a song and all the proceeds will go to women's education in Afghanistan. I'm so excited! It has to wait for a few months because everyone is all about re-building at the moment. But that's okay, gives me time to practise and make the whole thing perfect.

Kris

PS, and this is a big ps, you know how I said that Jess had a big brother. Well, his name is Matt and I think I'm in love.

IN LOVE!!!???!!

WHAT??

You're in love? I can't believe you have kept this from me. I would be so mad at you if I wasn't so desperate to hear all the juicy details! Tell me everything!

Also, I had a bit of tear when I read your email. I can't believe you are organizing that whole thing. And you are going to sing. For me. I can't tell you how happy it makes me. I don't even care if you make any money, just the fact you are doing it means so much.

Love Azzie

PS If you haven't kissed him yet you HAVE to kiss him after you sing. It will be so amazing and romantic. You have to tell me if you swoon!

I think I'm going to faint. My hands are shaking. How am I meant to hold a microphone if my hands are shaking? The band before me has almost finished their song. I take a deep breath and let myself steal a peek around the curtain. Panic slices through me: the place is full.

So full that kids are sitting on the floor at the front. Matt catches me looking and gives me a big thumbs up. But this just makes me feel even sicker. Oh God, they are playing the last verse now, I've heard them practise. I've only got seconds. There's still time. I could say I was sick, hide in the bathroom till everyone has left.

The band plays their last note, thanks the audience, and sidles off. The stage is empty. Hundreds of eyes staring at an empty square. I'm so scared I want to run, but I force myself to think of Azzie. This isn't about me, it's about her. I take a step onto the stage. And then another. I walk to the centre, pick up the microphone. Mrs Franklin the music teacher plays the first note on the piano. It's too late now. I'll have to do it. I bring the microphone to my lips, expecting no sound to come out, but it does. My voice comes out strong and clear. The jitters in my stomach turn to sparks; they pulse through my body as if I've been charged with an electrical current. I don't look at the audience as I sing, they don't matter right now. It's just me. I let the music take me over.

And then it's finished. The crowd applauds. Matt looks at me like no one ever has. I walk off the stage. I want to run into the dressing room, ask everyone if they heard it, if it was good. But instead I just let myself stop, be in the moment, take a breath. I was scared and I did it anyway and it was the best feeling ever.

I can't wait to tell Azzie.

# In the tower

*by Kate Forsyth*

Walled in my old stone tower
the bitter taste of tears
always in my throat
only a slit to put my eye to
yet how full of change is that sky
I watch the stars wheel past
seasons turning and turning
the one tree on that faraway hill
once more bursts into life
green in the shadows
golden in the light

Walled in my silent tower
how can I frame the words
to tell my story
my heart is a riddle
green sickness in my soul

loneliness the heaviest burden
how I long to slip free
of this empty shadowed tower
fly on muffled wings like the owl
white against the thorns
black against the moon

Walled in my cold stone tower
I conjure a steed from flame
an invisible cloak from ashes
a frail ladder from cobwebs
I make a dagger from ice
a key from bone and wishes
I spin a song from the silence
one day someone shall sing my refrain
green in the shadows
golden in the light

Free of my shadowy tower
we shall bind ourselves together
with tendrils of green
with tresses of gold
we shall build a castle of light and air
and banish silence with song
together we'll dance in the forest
white against the thorns
black against the moon

# Meatloaf soldiers

*by Susanne Gervay*

The news hums from the TV: *'Syrian Government forces bomb Aleppo. Thousands killed ... Human rights abuses, torture ...'* The newsreader's eyes, ringed with make-up, cake into mustard gas and war.

Mum cuts the meatloaf with two hard-boiled eggs in the middle. It's our family favourite.

'Tomato sauce,' my brother Joshua calls out while Milly sticks her fingers into the eggs.

I grab her hands. 'No, Milly.' Her bottom lips quivers and I hug her. A hug always works for her. Milly was born just after Dad left. Five years ago. He never calls us. Just seemed to disappear. Mum and I became the A-team. We organise everything. It's been easier since Joshua and Milly started at the school right next to my high school. Mum teaches there too.

*'Kofi Annan has resigned as the UN–Arab League joint special*

*envoy for Syria because of the lack of international support for his*
*efforts to end the bloodshed in the Syrian civil war and …*'

Mum looks up at the TV, then at me. I get it.

She taught World War I to my class. We saw photographs of soldiers in gas masks and burrowed trenches. The girls in my class sat eating chocolate behind their hands when black and white film of soldiers 'scaped' across sixteen-millimetre celluloid. They loved the Peter Weir film *Gallipoli*, where the hero was blond and brave, where Australians skylarked in Cairo and got drunk in Egyptian chaos. The girls stopped eating when the young soldiers trapped Turkish bullets, dying with their mates on a beach far from Australia. The boys watched.

Mum shouts at Milly and Joshua, who are arguing about the space between them at the dinner table. 'I've got no room!' Joshua shouts, shoving Milly's arm as she plops her teddy next to her plate.

I pull another chair next to Milly and put teddy on it. 'Teddy's happy there. She has her own spot now.'

Joshua spreads out his elbows as he scoffs his meatloaf.

There's always a solution if you look for it. Negotiate it. Fight for it. I learned that after Dad left.

Mum switches off the television. She'll watch the late night news tonight. It's dinner time and Milly and Joshua want to tell Mum their news. There's a show coming to school and Joshua needs a note signed so that he can attend. He drags it out of his pocket. Mum pours orange juice into

Milly's cup and I nod, preoccupied with World War II. It's the next history topic. A man with a moustache pointing at genocide. I've been reading William Shirer's *Rise and Fall of the Third Reich*, but history won't stay inside books. It jumps twisting, winding into the present. I lump chocolate ice-cream into Milly's Humpty Dumpty bowl.

An indignant spoon slams onto the table. 'I want chocolate sauce.'

Mum taps Milly's hand. 'Orders get you nothing.'

Milly's face crunches into tears. She runs to her room, crying.

Joshua laughs as he flashes his note in Mum's face.

'Stop laughing. It's not funny, Joshua.'

'It is, Mum.' He argues until Mum closes her eyes and there's silence.

'Orders get you nothing.' It's not true of course. If Milly shouts loudly enough, demands long enough, Mum gives in. I give in. If Joshua shouts loudly enough, demands long enough, Mum gives in. I give in. It's hard to fight, struggling against their wills. Milly can't be a dictator, demanding chocolate sauce. Joshua can't laugh, joining the crowd.

In Mum's first class today, she sent a boy to the Principal's office. She caught him with his arm extended, goose-stepping at the front of the room, pretending to be Hitler. The class was laughing when she came through the door. I laughed too, as the boy tried to lick away the blackberry jam from his top lip.

'No sense of humour,' I heard one girl mutter when Mum sent the goose-stepping Hitler to the Principal. I stopped laughing. A few kids called out insults at Mum, at me. I ignored them and walked away with my friends. Genocide wasn't funny today.

I wish it was eight-thirty, when the house is quiet, Joshua and Millie are asleep in their double bunk, and when Mum's preparing her class work. I can turn on my music and think. I loved it when Dad took us to the beach. Joshua was little and I was eleven. I'm fifteen now. Mum looked so beautiful in her sparkling wraparound cotton sarong with jasmine threaded in her hair. She'd threaded them in my hair too and the sun shone. But there were other times. He'd just get angry. He'd hit me for spilling my lemonade or laughing too loudly or just because I was there. He'd hit Mum, too.

Milly is calling out. Mum looks at me.

'I'll clear up the dishes, Mum.'

She smiles as she pads towards Milly's bedroom.

Joshua brings plates to the sink and I scrape them. 'How's cricket going?' I ask him as I stack the dishwasher. There's no answer. I glance at him. His face is flushed. 'Are you okay?' He looks down. 'Joshua?'

Mum's singing and Milly's giggles drift towards the kitchen.

I rub my hands on the dishcloth and wait. He looks up at me. 'Joshua?'

'You have to promise not to tell Mum.'

I don't feel good about secrets.

'Promise, otherwise I can't …' His voice peters out.

I nod. I look down at him. His eyes are like Dad's. I wish they weren't. There's silence. I wait. Slowly Joshua's words splash over me, some seeping in, before puddling onto the floor.

'Bill stole my cricket bat,' he stammers. 'He hit me.' Joshua bends his head. His Dad-like brown eyes disappear under his hair falling across his forehead. 'I can't play at lunchtime without my bat. I can't play.' Then he whispers, 'No one can play with me.'

I force away emotions. I've got to think. Anger has to be pushed away. I read history. I write essays. History demands rational analysis and deduction. I take a deep breath. My brother was attacked. His cricket bat stolen. He can't play cricket with his friends at lunchtime. He can't share a game, negotiate a play, make a winning hit, cheer his team. Joshua looks at me. I swallow hard. Instinct wants me to find this Bill, grab him by the collar, report him to the teacher, demand action from the Principal. Suddenly I press my hands on my heart. Mum didn't protect us when Dad was angry. I didn't protect Joshua then. But it's now and I'm his big sister. I'm different.

Joshua is in a battlefield. And there are dictators out there. 'I don't want to go to school any more.'

I catch my breath. 'Do you want to hide at home?'

He bends his head. I remember doing that when Dad was in a rage because I woke him too early or spoke when he didn't want to hear my voice or opened the door or shut the door. Mum would hide me behind her skirt or give me a book to read quietly. I'd watch Mum scurry around the corners of the kitchen making breakfast, setting plates, rubbing cleaner on the kitchen bench. Then she would wait, pressing against the wall, hunching her shoulders so that her neck disappeared into her chest. With me hunching behind her.

'I'm not hiding. I just want to stay at home.'

'I used to hide. From Dad. Mum used to hide.'

It took all Mum's courage that day. Mum stood away from the wall. When she told Dad he had to go, I was so scared. Scared to goose-step across the room. Scared to race into Arab bullets. Scared I'd die on a beach far away from home. But I have had to stand up, because I have a life.

Joshua waits for me to respond.

Closing my eyes tightly, I think of *The Rise and Fall of the Third Reich*. I think of Mum marching the boy to the Principal's office. I have to be a strategist, tactician, teacher. 'We need a plan. A very good plan.'

Joshua is scared.

Mum comes into the kitchen. 'The spoon basher is asleep.' Mum sees our faces. 'Is everything all right?'

I look at Joshua. 'We can't do this alone,' I say, and glance at Mum.

Joshua presses his lips together and eventually nods. He tells Mum.

She's silent at first, holding her breath until it seems she's going to burst. As the air gushes, she becomes emotional, angry, appears to want to attack, but finally she reaches into history. Planning, strategy, tactics. We're a team now.

'Hot chocolate?' She fossicks in the cupboards for the marshmallows and reaches for the tall glasses.

Armed with warm drinks, we sit at the table. Then we begin. Like generals, we work out troop movements, defences, mobilisations. We talk, discuss, negotiate. Joshua laughs when I dot chocolate sauce on my upper lip. Eventually the strategy is in place. Mum and I hug Joshua. 'Right?' He nods.

Joshua rings his friends, gathers supporters, argues his case. Enough kids agree that Joshua has the right to his cricket bat. They plan to group together on the school cricket pitch at lunchtime. They will surround, block, outnumber Bill. If he doesn't give back the bat, a runner had been nominated to call for teacher support. They know Mr Jones is on playground duty tomorrow. Mr Jones is fair and tough. Mr Jones won't stand for the cricket bat theft. D-Day is tomorrow. Everything is in place.

Bedtime is late. Tonight is different. Joshua is mining history. We're part of history and there's a battle ahead. Joshua is nervous about tomorrow. He whispers to me: 'I really didn't want to stay at home.'

Mum reads us all a story, about brave princes racing white horses across sandy beaches. Joshua pulls his blanket over him. 'It'll be all right,' I whisper.

The heater warms the lounge room and I open Bullock's *Hitler: A Study in Tyranny*. 'Hitler, a man who believed neither in God nor in conscience.'

It's dark outside. The trees look cold and I rub my hands. Mum turns on the late night news to watch missile attacks in Syria.

Joshua *has* to win. I hold Mum's hand. We're afraid. But it has to be better than hiding against a wall.

The face of Syria's President Assad looms large on the screen. The man takes up the whole picture, spitting 'necessity', 'God's will', 'rights', 'the good of all'. The late news ends with the weather. 'A cool but sunny day is expected.' I hope the weatherman is right.

I nestle into my bed. I lie silently, edging into sleep, thinking of history — thinking of dropping Milly off in the playground, waving goodbye to Joshua, walking with Mum to the high school.

Mum and I are working it out. I smile. Milly has stopped bashing her spoon in her Humpty Dumpty bowl. Joshua can do this because he isn't alone — I'm here. Mum's here, his friends, Mr Jones. And Joshua believes he can do it.

Joshua is going to be all right. We all are.

# Guantanamo boy

*by Anna Perera*

There's an oasis of silence and peace inside the house as
the door closes. The dark wall-hangings create a sense of
cave-like gloom. Though his temporary home is familiar, it
provides no comfort to Khalid as he pauses to gaze through
the open door of the dark back room to see Uncle Amir
curled up, asleep as usual, in the far corner.

Everyone else, he can tell, is in the other room, listening
hard. Knowing it's Khalid by the way he kicks off his
sandals before he heads towards them with hesitant steps.

Looking round at the sea of questioning faces, Khalid
thinks that the whole neighbourhood seems to have
crammed itself into the living room. There's barely space
on the small tables for another bowl of sugar cubes or
cup of half-drunk coffee. He suddenly has no idea where
to start. All at once, hundreds of enquiring voices fire
questions at him in Urdu and Punjabi, neighbours and
distant relatives crowding round him. The aunties wring

their hands, sobbing. Mum stands in the corner, wailing. Gul and Aadab, pale and shaken, are close to screaming.

'I dunno where Dad is,' Khalid says when everyone eventually falls silent. He goes over the chain of events as quickly as possible, not bothering to mention the demonstration and the hordes of angry men he'd come across.

The moment Khalid finishes, leaving people none the wiser, everyone begins sounding off with their own ideas and gesturing to heaven for help. A stream of desperate prayers begins to flow from their downturned mouths. No one notices Khalid slip away to grab a glass of water, wash his dusty face and hands and flop on the kitchen floor. At last, he gets to sit on his own in a state of total disbelief at his useless, wasted search.

He is tired out of his mind, head spinning from too many hours without rest. The wooden ceiling fan seems to loom over him as he builds a nest of red cushions on the floor, their gold tassels swinging as he lies down. Soon falling under the gentle hypnosis of the fan's whirring and faint clicks, he enjoys a moment's peace until people begin coming and going, stepping over him. Clattering cups, making coffee, whispering, trying not to be noisy, even though they can see he's not asleep.

In the end their constant interruptions force Khalid to get up again. He pads back to the living room, where Gul and Aadab stare from one sad face to another, wondering if anyone will notice if they eat the rest of the sugar cubes in the green glass bowl. Gul reaches to grab a handful and pass some to Aadab. Both try hard to enjoy the cloying sweetness while pretending not to be eating anything and, along with Khalid, gaze sadly at Mum. Fatima and Roshan stand with their backs to them at the window, looking out. Aunt Rehana listens blank-faced to a neighbour who's brought a pot of honey and some walnuts to cheer them up.

Everyone is in the same state of lonely grief, only half here in this room, their minds overloaded with stories they've read in the papers about people who've gone missing and are later found dead from bomb blasts, accidents, murders. It's easy to think the worst here.

Later, after a few hours tossing and turning in bed, Khalid gets up. He moves quickly, pulling on his jeans, hurrying to hear what's happened. Peeping into the living room, he sees the same faces, feels the same hopelessness, and steps back. Rushing instead to the computer cupboard, where he half expects an email from someone, anyone, who might be able to tell him what's happened to Dad.

He opens the door and is amazed to find Abdullah on the computer. 'What are you doing here?'

'What do you mean?' Abdullah clicks on the corner of the page he's looking at so it disappears. Quickly turns to face Khalid with a calm, unsurprised smile.

'That's our computer,' Khalid stutters.

'I have permission from the family to use this, but I have finished with it now so you may continue your game,' Abdullah says in his annoying formal English and scrapes the chair back.

The thought flashes through Khalid's mind that he's never told him about Tariq's game, but then anyone could see what he's been doing online because he didn't log off the last time he used the computer. From now on, he'll log off each time and shut it down properly.

'Don't worry. I am not interested in what you are doing on the World Wide Web. I am not a spy,' Abdullah says, reading his mind. 'Myself, I am only reading the newspapers, as I have always done. My brother and my sister's husband, they come here to do the same. We have not been doing this for some days because your family are here. I was looking to see if there was any news of your father.' He stands up and walks off, leaving Khalid standing there, unable to say anything back.

He feels guilty for a moment, but quickly forgets as he checks his emails. There are three: one from Tariq, suggesting the time to play *Bomber One* tonight; one from Nico, rambling on about how he's downloaded a bunch of songs for free on his MP3 player; plus one from a kid at school called Jamie, who's doing his history coursework on Galileo too.

'He could have had a stroke,' someone says from the hall, their thoughts clashing with the lovely smell of curry that's building in the air.

After a while Khalid closes the computer down and steps out of the dark cupboard, surprised to see Abdullah is back again with his wife. They are smiling at everyone and their arms are loaded with dishes of steaming food.

'Bottle gourd curry and chapattis. Chickpeas too for you!' Abdullah says.

Someone bangs on the door, too calmly for it to be urgent news about Dad. *Another neighbour*, Khalid thinks, heading down the hallway and opening the door to a familiar face.

'Hiya, how's it going?' Jim smiles. 'Just thought I'd pop in on my way to the airport. Everything OK?'

Khalid shakes his head. 'Nah, Dad's not here.' Mum and the aunties disappear from the hall after seeing it isn't anyone with important news.

'We still, like, don't know what happened,' Khalid says, hogging the doorway. Hearing Abdullah and his wife offer to put the food out in the kitchen, all of a sudden Khalid's stomach twitches with hunger.

'Have you checked the hospitals?' Jim asks.

'The neighbours have.' Khalid nods, all of a sudden wanting to talk about something else in case he gets worked up again. 'We're just about to have some food. Do you want to join us? One more mouth won't make a difference round here.'

'Nah, I've gotta go. Thanks, though. Just wanted to see how things were going. Wish it was better news.' Jim sighs.

'Well, best of luck, mate. Hope you enjoy the rest of your Easter holiday.'

'Thanks.' Khalid closes the door as Jim jumps back in his taxi. Remembering Easter at home, a picture of his town, Rochdale, flashes through Khalid's mind. Suddenly he's walking with his mates down a pretty cobbled street — York Street. The shops are crammed with chocolate Easter eggs as they make their way to the shopping arcade. He feels such a strong connection to the lovely old mill town that for the first time in his life he realises he loves it there. Then Abdullah's suddenly behind him with a suspicious look on his face.

'Yeah, what?' Khalid asks, feeling annoyed again.

'Who's that man?' he says, expecting an answer immediately.

'Just some bloke.' Khalid's tempted to tell him he's a grenade thrower, but stops himself, not trusting Abdullah to take it as a joke. 'I met him in the market. He's a student in London and he helped me find the address of the flat Dad went to.'

'What else?'

'Nothing else. What do you mean?' says Khalid, thinking, *None of your business.*

'What things did he tell you?' Abdullah asks.

'Things? What do you mean? Nothing. He's from Liverpool. He's English. Look, I'm starving. I haven't eaten anything proper since yesterday.' With that, Khalid wanders off. He suspects Abdullah knows more about his dad's disappearance than he's letting on. That suspicious look on his scarred face isn't right and the sick feeling Khalid has in his stomach won't go away. Luckily, when Abdullah comes to get some food he doesn't mention anything about Jim in front of the others.

Later in the evening, when the neighbours have gone home and the aunties and Mum have finally been persuaded to go to bed, the house falls silent once more. The latest decision is to go to the police in the morning. A group of male neighbours are preparing a list of questions to ask.

There were some questions Khalid wanted to ask Abdullah, but Mum stopped him by putting a finger to her mouth. She warned him not to speak out of turn, even though the knot in Khalid's stomach is still there. All this is on his mind as he switches on the computer. The familiar ping is the best sound he's heard all day.

'Hiya, cuz.' Tariq's already there waiting for him with a message.

'My dad's disappeared,' Khalid types immediately. Tells him the whole story without quite believing it himself.

'I heard from my father,' Tariq replies. 'Everyone is so worried. They're saying the War on Terror is getting worse each day.' Tariq sends Khalid some links to online articles written in English, knowing he hasn't seen any newspapers he can read since he's been here.

'Why my dad, though? He's no one,' Khalid questions after scanning the reports.

'He's a man, isn't he, you dorkhead,' Tariq types. 'That's good enough reason for them.'

'I don't get it,' Khalid answers wearily, worried sick again.

'Come on. Log on to *Bomber One*. Your dad might be back by the time we finish this game,' Tariq says. 'The others are ready and waiting.'

Khalid eventually clicks through to the game, hoping for a simple distraction. The other players quickly line up their soldiers, moving them to the target points to start. The fighter planes shift into view. All the points from the last game are quickly calculated to the highest fraction before the battle begins.

Losing himself in the desire to win, Khalid types wildly. His fingers start tapping to the beat of the pictures on the screen until the keyboard appears to be playing the game on its own. Spontaneously battering every plane in sight. Using up bombs to bust the targets with effortless ease. Blasting the enemy's boats out of the water, power surges through Khalid with every explosion. Finally he's not thinking about anything else but the game and suddenly his mind feels lighter, despite the complicated scoring system.

At last, coming up for air, Khalid pauses to dash to the loo. Hurrying, jeans half zipped, he's determined to get back to the computer before it's his turn to man the rockets, when the front door swings open. Immediately excited and distracted, Khalid rushes back down the dark hall to the door. Surely only his dad could be coming through the door without knocking at this time of night?

But he's badly mistaken. Blocking the hallway is a gang of fierce-looking men dressed in dark shalwar kameez. Black cloths wrapped around their heads. Black gloves on their hands. Two angry blue eyes, the rest brown, burn into Khalid as the figures move towards him like cartoon gangsters with square bodies. Confused by the image, he staggers, bumping backwards into the wall. Arms up to stop them getting nearer. Too shocked and terrified to react as they shoulder him to the kitchen and close the door before pushing him to his knees and waving a gun at him as if he's a violent criminal. Then vice-like hands clamp his mouth tight until they plaster it with duct tape. No chance to wonder what the hell is going on, let alone scream out loud.

Stunned and shaking, Khalid feels his world slow down to a second-by-second terrible nightmare as they grab at his ankles and arms, handcuffing them tight before dropping a rag of a hood over his head. Then, without missing a beat, someone kicks him in the back, ramming his body flat on the floor. A heavy boot lands firmly on his spine, forcing Khalid to moan with muffled pain, while dust from the rug works its way inside his nose, making him sneeze uncontrollably through the threadbare hood. This simple reaction makes the strangers add a sharp thrum of boots to his side and a fiery agony explodes over Khalid's body as, stunned and shaken, he snorts desperately, trying to get air in through the tape stuck fast across his mouth.

*Dad. Dad*, Khalid pleads silently. This must be what happened to him. Khalid twists and turns, unable to breathe or scream or stop his heart from thumping. He recoils in terror as they lift him like a crate, hot fists on his legs and shoulders, and silently carry him out. Dumped in the back of an open truck, he groans as his face and body smash hard against the floor. The sudden movement of the truck jolts him from side to side its it drives off, the men breathing heavily and crowding over him with their smells of warm flesh and tobacco. Paralysed by fear, Khalid wonders desperately where they are taking him. Who are they? Why him? What for? Questions he can't even speak out loud.

The sounds of the city die away as the truck speeds along a potholed road that sends Khalid rolling across the truck in agony. He breathes in oil stains and the stench of animals, knocking his head on the uneven metal floor. A hefty boot kicks him back to the centre each time he slides their way. Pictures of his kidnapping flash quickly, one after the other, through his mind, building to an overwhelming fear that he's going to be dumped at the side of the road any second and left there to die.

\* \* \*

Khalid thinks the worst when the heavy-built guard with eyes like moons stops outside his cage before the first prayers are called, rattling keys. His hair, still damp from an early shower, smells strongly of almonds and he seems in a bad mood.

'Your head's covered in baby hair, dude,' he says.

'Done for, am I? How sad.' Khalid rubs the thin clumps of hair on his head to check they're still growing. 'What's up, then, eh?'

'You get your things,' he adds. 'And cut it.'

'You're moving me back. Great!' Khalid grabs his sheets of paper and pen, unsent scribbles, postcard and precious letter from Dad. Then his Qur'an, quickly checking the cage for anything he might have missed. Oh yeah, his flip-flops.

'We ain't got all day.' The guard tries to hurry him up, without any luck.

'Hang on, what did I do with my flat-screen TV and iPod?' So glad to get out of there, Khalid's larking around, busy pulling apart the diamond-shaped wire to prove he's left nothing behind. One man starts waving and laughing at his antics.

It's only when they're outside the cage that Khalid, his arms full of papers, begins to realise something strange is going on.

'You forgot the shackles,' he tells the guard. 'You're going to get into trouble now.'

'Is that right?' He smiles.

Walking normally is something Khalid's only done inside his cell or that time he went to the hospital because of his ear. Unable to do more than three and a half unrestrained steps in all from one end of his cell to the other since he came here, he's pigeon-toed now.

Khalid manages to nod goodbye to each man as he goes past with his small steps, walking weirdly like an old man. They greet him with affectionate *salaams* and questions in various languages, wondering where he's going without his chains. The same thought occurs to Khalid, but all he can do is wave and try to concentrate on not tripping over as he's led to a nearby block, put in a small room and left there.

'Hey, there's no water in here!' Khalid yells as the guard clicks the lock shut. The sound of heavy boots fades away, leaving him with nothing to do but sit on the blue chair, his stuff in his lap, and wait for someone to come.

With no air conditioning, the room is hot and sticky. Khalid stares at the desk and chair opposite him and listens to the sound of a door opening and closing. More footsteps. Trucks starting up outside. Dogs barking. The call to prayer begins. Surely they're not going to leave him here for much longer without water? The more he thinks about it, the more convinced he becomes that he's been brought here because Harry has demanded to see him. And if he has been told to bring his stuff, they must be taking him to another block afterwards. Maybe they're playing another psychological game with him. All Khalid knows is he's thirsty. There's been no breakfast or lunch and the chair he's sitting on is made of rough, itchy material that feels like carpet. The next time he hears footsteps, Khalid jumps up to bang on the door.

'Hey, where's my water? Where's my water?'

The door opens at last. A female soldier with deep-set dark eyes passes him a warm plastic bottle and then an amazing thing happens. She nods, saying, 'Sorry, you should have been given this earlier this morning!'

Unbelievable.

Khalid is so flabbergasted, he takes the bottle and just stands there staring at her. No one has ever, ever, ever said sorry to him since he was kidnapped. Except for Lee-Andy, of course. That one time, yeah.

When the door closes and he sits down to drink, Khalid also realises, for the first time, that he might, just might be getting this special treatment because he's got a lawyer to hear his complaints.

It's past midnight when two guards come to take him away. One scoops up his Qur'an, papers and pen, the other clicks the shackles into place with unnecessary force. Khalid's eaten nothing since yesterday and he's feeling dizzy from the heat, so he doesn't care where he's going, but he's shocked they've taken all this trouble merely to walk him ten paces down the corridor to a room similar to the one he's just left.

Only this time two hot-shot American military men in smart uniform are waiting for him.

'I'm Major Donaldson. This is Major Leeth,' says the first man, holding out a palm to introduce the more important-looking man standing beside him. Both eye Khalid as if he's another nuisance they can't wait to get rid of, while the guard at the door watches his every move.

'We're here to tell you, number 256 …' Major Donaldson pauses.

Khalid shivers. *What? What?*

'You're,' Major Leeth butts in, 'yes, you're going home!'

'What?' Khalid swoons, going hot and cold at the same time. Overwhelmed as the length and breadth of Rochdale flashes before his eyes. Is this for real?

'You'll be given a bag for your things. Follow the guard.' Major Donaldson nods.

'That's all you've got to say?' Khalid narrows his eyes. 'That's the lamest thing I've ever heard.' This idiot is clearly a robot. He's no use as a major, that's for sure. 'How come you're letting me go all of a sudden? Are they going to put me in prison in England? Go on, tell me!'

'Let's just say you're no longer considered a threat,' Major Donaldson replies.

'You're the threat, mate, not me. I'm going to sue you for all of this. Just so you know,' Khalid says.

'I think you'll find you were never arrested,' Major Leeth tells him, smirking.

'No, that's right, I was kidnapped, wasn't I? You suckers better apologise for torturing me.'

At this, the guard grabs his shoulder to push him outside.

'Wait. I need to say goodbye to someone first,' Khalid begs. 'Please can I?'

'Take him directly to the exit gate.' Major Donaldson hands the guard a sealed brown envelope and closes the door.

'Thanks for nothing!' Khalid yells, elbowing the guard away. Two years' worth of anger in his eyes.

'Hey, man,' the guard says, trying to calm him down, not quite understanding. He raises his eyebrows. 'Be OK, you'll see.'

'Yeah, if they're telling the truth.' A number of conflicting emotions pass through Khalid as they walk out of the building. What are they up to now? Where's he going? How's he going to get home? Will anyone believe him? The idea of no longer being bound by shackles, barbed wire, soldiers, feels too frightening to imagine. Free? What does that mean?

Day after day he'd pictured being back in Rochdale — at home with his family and friends, at college, with Niamh even — but he'd never actually imagined walking out of here one day.

'I don't know where to go. I haven't got any money.' Khalid shudders.

'You're not done yet.' The guard smiles. 'Don't worry.'

'Look, will you do me a favour?'

This time the guard eyes him suspiciously. 'Depends what you want.'

'Find number 372. Tell him about me going. Say I won't stop trying until he's free too. Will you do that for me, man?' Khalid begs, desperate to let Tariq know what's happening.

* * *

'And now, this fine young man, Khalid Ahmed, who's been to hell and back in the last two years, has agreed to read out the letter he sent me from his cell in Guantanamo Bay. It was the only one among the many letters he wrote to me that arrived here for me to read. As you know, Guantanamo Bay is situated on the south-east corner of the island of Cuba …'

A group of teachers behind him shift in their chairs. Some with drooping, tired faces and untidy hair look half asleep, while others with eager eyes and polished shoes lean forward to listen.

Finally, Mr Tagg stops talking and nods for Khalid to get up from the seat at the side of the stage, which causes him to stop fiddling with his shirt cuffs and break out in a nervous sweat.

Scraping his chair back, Khalid looks down at the sea of faces watching him walk towards the microphone, the letter in his hand. Breathing heavily, heart thumping faster the closer he gets, Khalid becomes irritated with himself for shaking so much as he grabs the microphone. Seeing most of the kids he used to play football with all looking up at him now as if he's a hero, thinking because they know him they understand what he's been through, Khalid is suddenly put off. And all the time he's scanning the crowd for Niamh's pretty face, longing for it to jump out at him. To see her is all he wants now, her brown, wavy hair flicking up from her neck. The memory of her smile hypnotises Khalid for a second, blanking his mind completely. Now, two long years later, someone who looks a bit like her is smiling up at him from the front row and he knows she means nothing by it because she isn't Niamh.

Mr Tagg rushes to the microphone to cover for him while Khalid's heart and mind are lost in the memory of Niamh's pretty face — an image that has helped him make it to this point.

'Ahem. One. Two. Yes, it's fine. Go ahead, Khalid. Go on, lad. Speak.'

Then Nico, in the back row, suddenly cheers. Everyone turns to look at him, which makes Khalid laugh and gives him a moment's pause before he starts.

'Dear Mr Tagg,' Khalid begins shyly, voice trembling. 'I thought I'd let you know why I didn't finish my history coursework.' A raucous laugh rises from the hall resulting in a sudden burst of confidence. The second the noise dies down, Khalid clears his throat and lays into the letter again.

'It's a bit of a long story and beggars can't be choosers, as the man said. I asked my dad to fill you in about all the lies they've made up about me here so I won't go into that now. But I know one thing — even if I am an evil person that doesn't mean someone has the right to try and drown me by hanging me upside down and pouring water down my nose. They've beaten me. They've kicked me. They've bolted me to the floor like an animal. They've kept me awake night after night. Almost burst my eardrums with loud music. Some are suffering worse things than me, they've been badly damaged in so many ways you don't want to know, and my cousin Tariq is here too. They've put the finger on me for no reason is what I'm saying and I'll never understand why.'

A rumble of murmuring and spate of shuffling fill the hall as kids twist in their seats to catch every word. Shock, horror, disbelief passes over their surprised faces while Khalid takes a quick breath before continuing.

'Hurt is hurt. Harm is harm. Bullying is bullying. What everyone wants is the same thing — kindness. I'd like to see more kindness when I get out of here, because I'm sick of hearing about bombs and seeing pictures of people dying and terrorists doing this and that. I'm just a kid who wants to get A-levels and go to uni and make something of himself. I don't want to hang around waiting for someone to give me anything, but I do want to see the snow blowing over Rochdale again and get a game of footy going down the park with my mates. That's something I dream about every day locked up in Guantanamo. I hope you can help me get started again one day, that's if they ever let me go.

'I know one day, Mr Tagg, you will ask me what I've learned. Well, if I could advise anyone out there, I'd say the only way to prevent violence is to stop being violent, stop thinking nasty thoughts about other people. Stop hurting other people. Stop lying and cheating. How come the world doesn't get that? One day I'd like to go to Mount Snowdon in Wales or to the Lake District or out walking in one of those pretty villages with nice stone cottages in the Dales. I'd love to have that freedom. But you know what? I haven't got the nerve to go there because people might stare at me and the woman in the shop will maybe get her husband to serve me because she's scared.

'There're woods and streams and fields and nice places in England my family have never seen because people are so suss of anyone who looks different. When people do that, I shrink up, trying not to look like a wacko. I hide my face by pretending to find a shop or pavement that's interesting.

'I'm writing this because I would never have the nerve to say this stuff to your face. Yeah, and sorry about not having spellcheck and that to do this properly. Bet you a million pounds this won't get to you at the school anyway. By the way, you ought really to stop smoking. I've seen you light up two fags before you get to the main road.

'I've been a regular blatherer, I know. Sorry. I just want to get back and stop in my house, eat some decent food and see my mates. I suppose the main thing I've learned is that hatred changes nothing. It just adds to the hatred that's already there. The person who's hated has the choice to ignore it, while the hater is always overtaken by his violent feelings. So who's the loser? It's the person who hurts every time, who lies and cheats, and I'm never going to be like that, because then I'll have learned nothing.

'Yours sincerely,

'Khalid Ahmed (10G) (from two years ago)'

The minute he finishes, the hall erupts with cheering and clapping. Nico starts whistling, then shouting, 'Close down GUAN-TAN-AMO!' And then another burst of cheering, clapping, whistling and foot-stomping breaks out. Rocking the school hall until everyone joins in. Even a few of the staff.

'Close down GUAN-TAN-AMO!' The sound hits the roof, bouncing off the walls as Khalid returns to his seat. Shaking. Mr Tagg anxiously flaps his hands to calm them, while proudly nodding at his former student.

'Well read, Khalid. Well done. Thank you!' But his voice is drowned out by another burst of stamping feet.

'Words aren't enough,' Khalid whispers. Tired of everyone getting high on their own righteousness. Refusing to allow his heart to swell in case he starts sinking. In case he starts forgetting how to let go. Something no one else in the room will ever understand. How can he be blown away by the sound of their chanting? Their words are too far outside the hell he suffered.

Leaving the stage with Mr Tagg's arm round his shoulder, Khalid catches sight of a pretty girl smiling at him. A picture that lights up his mind for many days to come.

Prayer for the Strengthening Alliance and the Deepening Split.

God save us from the bad guys

God save us from the good guys

God save us from the madness

That carves up the world

Into us guys and them guys.

Leunig

# What we eat

*by Gary Crew*

It is 6.45 pm.

It is dinner time.

The mother takes a pizza from the oven.

It is a store-bought pizza.

The label on the box reads,

'OUR BRAND: CHICKEN AND ANCHOVY'.

The television is on.

The television screen shows a cartoon.

There is a teenage boy in a lounge chair in front of
the television.

He is a big boy.

He has a chocolate biscuit in his left hand.

He has a packet of chocolate biscuits in his right
hand.

He is watching the television.

'These biscuits are stale,' he announces.

'You should get a refund.'

The mother is setting the table behind the boy.

She puts the pizza on a blue plate on a red gingham
   cloth.

There are three white plates on the table.

The mother takes a bottle of Coke from the
   refrigerator.

She reaches for a glass.

'Put the biscuits away now,' she says.

'Your father is due any minute.'

The cartoon disappears.

Some political story is now on the screen.

It is a news clip about trouble,

Someplace ...

People with black skins are shouting.

There are guns.

There is sand —

desert, maybe.

The boy gets up.

He stuffs the remainder of the biscuit into his mouth.

He leaves the open packet on the lounge.

'Bring that packet over here,' the mother says.

'The dog will get it if you leave it there.'

'The dog can have it,' the boy says.

'Sit down and eat your pizza,' the mother says.

   'Your father is late.'

The boy looks at the empty box on the stove-top,

then at the pizza on the blue plate on the table.

'I hate pizza with anchovies,' he says. 'It tastes like
     shit.
You can give that to the dog too.'
The mother looks at the television screen.
She sees the ad with the black people and the guns
     and the desert.
She sees there are children in this place.
'Those black kids would eat it,' she says.
'Then mail it to them,' he says,
     opening the refrigerator.

# The two-month turnaround

*by Rose Foster*

**Week one**

'I ask new volunteers, before we get down to business, why they're here.' The coordinator took a seat at the table, a crudely carved slab on four tree stumps, sanded down and glossed with varnish. Half a dozen long-winged flies were making a meal out of a grain of rice wedged in a crack in the wood. I averted my eyes. Foul. Were they even flies? I'd never seen insects like these before. Or the sort caught in the spider web in the lamp shade above us, or the type dead in little clusters under the table. I caught sight of an ant making a bid for my big toe. It was red and I killed it beneath my sandal before it could get any further.

'So?'

I looked up at the coordinator, an American man, tanned, and badly in need of a haircut.

'What inspired you to come here?'

Inspired? Oh God. So that was the tone of this place. You had to have been *inspired* to come here. I took a swift look at the dirt road at the end of the path. The bus I arrived on had well and truly disappeared. It'd be back tomorrow, surely.

'Yeah, you know,' I muttered. 'Wanted to do something different. Something ...' A girl in cargo pants was collecting fallen mangoes in my line of vision. 'Something helpful.'

A complete lie. This was the lesser of two evils. A recommendation, rather than a moment of inspiration. A choice, even. I could do this, or I could sit in an office with mass-produced furniture and think of more random introspections to feed to people for two months.

'Right,' said Sam, the coordinator. 'Well, you're on elephants. Ever been around an elephant?'

'Excuse me?'

'That's a no,' he said. 'We'll get the tour out of the way now.'

To the right of the volunteer house, an open-air hut with a kitchen and another varnished table, were a number of massive enclosures, not on the ground but on stilts, set high into the trees. I shuddered. Monkeys.

'These are gibbons,' Sam explained. A horrific creature with black skin and orange fur jerked its squashed face to look down at me. It had long arms and fingers, and sat crouched on its legs, clutching onto a trapeze dangling from the wire ceiling of its home. It gave a curious hoot, a sound I wasn't expecting it to produce. It seemed like the sort of animal that would screech.

'They'll do that,' Sam said. 'They sound like owls, or sirens. Nothing in between.'

'Sirens?' I asked.

'Yeah, you'll know exactly what I mean tomorrow morning. They start early. These guys will never be released back into the wild; they don't how to look after themselves. They'll be here for the rest of their lives.'

The next wire tree house held a black version of the same beast. It, too, studied me for a few seconds from its wooden perch, before diving for the floor of its enclosure with a crash and baring its teeth. I stumbled backward, terrified.

'He's a boy, so he already hates you. We only let the girls look after him.'

'Great,' I said. I'd been there half an hour, and already had an enemy.

'They've all been rescued,' Sam told me later. 'The bears are from bear bile factories. They pump the bile from their stomachs, but they keep them alive for it for years in cages barely big enough to hold them. Apparently bile has medicinal properties. The gibbons and macaques were pets, or props for tourists to have photos with. Some come from circuses. The elephants are from camps. Six tourists on their backs, ten hours a day. She has a dip in her back, see it?'

We stood on an open plain at the back of the centre, far from the other volunteers, well away from the hoots and shrieks and caws of the other animals. An elephant stood in her own enclosure, so old her grey skin was beginning to whiten. Her face was marked with pink lines — scars, I guessed — and Sam was right; there was a cavity in her back where there should have been a ridge.

'She's our oldest. She the one who's spent her entire life in a camp, until we brought her here.'

'And them?'

Three more female elephants resided in an enclosure down the hill.

'Two were street elephants. More tourist riding, but from the city. They're more volatile. The third's from a camp.'

He led me down the hill.

'Our two babies.' He gestured toward a slightly smaller enclosure, where two elephants, mini in comparison to the ones he'd just shown me, were together by their massive water trough. The smaller of the two was swaying from side to side, its ears flapping, its trunk curling.

'Cool,' I said. 'He's dancing.'

'All these elephants have experienced something called phajaan,' Sam said. His arms were crossed, and there was an edge to his voice. 'Translates literally to "crush". It's when an elephant's owner breaks its spirit through torture when it's a calf. It's strung up in chains, denied food and water, taught to fear pain and obey its owner's commands. It's brutal. He's dancing because he's been crushed. They all have. His owner taught him that if he dances, tourists will be delighted, his owner will get money, and he won't be harmed. He learned that notion through fear. We're trying to discourage it, so we don't reward the dancing. Maybe don't call it "cool", okay?'

'Okay,' I said, annoyed. How was I supposed to know that without being told?

Sam strode off.

'I've put you in room 8,' he said. 'You don't have a roommate.'

## Week two

I've realised I want to go home. Every day I wake up at six in the morning to the siren calls of the gibbons. I climb into a tractor and ride into the jungle on the steel seat of the tractor tray to find the elephants from their night spots beyond their enclosures. Every morning I find this more and more unnecessary. Why not just keep them in their enclosures overnight? What's the point in moving them for just a few hours? They'll only have to come back anyway.

I don't like the other volunteers. Three guys and two girls. They've been here for a while. They seem to enjoy every moment in the pelting rain, every second in the sun. They know the elephants' names and have in-jokes from two weeks ago and run around laughing when we're forced to go on harvest. Harvest is maybe the worst thing I've ever experienced. They drag us out to a field and slash down banana trees. It's our job to heave these logs of sap onto our shoulders and haul them back onto a truck. This goes on for hours. I get banana tree sap in places where banana tree sap doesn't belong just to bring it all back and watch the elephants chew through it in two days flat. Then its harvest time again. Between that, there's cleaning out the enclosures. Which means elephant shit. Lots and lots of it. I hate it here.

### Week three

'What you doing?'

The girl in cargo pants was observing me from the smokers' table between the volunteer houses. She was alone, between chores, and had been watching me for a while.

'Uh, a broom,' I said, distractedly. 'I need a broom.'

She wasn't smoking. She was just sitting. Go collect your mangoes, I thought angrily.

'What for?'

'For sweeping.'

'Sweeping what?'

'I left the light on in my bathroom overnight,' I said, as annoyed at myself as I was with her. The bathrooms were open air. 'I need to sweep up the moths.'

The tiles were completely obscured by a blanket of the insects, all dead, all stewing in the couple of millimetres of water left over from my freezing shower the previous night.

'Here,' she said. She left the table, went to the nearest tree and stuck her hand in a hollow at its base. She extracted two fat, flabby toads and brought them toward me. They struggled in her grip, little legs writhing from between her fingers. I backed away.

'What are you —?'

'You're in 8, yeah?' she said. She entered my room without asking. I followed her. She dropped the toads in the bathroom and shut the door.

'Put them back in their tree in a few hours.'

That afternoon, all but a couple of the dead moths had disappeared. I needed gloves to bring myself to grab the engorged toads and return them. I wasn't sure if I was more revolted or impressed with the girl.

'Do you know what to do about these?'

This time she was in a bear enclosure, by herself, scrubbing the walls of a drained-out pool where the animals usually whiled away their time. The two black bears were quarantined in their side enclosure. One was watching her scrape the filth away, the other was clawing at the scar across its stomach. The scrubbing brush stilled.

'What?' she asked, blinking at me in the glare in the mid-afternoon sun.

I showed her my leg. Three mosquito bites had gone white. They were beginning to put out pus.

'Infections?' she asked. To her credit, she didn't look sickened by the sight of them.

'Yeah.'

She threw down the brush and got to her feet.

'Let me wash my hands,' she said.

She dumped a tiny canister on the table at the volunteer house. It was between meals, and the other volunteers were on cleaning duties of their own. She opened the canister and showed me the yellowish goo inside.

'Tiger balm,' she explained. 'You can get antibiotics from the chemist in the village.'

'The chemist in the village stocks antibiotics?' I asked.

'Of course,' she said. She tossed her blonde rope of hair over her shoulder, and looked very much like she was trying not to smile. 'For us and our precious skin and weak immune systems. The locals don't need them like we do.'

'Right,' I said, taking the balm from her. The instant it was applied my flesh seemed to cool.

She took some of her own on her finger and glossed it over a gash on her hand.

'God, that's awful,' I said, staring at it. A scab was forming, thick and black.

'Mmm,' she agreed. 'Macaque got me during feeding time.'

I suppressed my shudder, and could almost feel the monkey's unnaturally long fingernail scraping at my own skin as I took in the cut.

'Don't you kinda hate them?'

'Hate them?'

'You're just trying to give it its food,' I muttered bitterly. I rubbed in more tiger balm. The cooling effect was short lived. 'You're just doing it a favour, and the stupid thing thanks you with that.'

'I think you might be looking at this the wrong way,' she said softly.

**Week four**

New volunteers came in today. Two girls, who arrived together but didn't know each other. I was shovelling elephant shit out of an enclosure when they came by on their tour and they gave me a pitying look. I found I didn't care and turned back to shovelling, skin browning in the sun, sweat dribbling down my back.

In the corner of the enclosure the baby boy was swaying on the spot, watching me hopefully out of one glossy brown eye.

'Don't,' I said. His dancing jumped in tempo when he realised he had my attention. I was aware, quite suddenly, that it was one of the saddest things I'd ever seen. 'It's not going to happen. You'll get food later. So stop dancing.'

The two new girls were struggling, and I was enjoying it. They complained about the cold showers, and the giant geckos in their room. They bitched about scrubbing out scungy water troughs, and lugging barrels of papaya and lychees to the nocturnals, and eating local food night after night. I wondered if anyone enjoyed watching me struggle my first week. Carly, the girl in cargo pants, probably had.

The truth was, I was still struggling, only now I'd leaned into it. I wondered how long it would take them.

One of the new girls was bone thin and so pale her face had grey undertones. I knew she was on some sort of recovery thing like me. I didn't have any plans to talk to her. I was making my way here, wading into the manual labour and staying there, enjoying the physical strain of my chores and the first jolt of my cold shower each night.

**Week five**

I uncoiled a hose and stuck it through the fencing around the enclosure. One of the female elephants turned her trunk upward and found the stream. She sucked the water away, and then curled her trunk inward to deliver it into her mouth. She watched me throughout the process, and returned her trunk to the hose.

'More?' I asked.

I wondered if she found me pathetic. Of course she wanted more. It was the hottest day so far, and I'd selfishly forgotten to come down and offer her water until now. After her last drink she let me fill her trunk and then tossed the water over herself to wash the grit and perspiration off her back.

I was turning to go when I felt her tap my arm through the fencing.

'I thought you were done,' I said, and returned the hose. But it wasn't water she wanted. I scratched the back of my neck.

'Hold on.'

I bent to grab a spotty mango from the ground. She plucked it from my hand, ate it whole and ambled away, limping as she did. She was one of the street elephants from the city. She'd been hit by a car there years ago.

'Okay,' I said. 'Mangoes. Got it.'

## Week six

'Pineapple plants?' one of the new girls complained. She stuck out her hand. A dozen tiny needles dotted her palm. 'Oh my God!'

We were deep in a valley an hour from the centre, grabbing the serrated fleshy leaves and yanking the plants from the ground. It was hard work, and gloves were required. The new girl hadn't brought them. She spent the rest of the expedition sulking against the truck as we worked, picking the needles from her hand. I neglected to tell her the switch from banana trees to pineapple plants had been my idea.

'Eating the same thing every day would get old fast,' I told Sam over dinner. It was the third night in a row for green curry. I didn't mind. 'A bit of variety could be good.'

Sam considered the idea, looking impressed. I was annoyed by it. He didn't need to be impressed. I hadn't said anything groundbreaking. A storm had cut the power in the volunteer house and we were eating dinner in the dark. The glow from someone's mobile phone reflected off our cutlery. I squinted at his plate.

'Sam,' I said, as he shovelled some rice into his mouth, 'I think a fly just flew into your food.'

'And?'

'And you just ate it.'

He shrugged.

'Protein,' he said. 'We can organise variety tomorrow.'

Yanking pineapple plants from the ground was considerably more work than lifting banana trees. I had remembered gloves, but not long pants, and I was walking around with dozens of the fine needles sticking out of my legs. They seemed to fit in well with the scars from my infections and the assorted scrapes and bruises that had accumulated there and so I didn't worry about it. I'd get them out later. A giant centipede scurried out from under my sandal and for a moment I wanted to catch the thing and drop it into the new girl's lap. I didn't, only because I knew centipedes could sting.

**Week seven**

I went down to the nocturnals today for no other reason than to see them. Next week was my last. I'd heard the other volunteers raving about some creature called a slow loris, and didn't want to leave before I got the chance to rave too. I'd never seen one before. Carly was down there, standing beside a shady enclosure with a tree inside, talking to a little ball of fluff clinging to the wire.

'He's my favourite,' she told me, and pushed a slice of apple into the loris's fingers. It was a tiny tree-dwelling animal, with huge eyes and a sweet little nose. It moved in slow motion. Carly stuck her fingers into the enclosure, and scratched its stomach. The little thing closed its eyes, and stayed perfectly still, adoring the contact.

'He was a tourist prop too.' She removed her fingers, and the loris opened its eyes, disappointed. She soothed it with another bit of apple. 'They used to put him in a doll's dress. Stick him on tourists' shoulders for photos all day. He's nocturnal. His eyes are damaged by daylight. He's partially blind now.'

The top of his home was piled with palm leaves.

'Are you here for some reason?' I asked her.

She grinned.

'What, like Eliza?' She was referring to the new girl, the bone-thin one who complained too much. 'Like you?'

I didn't mind that she knew I wasn't here because I was a good person, because I'd decided I wanted to help.

'I came here for the wrong reasons,' she admitted freely. 'I wanted to feel like I was the best person I knew. I wanted my friends to admire me for doing something as intense as coming to the middle of nowhere and volunteering with rescued wildlife.'

Another bit of apple, another stomach scratch.

'At some point — I don't know when — what my friends thought, what I even thought, didn't really matter.'

The scab on her hand was coming away from the new pink skin beneath. It had healed well. She caught me looking at it.

'I can help myself,' she said. 'I can change things if I want, do what I feel like, go wherever I want. These guys can't. That macaque doesn't understand gratitude. Why should he? Why is he supposed to give a damn about me, or how long it would take my hand to heal? I didn't do anything wrong, and he hurt me for it. Then again, he's never done anything wrong, and he's been punished his whole life.'

## Week eight

I don't want to go. I'm beginning to think this was the wrong choice. Maybe that room with its mass-produced furniture would've been the right idea after all. That way I could wake up late in the morning and pick at a piece of toast and feel completely justified in my habits. There was still work to be done here. A reason to get up that was so much bigger than myself.

Carly left yesterday. She hugged me and chucked her bag in the bus and disappeared down the dirt track. She cried, but she wasn't unhappy.

I desperately wanted to tell her I was looking at things the right way now, but she'd already moved onto her goodbyes with another volunteer, and I knew it should only matter to me anyway.

This morning, I got in the tractor and went out to find the elephants and no part of it struck me as unnecessary. How boring it must be, I realised, to exist in the same enclosure, the same spot, every moment of the day.

# Nui Dat: Australian Task Force headquarters

*by Libby Hathorn*

The young woman
being led away for interrogation
with her heart-shaped face
and sweep of dark hair,
looks like an old school friend.

What would they do to her?
How would they make her,
captive as she is in that place
that is her country,
Captive, say what it is they
want to hear her say?

The young man beside her
except for the glaze
in his young soldier eyes,

who holds her arm so lightly,
could be leading her somewhere,
kindly.
It's permissible to think,
in some other time, soon,
could be bending to embrace
the girl with the heart-shaped face,
familiar like a school friend.
But something is shining in his eyes:
anticipation, victory, duty,
and in hers,
and there is something terrible
not of their doing
between them.

# From the shadows

*by Graeme Base*


A world of ashes, leached of life.
The colours swept away.
A paradise lies lost beneath
A shroud of ashen grey.

And yet in time the veil will fall
The streams once more will flow
And from the shadows 'tween the trees
New life will surely grow.

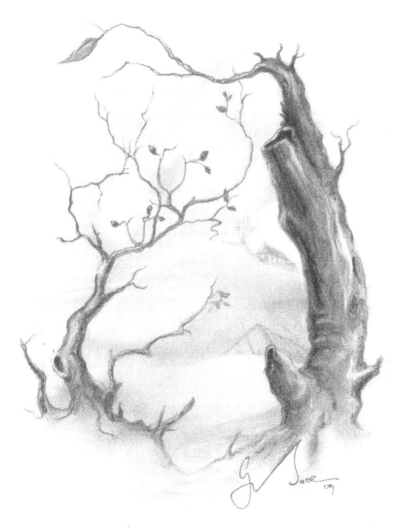

"FROM THE SHADOWS"

# The pain is never over

*David Nyuol Vincent*

*While the rest of the children in the world were playing with toys, I was busy playing with an AK-47, the only toy I knew during my entire childhood.*

I lay on my back on the new mattress provided to me when I first arrived in Melbourne, staring up at the ceiling. It was very difficult to hold back the thoughts flowing through my mind. I tossed my skinny body back and forth, trying to find a comfortable position so I could rest. More than twenty years of memories started to come back. It was as if I was watching a horror movie in which I played the lead. It was painful but I wasn't able to stop it. I couldn't find a stop button. I tried to cover my face, which made it even worse. I wanted to scream but I was afraid — afraid of not knowing what to say if asked what was wrong with me. My whole body felt as if it was on fire. What was happening to me? I wondered for a moment if I was possessed by demons. Why now? I was better off in the refugee camp, I thought. This never happened to me there. I tried hard to stop myself from going deeper. The more I tried the worse it became.

That was the first time. From then on, I was in nightly torment. Because I worried what my roommates would think of me, I kept to myself and tried different things to disengage my brain from the flashbacks. I tried many things: I sang, I jumped, I ate and I switched on the television. I even took off the fire alarm that was right above my bed, thinking it could be the cause of my disturbances. I showered with really hot water and nearly scalded my body; I tried cold water. Nothing gave me the comfort and peace of mind I craved.

For nearly two weeks I tried to figure out what to do with this new development in my life. I was raised to endure any sort of pain, but this particular pain was too much to bear. It was an internal pain, a result of memories stored away. Now they were back to haunt me. I could see it and feel it but I couldn't do anything about it. I could see my friend Jacob in his last days in the refugee camp trying hard to remain alive. I could visualise all the military drills we went through during our training days. I remembered the trainer stepping hard on my back, pressing me to the ground and calling me names. I remembered dragging our comrades to the cemetery each morning to bury them. And I remembered coming back the following morning to find the hyenas had dug up them up again. The debris of their bodies was everywhere. I blamed myself for not giving my friends a decent burial but I was a child and weak. I remembered the times when we had nothing to eat and were forced to steal from the locals. I remembered the days when we had to live under the bunkers for protection from aerial bombardment and only crawled out in the evening to find something to eat. I remembered I was once reduced to believing we were cursed by God. I even believed that we were lesser humans.

No one spoke to me about these things prior to my arrival in Australia. I thought I was going to start over. I wanted so much not to be reminded of my previous life. I thought my past belonged to me and it belonged to the refugee camp. But now I was being haunted. I carried with me all the memories and flew miles and miles until I got to Australia. Since I was eight years old, I had been a responsible child looking after myself. I had been raised to be tough and to confront things as they came. But I couldn't find a name for what was happening to me. I couldn't even describe it — could only express it through the pain I was experiencing. I was fighting a battle in unfamiliar territory. During the day I would be just fine. The moment the dark approached I would be reminded of the hours of sleepless nights. Deep down in my heart I wanted to give in and ask for help. My worry was I couldn't even name what was troubling me. I was ashamed to even think about it. To me this was close to going crazy. I thought I was just moments away from stripping and running around naked.

During one of our regular catch-ups my support worker finally noticed that I was yawning and looking restless. She asked if I was getting enough sleep. I nearly opened up but then I dodged the subject and that was it. I was disappointed with myself for not being courageous enough to speak out. After that, I thought if I wasn't going to talk to anyone about it I might as well find a solution to the problem. I thought I had to play two versions of myself: there was me as David, and there was another me as an elder who assumed the role of advising — or call it 'counselling' — me. I threw myself into activities: playing soccer, hanging out with my friends, reading books. This helped to occupy all my time. I kept myself busy and that was the only way that I managed to cope with my trauma. The support needed to deal with a condition such as mine was available, but I had no idea how to access it.

Although I haven't spoken about this for many years until now, I wonder how many refugees have come to this country and have had to go through what I experienced. At first I felt unwelcome — not because anything was said to me but because everything felt strange and I saw myself not fitting in. I wanted familiar territory. Despite the glamorous life available here in Australia, it wasn't what I needed. I just wanted a simple refugee life. A life where I had to struggle to find food to eat and clean water to drink. A life where I would not know if I'd live to see tomorrow; a life filled with uncertainties. That was the life I was familiar with and wanted back. People would wonder why, when Australia can give you all you need? Yes, indeed it is true that when I came to this country I was presented with everything, more than I wanted. I felt life was too easy here: just by the click of a button you could have almost anything you wanted. I wasn't used to that at all. Would that be the reason why I was not uncovering my past?

At the camp we drank, cooked and washed with water from the nearby river. Imagine how many people died as a result of waterborne diseases. Imagine if someone told us to boil all our drinking water first —a simple solution that would have saved lives. This knowledge isn't rocket science. It's the same thing with the flashbacks: I was traumatised and I didn't want to believe it because I didn't know what it was. No one talked about it and I thought it would be shameful to tell people. Instead I wasted time trying to cure it. Imagine if information about how to deal with trauma was readily available to refugees as they arrived. It would make life much easier.

The more I was exposed to the beauty of this country and the opportunities that were presented to me, the more I started to embrace it and make the best of it. I have shouldered the pain from my past and it is now time for me to let go. The moment I arrived in Australia I wanted to become a better person so I could help others in a similar situation. It is time to give back.

I lost my childhood but I have no regrets. I now find joy in helping others and I forgive all those who in one way or another caused us such unbearable pain.

# wikipedia leaks war list by death toll*

*by Janine Fraser*

### for samantha

war in the news making headline the headcount
two thousand american our thirty-nine
our bright and shining tallied like medal
our ran the good race our fought good for right
out for the count now their number called up
flag folded on coffin last post sound of night-fall
the bloods of their poppies spatter the wall —it's just

war and my daughter is asking who's naming
who's counting their dead how many of theirs are
struck down in their streets in terror for terror
red shredded limbs in shelled shells of houses
ravaged by bomb-blast savaged by shrapnel
three million dead in the soviet trouble
two million more now afghanistan rubble — it's just

war and my daughter prints off the numbers
the columns of figures black leak of horror
long list of wars by death toll by long bow
by arrow and sword by draw and no quarter by
un-given inch for the pinch of an acre
by land mine by u-boat by hail down the sky
by mud in the fox-hole flesh rotting alive — it's just

war she figures killed millions killed millions
her hands laying shield on the round of her belly
the dead mounting up by nice rounded number
one hundred million the tai ping rebellion
thirty the ming twenty-five in the quing
sixty by horde of mongolian marauder
seven undone by napoleons order — it's just

wars of religion waged *bellum sacrum*
the go by the good book god blessed crusaders
converted by sword three bloody million
while the pious of france the right mighty of rome
for sake of the son under sign of their cross
in name of the father made holy slaughter
fifteen million of brother and daughter — it's just

war the first world tolled sixty-five million
dispatched by the bullet the weather the flu
then seventy snatched by the horrors of two

vietnam six million three million korea
more in the congo more in sudan
paraguay mexico iraq iran
thirteen million racked up between them — it's just

war from the garden to wars of the roses
clansmen and tribesmen for unlike of other
good neighbour and brother in red coat and blue
    coat
turning civil uncivil in wrest of a nation
revoltings rebellions military coups
overlord overthrows overkill bill
spilled oceans to raise his flag on the hill — it's just

war down the ages to news page today
millions of dead crying out from the ground
hear sound of the millions killed millions killed
    millions
crying for future crying for children
for mother with hands on the round of her belly
for unborn folded like hope in a bottle
floating towards the blood-soaked shore.

*Wikipedia: 'List of wars and anthropogenic
    disasters by death toll'

*Author's note*

This poem was written in September 2012 after a further five Australian soldiers were killed in Afghanistan, bringing the number of Australians killed in the current conflict to thirty-nine at that time. My daughter wondered about the Afghani death toll, and in a search came across the Wikipedia article, 'List of wars and anthropogenic disasters by death toll'. The list cites both a lowest and a highest estimate, but for the purposes of the poem, the highest estimate has been used. The list itself is by no means complete, but total of the highest estimates puts the number at around 500,000,000 killed by war in approximately 1,800 years.

# Just a schoolgirl

*by Rosanne Hawke*

A girl once asked me if my parents sweep the streets and gutters like most Christians. If that was what the other girls thought of me, it's no wonder they didn't speak to me. They would be afraid of getting diseases. Maybe they thought I cleaned rich people's latrines after school. I have seen poor Christian people do these menial tasks down at the bazaar, but my mother went to school, perhaps not for as long as my father but they both had respectable jobs. We lived in a small Christian village out of the town. My father brought me to school in his rickshaw, found passengers during the day, and took me home after school. My mother cleaned for a good Muslim family. When I started high school this year, however, she couldn't help me with my homework. Arabic and Islamic Studies were the worst. I tried but Mrs Abdul was always reprimanding me. It was as if she knew I was going to get it wrong.

'Aster, didn't you do your homework, you stupid girl?' She hit me over the ear and my glasses fell onto the desk.

'*Ji*, yes, Miss.' I was careful to sound respectful. 'I my best.' I wanted to say I never grew up with Arabic, never heard my father read the Quran aloud like other girls in the class. I was told different stories in Punjabi. Even my Injeel, New Testament, is printed in Urdu. Abu reads it after we've eaten at night, before Ummie and I clean the dishes and he watches a drama on TV.

'It is not enough, lazy girl. If you did your homework properly you would understand the lesson today.'

A few of the girls sniggered as I replaced my glasses, blinking too much. I rarely show my feelings; I've spent too long keeping my head down, not giving anyone reason to take issue with me. When I glanced up I saw Rabia watching me with pity in her eyes. I look like them, though my skin is darker; I wear a scarf too, but I have a name no Muslim girl in the school has. I was named after a Jewish girl who married a Persian king. At the time, Jews were a minority in Persia and she saved them from annihilation.

At lunch time, Rabia sought me out. I was eating leftover curry and rice from my three-tiered lunch tin. 'Aster, I'm sorry about what happened in class. Mrs Abdul will always be upset with you because you are the only Christian and you haven't said the Kalima.'

I swallowed my mouthful in a rush. 'The principal assured my parents I wouldn't have to convert to attend school.' I sighed. 'I wish I didn't have to do Islamic Studies — it's mostly Arabic and I will never manage the answers that Mrs Abdul wants.'

Rabia sat beside me. 'Why don't you say the Kalima for her? All you have to do is say "There is only one God and Muhammad is his messenger". Say it in Arabic and it won't mean a thing. Then she will stop bothering you.'

My breaths grew short and fast. 'I couldn't. Certainly, I believe there is one God, but I can't say that about Muhammad. Yesu Masih is the last prophet. He's the son of —'

'*Chup*! Quiet!' Rabia cut me off and checked behind us. 'Don't say that here. It will be misunderstood and you could be accused of blasphemy.'

'But I'm only saying what I believe. I'm not meaning to blaspheme.'

'All the same, be more careful.'

I decided the kindness in her eyes was genuine. 'Why do you care?'

Rabia stuck her bottom lip between her teeth and shifted closer. 'My father wasn't always Muslim. He was a Christian like you, but he couldn't get a good job. He was offered land, and money to build a house on it if he said the Kalima.'

I had no words to say; I just stared at her. Was my father capable of something like that?

'You mightn't understand,' she said as she sat back a little, 'but he did it for us, for his family. My brother is in university now. My father works in an office instead of some menial job. I will have a good marriage.' Then she narrowed her eyes at me. 'You won't tell?'

I shook my head. 'Thank you,' I managed to say. She was the first girl in the class to talk to me for any length of time.

After that, Rabia helped me during breaks. Arabic was the most difficult. I rarely knew what the words meant; I just had to try to remember how they were spelled, and if I put a dot in the wrong place it could change the meaning entirely and earn a cuff over the head from Mrs Abdul. But I was beginning to improve. Even Mrs Abdul noticed. She praised Rabia, not me, and that made other girls want to help me as well. Rabia was the only one I trusted though. Saleema, one of the sharp girls in class, told me how to spell some words and when I handed them up Mrs Abdul slapped me. 'This is not correct. Are you slipping again, Aster?' It was too easy to earn Mrs Abdul's ire.

When I glanced at Saleema, she shrugged her shoulders as if she hadn't known. Fortunately, I was good at Urdu and maths, and Miss Rehmat, the maths teacher, didn't hit anyone. Rabia soon realised I could help with her algebra equations and we became friends on equal terms.

Too soon the day of the end-of-term exams arrived. I was nervous, but so was everyone. Rabia had been to a shrine the day before to pray for success. 'I want to be a teacher,' she said. 'I have to get good results.'

She wasn't the only one: we all had to do well, not only to satisfy the teachers but also our families. It cost my parents dearly to send me to high school. My brother died when I was young and I instantly became my parents' hope for the future. 'You must earn a profession, Aster. Then you will be able to marry a man with a good wage, a man kind enough to support us as well as his own parents when we are old.' This was the plan for my life.

Later that morning I sat in the Islamic Studies exam. I managed to complete all the answers that were required in Urdu. I approached it clinically, telling myself that I was just repeating information for an exam. *I don't believe all this*, I reminded myself. Then the Arabic questions began. A question called for a passage praising the Prophet Muhammad. I tried to write the correct text from the Quran, but I couldn't remember exactly how to spell a word. Was it a *baab* or a *taab*, one dot or two? If I understood the meanings of the words it would have been easier. The bell to put down our pens sounded and I quickly wrote in the word. After we handed in the papers we were allowed a break before the next exam.

I sat with Rabia outside and we went over the questions. It seemed as though I had answered most things correctly and I smiled at her in relief. She was about to speak but her gaze slipped above my shoulder and her face froze, her mouth still open. I looked behind me to see what was wrong. Mrs Abdul and a man in a blue shirt and khaki trousers were walking towards us. *A police officer?* It was as if all the girls in the yard became statues; only their eyes moved, watching. What could a policeman want at school?

Mrs Abdul stood in front of me. 'Stand up, girl!' She had been angry with me many times but she had never spat words out at me like she did then, as if I was a bazaar dog with rabies.

'This is the girl, officer, who has blasphemed the Holy Prophet, Peace be upon Him.'

Rabia gave a cry. I couldn't: I was too shocked.

'There must be some mistake, she wouldn't …' Rabia's voice trailed away as Mrs Abdul's gaze bored into her.

'Be careful, Rabia. If you support her you could be arrested too. This malaise is catching.'

Rabia shut her mouth but I finally found my voice. 'Why is this happening? Is it the exam? I tried my best.' Surely they couldn't arrest me for doing badly in an exam.

'Dirty kafir, you finally showed your true colours. You insulted the Holy Prophet in your paper.'

Tears welled in my eyes. 'I'm sorry, I didn't mean to. W-what did I write?' But Mrs Abdul wouldn't tell me. Was it the spelling? Should it have been two dots after all? I couldn't even remember what I dashed down at the end, but surely it wouldn't have made a blasphemous word.

Tears fell onto my hands as the officer put handcuffs on me. None of the other girls spoke on my behalf. Their fear was as palpable as mine. Rabia was weeping. I could still hear her as I walked with the police officer towards the outside gate. We had just passed the staffroom when Miss Rehmat stepped in front of us. 'There must be an explanation,' she said. 'This girl is law-abiding. She would not wilfully blaspheme.'

We were too close to the gate. A man on the street heard her words. By the time the principal had joined us and Mrs Abdul had finished explaining to Miss Rehmat how bad I was, there was a crowd gathering on the road. 'Try her under Sharia law, kill her!' one man called out.

'We don't want blasphemers here!' another said.

The officer called for reinforcements on his mobile. Within minutes there were a dozen police at the gate, pushing men away.

'We will have to take her to the jail now whether we want to or not,' the first officer told the principal. 'There will be a riot otherwise.'

One of the younger policemen bundled me into the police van; he actually pushed me from behind with his hand squeezing under my buttocks. He locked me in, and that was when I wept in earnest. I have never been touched like that by a man and the shock of it shamed me. I thought of my father, and my more pressing problem took over. He would come to collect me in a few hours, what would they tell him about me? But what could he do? Everyone knows once a Christian goes to jail they rarely come out.

It took a long time for the senior officer to fill out a First Investigation Report. A few of the policemen stood near me as if I needed guarding. The senior officer left the room and the man who had bundled me into the van said to me, 'I know you Christian girls go with men before you're married. I've seen how women in America act on DVD.' He slipped closer to me and I tried to step backwards but the wall was behind me. He shoved me so that my head hit the bricks too hard. I felt I was spinning in circles but not one of the other men intervened. He pressed himself against me as if he was hugging me. But it was nothing like my father's hugs and I screamed. He slapped me just as the senior officer returned.

'Leave her alone,' he snapped.

'She's nothing, who cares what happens to her?'

The older police officer stared at the younger man until he stepped away from me, but no one apologised. The senior officer only asked for my signature. I didn't want to think what could have happened if he had taken longer to return.

I was transported to a high-security women's jail in Rawalpindi. It was so far from my home. I still had my blue-and-white school uniform on. At least I had my red cardigan. It was too cool in the brick cell and there was no toilet, just a bucket, a string bed and blanket. Some of the cells had many beds and I was glad to be alone. What if the other women beat me for being a blasphemer? I couldn't eat the vegetable curry they gave me that first evening, although I managed to swallow some chapatti. A young woman in a cell opposite called out to me: 'What are you in here for? You're just a schoolgirl.' She had a small child with her and he stared at me through the bars.

I didn't want to say. Maybe she'd be Muslim and think I deserved it. But a heavy female officer walking past told her 'blasphemy'. She sounded smug, as though she'd found me out herself.

The woman with the child didn't say another word. She sang in a low voice to the boy and cuddled him. The corridor fell quiet and I lay on my bed, trying to keep my weeping quiet.

In the morning there was someone asking to see me. Her voice was bossier than any of our teachers, even Mrs Abdul's. 'You can't keep her in here,' she was saying to one of the female officers. 'She's only fourteen. I want to see the exam she wrote.' The officer must have said something for the woman replied, 'Then get it, if the teacher still has it. It's stupid to compel Christian kids to take Islamic Studies. Of course they'll get it wrong.' Her voice came closer and then the woman was being let into my cell.

I sat up on the bed, while the disapproving officer brought in a chair. The woman was young, wore a scarf on her head and sat very straight.

'*Asalaam alaikum*,' she said. 'My name is Mrs Jamal Khan, but please call me Mrs Jamal.'

'*Walikum asalaam*.' I returned the greeting. This much Arabic I knew.

'So, you have yourself in a pit of tigers, I see.'

I wanted her to understand. 'I didn't blaspheme.' I brushed at my eyes. I suspected Mrs Jamal would be impatient with tears.

'Listen,' she said. 'A Christian blasphemes just by breathing, by not saying the Kalima. It's the blasphemy law we need to reform.'

She sounded like my father when he was with his friends. 'Are you Muslim?' I ventured, even though I knew she must be.

'Certainly. Not all Muslims believe kids like you should be locked up because they can't spell.' She leaned down to her handbag and took out a notebook. 'Now, I need details. I am your lawyer.'

It took a moment for her statement to sink into my head. *A lawyer?*

'But how can we pay?'

Mrs Jamal gave me her first smile. 'Let's just say the firm I work for has an interest in cases like yours. You will not need to pay.'

It looked like a dangerous occupation to me. 'Thank you, but how can you do this?' I asked. What power could she have? Even a leading politician and a cabinet minister were assassinated last year for trying to change the blasphemy law. My whole church went into mourning for them.

'First we must ascertain your innocence. Your full name?'

'Aster Suleiman Masih.'

I watched her write 'Aster Suleiman Masih, student' at the top of her pad.

'And you did a Year 8 Islamic Studies exam?'

'*Ji*,' I said miserably.

She looked over at me. 'You don't know Arabic at all, do you?'

'*Nay*, Miss. I didn't learn it in the village school. Abu reads from the Bible in Urdu. I've never heard the Quran other than on TV.'

'And your father switches the channel?'

I hung my head, for it was true.

Mrs Jamal sighed. 'It is your right to follow your own faith; it is in our constitution. However, since the blasphemy law was changed in the 1980s to include the death sentence, we've had thousands of arrests.' She gazed at me. 'They need to prosecute the people who wrongly accuse.'

This was an encouraging thought and I said, 'I am afraid I must have spelled a word wrong but I didn't mean it to be offensive.'

'Of course not. Any educated and sensible person will understand that.'

Her words silenced me. Crowds of men at gates were not made up of sensible, educated people. Would it come to court? Those people are supposed to be educated. I had a sinking feeling that education wasn't always what mattered, but conviction. Mrs Abdul was educated but she was convinced I was evil.

'Now you keep a strong heart, Aster. There are people, some leading mullahs also, who don't agree with this. I'll make sure your parents know how you are, and they can send more clothes.' She looked at me as she put the pen away. 'But don't expect your parents to be able to come straight away.'

My heart sank but I voiced what was worrying me the most. 'How long do you think I will be here?' I knew of many Christians who were jailed for blasphemy; my father prayed constantly for their release.

That was the first time Mrs Jamal hesitated, and the first indication of how difficult this situation might turn out to be.

'Aster, this must be terrifying for you, but I will not lie to save your feelings.' She watched me as if gauging how I would react. 'It may be a long time. I have not been able to secure your bail.'

I opened my mouth to protest my innocence again but she cut me off. 'If you are released now, the mob will rip you apart with their hands. You are safer in here. Also …' she paused, 'your village has been threatened.'

I felt coils of fear tighten around my chest. The thought of my village burning and my family killed stopped any more protests I may have made. I told myself I could endure jail if only they were safe.

Mrs Jamal ripped off the pages she'd written on and gave me the pad and another pen. She looked around the cell. 'So they didn't even think to send your school bag. I'll see what I can do. You can still study here, so you are not behind when you are released.'

She pressed her lips together after she said 'released' and I knew she had slipped in her resolve not to lie to me.


Two shalwar kameez and a shawl came for me, also my glasses case, and my Injeel. Mrs Jamal brought wool, knitting needles and embroidery for me to do. She also brought me snacks. I liked the channa dhal the best. My school bag arrived with my books, but I never opened the Islamic texts again. The school had expelled me — there was too much pressure from the other parents and students.

There were other Christians in the jail. One lady had been sentenced to death for blasphemy the year before but was still alive. That gave me hope. The woman who called to me the first night had been imprisoned for adultery. Her name was Kamilah and she told me how to live in the jail, and helped with my washing since my family couldn't come. She told me she had been raped but was too ashamed to report it. When it became obvious she was pregnant, her mother couldn't hide her any more. Nor could Kamilah find enough male witnesses to vouch that she had been raped and so she was arrested. It was her father who informed the police.

My parents sent a letter. They sounded distraught but it still wasn't safe for them to visit — they had to think of the whole family and community. Some of our extended family and neighbours had fled into hiding until it blew over. Would it ever? Even if I was released my family would have to be relocated. My parents' words were heartbreaking — they knew they had lost me. The blasphemy law in Pakistan is like a huge machine that has no brakes. It squashes everything in its path.

My time in court was short: just long enough for Mrs Abdul to say she had to do her duty — she had destroyed my exam as she didn't want the evil thing in her classroom — and for Mrs Jamal to lose the case. I felt strange, as if I was standing on a cloud and could see a bright light, like Astafaan did when he was being stoned. The cloud disappeared and I was left staring at the floor. I could hear the judge pronouncing me wilful and guilty; then sentencing me to death. I grabbed hold of the chair so I wouldn't fall. My chest heaved; I couldn't stop the sobs. Mrs Jamal actually put an arm around me and I wept into her shoulder. None of my family was there — it would have been too dangerous. As it was, there were many policemen, not only to guard Mrs Jamal and me but to contain the crowd. One policeman leaned closer to me. 'Do not cry,' he said. 'It is just to keep you safe. No need to cry.' I looked up, sniffing. He had dark skin like mine and looked as if he would weep himself.

There was so much shouting it sounded like the end of Ramadan, as if the people had so much to celebrate. There was even shouting in the streets. I hoped they wouldn't stone me. Shooting or even hanging would be quicker. If I had said the Kalima I might have been saved, but Mrs Jamal said I shouldn't have to, and I agreed. I don't think she ever imagined she would lose.

I dreamed that night. Yesu Masih was holding his hand out to me. He wore a long yellow robe and shawl. He looked strong, as if he could overthrow a government if he wished it, but it was me he wanted. His dark eyes were brimming with compassion. 'Faithful Aster.' His voice reverberated in the sky and his love settled around me like a blanket made of peacock feathers. Such power and light I had never experienced. I knew Yesu had delivered me, although in a different way than I had expected, for when I woke I was not so afraid.


It has been months since the court. I have learned too much here; I don't feel fourteen any more. I feel old, as if I have lived my whole life but just can't remember it. At least I am safe, although the fat officer beats me if I don't tidy up quick enough or stay in bed too long.

At night I often wish they'd get the sentence over with. I used to sometimes hope that something could be done, an appeal maybe, but those hopes of appeal are dashed now. Yesterday I discovered that Mrs Jamal has been shot outside her house. The fat officer threw the *Dawn* paper into my cell. 'See what good that stupid lawyer was.'

On the front page was a picture of a young man with blood on his face holding Mrs Jamal and weeping.

Underneath the picture was an article. It said the Khan family would not let this go. Even though the country needs the blasphemy law to protect religious beliefs, they would work to help reform the law so it is just and protects minority groups.

A friend of Mrs Jamal visited me in the afternoon. Her name is Seema, but I doubt that is her real name.

'I am sorry to hear about Mrs Jamal,' I said after we exchanged greetings. Then I added, still seeing the image from the paper, 'Her husband must hate me.'

Seema was quick. 'It is not your fault. Her husband is a lawyer also and his father has a law firm interested in social justice. They will not give up.'

'What can they do?' I said without thinking how hopeless it would sound.

Seema didn't deny it. In her eyes was the same sad pity I had seen in Rabia's. Instead, she said, 'I am a journalist and I need a story from you.'

That is why I am writing this. Seema will publish it in a safe place under a different name. When Queen Aster approached the Persian king to ask for her people to be saved from a cruel law that targeted them, she knew she and her people might perish. Yet she took the risk and moved the heart of a king. I pray my story will do this also, whether I live or whether I die.

# The glass collector

*by Anna Perera*

'Cairo treats the dead better than the living.'

Aaron is overwhelmed by the truth of what the man says as he pushes past. The words roll into him in a blind-person-seeing kind of way, because the stranger in the dark suit is right — the mummies and old bones in the Egyptian Museum are better cared for than he is. Inside there are plush rooms with air conditioning and marble floors for the sacred dead, while the despised Zabbaleen people are treated like the lowest of the low, left to live like pigs, scrabbling through the city streets for garbage to recycle.

Aaron walks slowly and painfully, trying hard to take the weight off his left knee, which is throbbing badly after a fall this morning from the pony and cart. The toe he jabbed and the elbow he bashed when he landed on the hot, potholed road hurt almost as badly and, for one awful moment, he thinks he'll just sink down on the pavement and give up.

He stops beside a stall selling King Tut replicas and papyrus pictures of blue flying birds, and stretches his leg, which eases the pain a little. If Aaron has broken a bone, it'll be too bad. When he gets home, the best he can hope for is to sleep despite the pain, because the health clinic isn't open every day. When it's closed, the Zabbaleen have to visit the hospital, and Aaron won't go there after hearing his best friend Jacob's stories about patients dying from little things like a nosebleed or an ingrowing toenail.

'And sometimes the doctors take one of your kidneys without you knowing,' Jacob once told him.

Aaron has no idea where his kidneys are. Are they at the front or the back of his body? Through his dirty green shirt he presses down on the sponges of skin either side of his navel but finds only soft flesh and a tender spot that wasn't there before. Another bruise from this morning, he decides, as it sparks the old ones to life and his whole body begins to throb more than ever.

He checks for the industrial-strength plastic bag that's safely tucked under his arm, then straightens his back and sighs. If he doesn't get on with clearing the last alley, which is still more than fifteen minutes' walk away at this slow pace, he'll have to find his own way home because his stepbrother Lijah can't be bothered to hang around for him.

Four young African refugees are sharing a glass of pink hibiscus tea outside a bar and glance at Aaron as he turns towards the busy shops. Their gaze follows him as he moves through the sunshine, bouncing past windows displaying tablecloths, tent material, galabeyas, black lace, bright cardigans and enough shoes for everyone in Egypt. Young women in headscarves saunter by without seeing the thin boy hobbling towards the main road, while tourists force him to step out of their way as they stream past with open maps and sharp voices.

The thought of being late and making Lijah even angrier adds to the feeling that there's a snake in Aaron's stomach reaching for his throat. Who knows how he's going to manage walking the streets of Cairo tomorrow and the next day with his knee hurting like this.

With a grubby hand, he wipes hot tears from his face and makes a silent promise to get even. Lijah — the creep, the bully. What did he say to make his stepbrother shove him off the cart and into the path of a passing car this morning, almost killing him? If it hadn't been for the quick reactions of the man in the silver BMW, he'd be dead now.

'You all right?' The man had slammed on the brakes and jumped out of the car to stand over Aaron, who was already on his feet by that time.

Aaron's insides shake at the memory. The man had a nervous face — the vein in his forehead was sticking out and he kept glancing at his jewelled gold watch. He was rich and Aaron regrets leaping up from the road so quickly. He should have stayed where he was, pretended to be hurt and asked for fifty piastres — at least. Instead he took to his heels to catch up with Lijah, who was ages away by then, not caring if he was dead or alive.

Aaron hadn't noticed the trouble with his knee at first. It was only when he tried to climb back on the cart that it started aching, and his toe began to throb and the pain in his elbow kicked in. All the while Lijah was staring ahead, as if nothing had happened. He was squinting at the road with his hard insect eyes and, when Aaron finally turned to face him, Lijah said, 'Keep your mouth shut or I'll kill you.'

But Aaron wasn't worried by the idle threat. When Lijah was really angry, his eyes popped out like bubbles. Only then was it time to run.

Jacob had once said, 'The trouble with Lijah is he never dreams.'

Aaron sort of knew what his friend meant and had agreed, saying, 'Yeah, he's useless.' It made sense that Lijah was stupid because he didn't have an imagination.

'He has got a bit of a brain, though,' Jacob went on, backtracking, cushioning his comment.

'But it's up his backside,' Aaron told him, 'so it doesn't count.'

Aaron smiles at the memory of Jacob laughing, his Adam's apple jack-hammering in his throat. At least his friend understood something of what he was going through, of how tough life could be. These people around him on the streets of Cairo now, they have no idea.

Aaron glances at the sky to catch his breath. The closer he gets to the main road, the more it seems as if every car horn in the city is honking at once and the curling exhaust fumes are out to gas him to death. A blue tourist coach, with the pyramids of Giza painted on the side, moves alongside him as he limps past a burger bar and, when he looks up, he sees a middle-aged woman staring down at him. She eyes him with a cool expression and he knows what she's thinking. He's seen that look a million times before. She's wondering if he's an innocent street kid or a homeless refugee, ex-mental patient or some other kind of reject.

She probably thinks he's stupid and can't read or add up.

She doesn't know that there's a primary school in Mokattam, where he lives, and that the clever kids can continue with their education elsewhere while the rest have to leave at the age of eleven to collect and recycle waste. She doesn't know Aaron wanted to stay on but had to help his mother instead.

Aaron stares back at the woman — at the slow way she flicks her fair hair behind her ears. He stops dead in his tracks to watch the coach overtake him.

'I know who you are, lady, but you don't know anything about me,' he mutters.

The coach pushes on and Aaron starts limping again as a sudden burst of exhaust fumes intensifies the feeling that his knee is about to give way.

This part of the city is always busy and, when he finally reaches the main road, he heads for the only safe spot to cross, which is a distance from the backed-up cars queuing to get on the flyover. Aaron gazes at the road as the traffic echoes round him. He could be standing on a thousand streets in Cairo, with the same four lanes of taxis, cars and buses hurrying to nowhere, the same blank faces between him and the dark alley opposite. He checks that the plastic bag is still under his arm and the sudden movement aggravates the pain in his elbow.

He screws up his face in agony. But at least the bag's still there. A couple of weeks ago he'd dropped it without noticing and Hosi, his stepfather, went crazy when he came home with one less bag of garbage.

'Those bags cost money, you idiot,' he yelled.

'Someone stole it from me,' Aaron tried to explain. But it was no use; Hosi screamed anyway.

Staring out at the dirty traffic, Aaron's fury moves from the picture in his head of Hosi yelling, to the cars, then to the businessman beside him, who's puffing on a cigarette and tapping his scuffed-up leather shoes — as if he's worried but weirdly calm at the same time. Aaron shakes his head to disperse the smell of tobacco. It's repulsive, that smell, and the small movements of the man's tan shoes with their fake gold buckles make him feel suddenly closed in. Stuck. Maybe he should pick another place to cross the street. By now Lijah has probably given up and gone back to

Mokattam without him. While part of Aaron hopes Lijah will turn up, another part is too tired and in too much pain to care any more.

Aaron turns his attention to the crowd gathering behind him. Emerald-green light shimmers off their dark clothes, sequins reflecting in the sun's rays. It's normal in Cairo — this city of magic and ancient mysteries — for rich and poor to stand side by side, to share the same doorways and buildings, the same streets, without ever really seeing each other. The congestion is building and Aaron's thin body aches with the impulse to hit out at something. Something big. Something that looks and feels like Lijah would be great. What would the priest back in Mokattam say to that, Aaron wonders? *Say a prayer? Ask for forgiveness?*

He turns to look at a woman in a blue headscarf. She's smiling down at her little boy as if she loves him more than anything in the world. As if he's the only kid who was ever born. The little boy clutches his mother's hand tightly. Aaron's mind travels back to when he was younger, because the woman looks a bit like his mother. Except she's dressed in a new galabeya, while his mother wore dirty rags every day of her life but one.

The woman smiles and Aaron is suddenly floored by the memory of the day his mother married nasty Hosi. For a second he brings up the picture of her wedding day — the only time she was able to rent a pretty dress. It was cream with lace at the hem and gold edging, and she looked like someone else in it. Someone he didn't know. Someone younger. It was hard to look away from her in that dress, dancing and smiling at Hosi, white ribbons swinging from her hair to her eyes. Aaron saw clearly then that she loved her new husband more than she loved him, her own son. That was the day she ruined his life. And, when she died, she left Aaron with a stone in his heart. A stone he's kept hard by returning to the picture of her on her wedding day, again and again.

But now she's dead, and he's stuck with Hosi and two stepbrothers. Stuck with a family he hates and it's all her fault. Lijah's her fault.

Lijah. How Aaron detests that name.

Aaron thinks back on himself as a sad younger brother. Someone to feel sorry for. Someone who could do with a hug. And because he never gets one, his heart fills with the kind of pain that becomes a fixed place from where all other feelings travel back and forth, but always find their way home.

The sun burns into Aaron as if on purpose. Deliberately hurting him while he still waits for a gap in the traffic. The businessman steps on his cigarette and pats sweat from his neck, while the woman runs a red-nailed hand through her son's hair, pulling him closer to her.

The crowd pulses with irritation.

Everyone stops breathing for a moment when a black-and-white taxi screeches to a halt behind a yellow bus, but the gap's not big enough for anyone to get through. Aaron feels sick to his stomach. He can't breathe. He can't escape the sun. His bones seem to thump under the pressure of the heat and noise, and sickly smells, ugly shoes and memories that won't leave him alone.

*Come on.* There's just one more alley to clear, if he can reach it. Another filthy alley in a city of tourists and people who'll never know him or how and where he lives. Yet Aaron has touched their dead skin cells on sauce bottles, tins and old socks. He's wiped lipstick prints off wine glasses and tried on their old shoes. He can imagine their whole lives from the way they crush white plastic cups until they crack and split.

Sometimes he can feel them. Feel their breath on his neck.

Close by, the traffic on the flyover has come to a complete stop. Automatically, Aaron reaches to check for the folded bag under his arm again, then glances at the tall hotel on the opposite side of the road. With its plain brown windows and discreet entrance, it radiates peace and quiet. He's never been through the dark revolving glass doors, and he probably never will, but the sight of them cools him for a moment as he imagines the air conditioning inside.

Aaron rubs the sting of exhaust fumes from his eyes — then blinks. Instantly his life stops. He blinks again, hardly believing what he sees. What is that? That — something —

a woman — flashing on the hotel doors? A beautiful face on the dark glass, lighting up, then moving, now staring out at him. It's making him feel as if he's being lifted from his body and taken to heaven.

The traffic disappears as separate pieces — a face, a wing, a headscarf — float past him with a power so strong he can't look away. It's her, Mary, and it feels as if she's wrapping her arms round him as he gazes in awe at her soft face. But he knows that hotel well. He knows those dark swinging glass doors. There's nothing etched on the glass. No marks.

Nothing. But her ghostly face floats from the door again and a powerful feeling that she's real, she exists, she's part of this life, part of him, overtakes Aaron and he falters.

The Virgin Mary, Queen of Heaven, is here in Cairo, on the glass doors of the Imperial Hotel.

And only he knows.

How can he explain what he's seeing? Who would believe him? He hardly believes it himself, and at the same time he also knows he's seeing something that doesn't really exist. Maybe the pain is affecting his mind. He never thought she was real — just a story, an old story — until now. Shocked and confused, he thinks it's as if another version of himself is looking at a different world. A world that's changing shape right in front of his eyes. Her appearance must be a message. But what? And why him? He's nobody. He doesn't go to church. He never listens to the priest. Being constantly told what to believe, how to live, who to follow — all that gets on his nerves.

A shrieking truck shoots by, blocking his sight for a second. The sudden draught shaves his sore knee and he steps back, forcing his bare feet against the edge of the pavement. Aaron tries to make the vision disappear from his mind. *Go away!* It scares him.

# The leaving

*by Lili Wilkinson*

It's been thirty-seven days since I saw the sun.

The three of us huddle together in old bomb shelters and cellars — hoping that walls of brick and tin will protect us from the smoke and fire. The ground shudders every few minutes as another missile hits, ripping into the earth and fraying our world at the seams. The radio went dead two weeks ago. But still the bombs fall. They won't stop until nothing is left but ashes and dust.

This morning Archer looked at me like I wasn't even there.

'Mama?' he said, with a little frown. 'Where's my mama?'

I glanced at Reuben, but he looked away, busying himself with folding a dirty brown blanket.

I swallowed. 'Mama's gone,' I told Archer. 'Don't you remember?'

He looked confused, and started to cry. 'I don't want to remember.'

Neither do I. Mama was taken away in the third round of trials because she worked at the university. She told me that everything would be fine, that the Resistance would fight back and she would come home within a few days.

She didn't.

We heard rumours about the trials. That faceless men in white hoods delivered sentences without hearing any defence. That no one accused of sedition was ever found innocent. That some prisoners were sent to the labour camps, and others were publicly executed. Some, it was said, were burnt in fires made of their own books.

We burnt our own books before the soldiers came. It was safer that way, said Mama, as she tossed another volume onto the fire. She said it was the smoke, making her eyes sting, but I could see the tightness in her shoulders, and the despair in her eyes.

When the Resistance began, we hoped that Mama might come home. Every night we listened for her key turning in the door, her step in the hall. But she didn't come. The Resistance was too weak, and it only made things worse. The labour camps were closed, the trials suspended. The white-hooded men disappeared to safety. And the bombs came. After the first one fell near us, our windows shattered, spraying glass into the house like it was raining diamonds. A shard of glass wedged in poor Archer's cheek, and I had to pull it out with tweezers. We retreated to the brick shelter in the backyard, reinforcing it with planks of wood and sheets of corrugated fibreglass we found nearby. We have been here now for over a month.

At first, Reuben went out every day, to speak to the other huddling souls and to trade. He'd come back with warm, funny stories about how Biddy Silver talked in her sleep, or little Pisky took his first wobbly steps across a damp coal cellar. When Reuben was gone, I sang songs to Archer and tried to pretend I wasn't worried about whether he'd come back. Reuben went out with jars of paraffin or bags of flour and came back with little bottles of cinnamon and tins of some suspicious-looking meatstuff that looked like pink jelly and tasted like nothing much at all. We ate the meatstuff cold from the tin, and sprinkled the cinnamon on our tongues afterwards to try and take away the waxy nothingness.

Five days ago, Reuben went outside to find water, but came back after only a few minutes. The smoke and dust is so thick, he said, you can't see your hand in front of you. There is no water to be found anywhere. Everything is poisoned with the choking yellow smoke. We have only one bottle of water left, to share between the three of us. One bottle of water, one tin of beans, and two tins of the suspicious meatstuff.

We have grown terribly thin, and Archer is sleeping too much, his cheeks hollow and his eyes unfocussed. He doesn't seem interested in my funny stories any more, and refuses to play marbles. My ears ring with a never-ending whine, and we mouth our words to each other in an exaggerated fashion, so we can be understood. My nails are filthy and ragged, my hair a matted clump. I can't remember when I last washed, or slept for more than an hour, or felt warm. Everything is cold and damp and tainted with the sour yellow smoke.

Staying is not an option.

The last radio report we heard said that the airports were choked with people, pushing and clamouring to leave. And yet no planes took off. It was too dangerous — and even if a plane did manage to escape, which country would have us? Other nations have their own problems — ours is not the only one being torn apart.

People are slipping away quietly, in twos and threes, silent, creeping things. Some set off on foot, scarves wrapped around their faces to protect them from the smoke. They are heading for the mountains, where the air is clearer. The bombs don't bother to fall on the mountains, because the ice and wind kill all living things up there before long.

Reuben says he saw some people float away in a silk balloon, drifting silently into the sky except for an occasional huff of helium and splash of flame.

We have no silks to build a balloon, and we are not strong enough for the mountains. But we know the sea.

Silent as mice, we take apart our makeshift shelter, stacking the sheets of corrugated fibreglass and tying up our last few belongings and blankets. I prise up the damp wooden boards of the floor and retrieve our most precious treasures — our last three books wrapped in hessian sacking. I hid them from Mama when she burnt all our books. It was easy because her tears made it difficult for her to see. I kept our three favourites — fairy stories of magic and excitement, where every adventure had a happy ending. These I tie to my back, underneath my clothes. I bundle up Archer the best I can, and he watches me silently with giant, dark eyes. For the past two days he has been refusing to eat the meatstuff. I tried to tempt him with my last great luxury — a small tin of condensed milk I'd been saving for Reuben's birthday — but he refused even that. Reuben and I ate it ourselves, but the sticky sweetness sat in my stomach like cement, and my mouth filled with acid.

We leave without ceremony. Our home stopped being home weeks ago, and we are not sorry to leave. We slip through backyards and over splintered fences. I don't recognise anything — what was once green lawns and washing lines is now just rubble and ash. The yellow clouds hang low and dangerous, and even though I have a scarf wrapped around my face, I can still feel my lungs burn with every breath. There is a sudden flash and the earth groans and shakes, and we fall to our knees, crouching and covering our heads as sparks rain down and more yellow clouds billow up from the ground. When the shuddering and groaning stops, we get to our feet and continue on. I squeeze Archer's hand as we pick our way through still-glowing embers, and he weakly squeezes back. I can feel every bone in his ice-cold hand. I can feel the sea tugging us forward, calling us away.

The fishing boats are all destroyed, the harbour choked with splintered wood and debris. We see no one. There are no birds circling over the ocean. No bees or beetles or crawling things. Even the sturdy grey-green grasses and shrubs that used to crowd the dunes have withered and died, leaving behind dry yellow sticks that spike into our feet. The world is dull, silent, dead. The jetty is gone, leaving only splintered stumps rising from the sea. The water looks filthy, with great clumps of brown foam floating on top and clinging greasily to everything it touches.

This is not the ocean that we used to swim in, the ocean that provided us with endless riches — wriggling fish, bundles of seaweed, pink-lipped clams and mussels. This is not the beach where Archer and I once built sand forts for scuttling crabs. This wasteland is unfamiliar to me. But I can still feel the ocean, far off, beyond this greasy brown wetness. The ocean still calls to us. Beyond this harbour, there is a world where there are no bombs and no yellow clouds.

We have to believe this.

After hours of picking through the stinking foam on the beach, Reuben finds a canvas sheet tucked away in the stubbly dunes, and under the sheet is a little wooden dinghy, barely big enough to carry the three of us. But to us it is perfect, the very finest vessel we ever laid eyes on. Reuben stacks the fibreglass sheets on the dinghy, making a little roof for us to shelter under, and I fold up our belongings in the canvas sheet to protect them from water and the yellow clouds. Archer sits on a dune, running ashy sand through his fingers, his lips twitching.

We wait until nightfall, in case there are any watching drones. It never really gets dark any more, but the yellow clouds fade to a dark, dusty brown. I lift Archer into the dinghy, and Reuben and I push it down the dune, creating a deep furrow in the sand. I shudder as I step into the slimy brown foam, and the skin on my feet starts to burn. But then my toes splash through the foam into the icy shallows of the harbour, and my heart starts to beat faster. We are leaving. We are really leaving.

I pull myself into the dinghy, and Reuben wades deep into the water before hauling himself in as well. The dinghy rocks from side to side, slapping the waves and creaking loudly. We hold our breath, but nothing happens. There are no drones nearby tonight, and we start to breathe again. I settle myself into the stern with Archer pressed up against me, a blanket wrapped tightly around us both. Reuben sits at the other end, his knees tucked up, watching the black water as we drift slowly away from the shore. The foam clings to the sides of the boats, its acid stench filling our nostrils. Reuben leans over and scrapes it off with a stick.

# The Chinks

*by Bette Greene*

Now that August is here, my father says that our town is so hot, so quiet, that you could shoot a cannon down the Main Street of Jenkinsville, Arkansas, and not hit a single soul. Actually, you'd need two cannons, because our two main streets are T-shaped. Not capital T-shaped, but only lower-case t-shaped.

All the best stores — like our store, Bergen's Department Store, and the Sav-Mor Market and, directly across the street, the Victory Café — are on the up and down part of the t. Mr James Gilmore Jackson (the richest man in town, everybody says), has his cotton-gin office there on the cross street. Ditto Mr Clyde Barnes, whose furniture store is only open on some days and closed on others. Both those businesses, along with Chu Lee's new grocery, are located on the sideways part of the t.

The school library is closed for the summer and all my friends have left town to go chilling out at Baptist Training

Camp in the Ozark Mountains. And what that means —
I guess what it means — is that what they're all doing is
going into training to become what I thought that they
already were: Baptists.

You might wonder why I'm here and not there? Here
with nothing to do and nobody to do it with? Well, if you
knew anything at all about me you'd never ever have to ask
a question that dumb.

Okay, I didn't mean to insult you, but if you're really
not smart enough to already know, then I'll have to start
at the beginning. Well, here it is: the beginning. The very
beginning!

Outside of my parents, Pearl and Harry Bergen, I'm the
only Jewish person in our town. Probably the only Jew that
anybody in Jenkinsville has ever seen. At least up close.
Anyway, I'm going to say something now that I've never
said to anybody before — because if my parents heard,
they'd get mad and shake their heads wondering how
stupid some people in this town can really be. In the next
moment, they'd go delivering up this answer: '*Very* stupid!'

And if I told anybody else in Jenkinsville, they might
have trouble understanding what Grady did that was so
very wrong in the first place. To their mind, he only asked
the question that lots of inquiring minds wanted to know.

Well, it wasn't all that long ago, either, when the thing
that happened happened. I remember it was cold, so it
could have been around Christmas. Yeah, last Christmas.

And I'll have to, you know, give him credit, because Grady Lee Johnson was real polite when he came up to me with a smile on his not-all-that-bad-looking-face to ask if I'd let him feel my head.

'You want to do what?!'

He thrust his hands out for my inspection. 'See, I washed them real good.'

'What do you want to do that for?'

'To feel your horns. I'm not going to hurt them. I just want to feel them!'

'Grady, are you crazy?'

'No. I promise, on a stack of Bibles, not to hurt your horns. I only want to feel them. Feel what I can't see under all that hair.'

'Where did you get that from?'

'Nobody! It's just that you being a Jew person and all …'

'Who told you that? That I have horns.'

'I can't tell you.'

'Yes, you can!'

'No, I can't.'

'Why can't you?'

'Because I just can't.'

'Why not?'

'Because I made a promise. A hand-on-the-Bible promise.'

I heard myself sigh just as if suddenly appearing before me was this million-mile high mountain blocking my way to knowing what I needed to know. After a moment that seemed like an awful lot of moments it came to me that what you can't climb over, you can sometimes find a way around! This time I wanted to make it sound like there was no more breath or fight left in me because he had just scored this amazing knockout blow.

I sighed a sigh of defeat. 'Okay, Grady, I guess you win.'

He looked confused. 'I do?'

'Yes, you win. You don't have to break your hand-on-the-Bible promise and tell me who told you that I have horns.'

He smiled a winner's smile. 'I don't?'

'No, not if you don't want to,' I said.

As I saw his hands reaching up towards my head, I took a quick step backwards, saying: 'You don't ever have to tell me who told you that I have horns, you only have to tell me who was with you when you put your hand on the Bible.'

'Wasn't nobody but him!' Grady protested. 'Nobody but Pastor Paul Whaley. He held the Bible real steady like when I put my hand on it, too.'

To tell the truth, it was really lonesome here with everybody gone to camp, but that was before — wait! What I'm going to tell you next is not really a secret, but just the same, you must promise, promise me on your mother's grave that you'll not tell. Not another living soul!

Now don't get me wrong; I'm not doing anything bad. Least ways not to my mind. But just the same, you must never ever tell because folks hereabouts wouldn't even begin to understand.

If you must know, it's about the Chinks, and how we became friends. It may be hard for some people to understand, because, it's true, they really do talk funny. Their eyes slide upward and their skin is not what anybody around here is used to. I mean not colored skin and not at all white skin. Their skin — let's see — it's like maybe like they grew up eating way too much lemon meringue pie without watering the lemony part down with a little meringue.

But these are things that everybody already knows about the Lees. It's what they don't know (and I don't talk!) that's stranger still. The Lees, for example, never use forks and knives when they eat, but only sticks. Two little wooden sticks to pick up their bite-size pieces of food.

Then there's this other thing that our town isn't going to like. You know how every wife in this town knows better than serve her husband a plate of food where the mashed potatoes are touching (never mind mingling) with the peas? And how the pork chops are always placed untouched, like royalty, at the very top of the plate?

Well, if only the good ladies of Jenkinsville heard about what I'm going to tell next, they'd really have a lot of something to say and what they'd have to say wouldn't be nice. Okay, here goes.

Mrs Lee chops up everything into half-a-thumb sized pieces before throwing them into a sizzling hot pot that the Lees brought with them all the way from China. So, not only does all the food meet, all the food also mingles. Maybe it doesn't sound all that good. But what it tastes like is, well … awesome!

When I was on the street crossing Main, I saw this pitiful looking homeless dog stretched out in front of the Lees' store. Probably that's why I wasn't doing my usual eye scanning, making sure that nobody would catch me either going in or coming out of the Lees.

But then just as I reached out for the door, somebody did catch me. Mr James Gilmore Jackson himself was staring down at me just as though I was nothing more than a bug-size critter waiting to be stomped on. 'You going in there?' he asked, while allowing his damp cigar-smelling breath to attack my nostrils.

At this moment, I could think of nothing that would be believable, but the truth. So that's what I gave him. 'Yes, sir.'

'You and your folks now doing all your trading with the Chink? That what you're telling me?'

'Oh, no sir, that's not what I'm telling you!'

He gave me a half nod as though I might just possibly be telling the truth.

'I'm going in there only because the Sav-Mor is all out of Dr Pepper.' Then I added, just in case he got it into his head to go check, 'A really cold bottle of Dr Pepper.'

For a moment, I thought he was going to give my head a pat, but then, at the last moment, he didn't. He did smile though or at least as close as Mr Jackson could ever come to smiling. 'Glad to hear it, 'cause none of us want our good American money to go a bunch of foreigners, now do we?'

'Oh, no, sir, we positively surely don't,' I said, while trying to ratchet up enough enthusiasm to be believable.

He turned, and with every step his save-the-world gait took him further and further away from me. But his words — actually, it was *my* words, and *my* sheep-like actions, that struck a knot in my stomach. What good is a person, I asked myself silently, if they won't stick up for their friends? If they're too cowardly — if … if *I'm* too cowardly to even do that?

Then, trying to explain myself to myself, I began rummaging through my heart and my mind for answers. 'Yes, but it's so hard! Why can't I be like everybody else and have friends who are like everybody else? Why can't I at least do that, instead of caring so much for people who everybody else thinks are weirdos? And, if being weird and doing weird things wasn't bad enough, they aren't even my age, my colour, my religion or … or my anything!

I promised myself, on my most sacred honour, that no matter what, I would not move from this very spot in front of Chu Lee's until I had supplied all my questions with answers. One minute followed and then another. Problem was that my brains were dashing off in search of answers that were hiding in places way too dark for the seeing.

First the dog ambled off, and then breaking my most solemn of all promises to myself, I threw open the door of Mr Chu Lee's grocery store and walked on in.

Mr Lee smiled at me without showing any of his teeth, while Mrs Lee smiled at me showing all of hers. Then in unison, they called out, 'Hello. Can I help you?'

This time we all laughed together because those were just about the first five English words that I taught them. Those are the same words they use to greet every one of their customers when they are lucky enough to have customers.

The customers that they do have are mostly coloured sharecroppers driving their battered trucks in from the country. Seems like they're the only ones who don't seem to mind the Lees not being white. But now that I think of it, I don't think that Jenkinsville's coloured people are all that impressed with us Jenkinsville whites.

I answered the English words that I taught the Lees with the Chinese words that they taught me. In rapid order, and in their own language I called out every single word in my Chinese vocabulary. All five of them. *Hello ... Goodbye ... Yes ... No ... Thanks.*

Both the Lees burst out laughing. I know they're laughing at me because my pronunciation isn't all that good. But I don't mind their laughing, because anyone can tell that it's a friendly laugh. Besides, I'm laughing too.

Probably it's hard for people to understand how I, being only in the sixth grade and all, and not what you'd call a good student (what nobody in their right mind would call a good student!), can teach grown-up people. But I can and I do. I'm also a very good writer.

The next thing I'm going to say is going to sound as though I'm just bragging about something that's not even true. Well, I guess I'm bragging, but it is true and I can prove it. Four years ago, at age eight, I became a professional writer. The *Memphis Commercial Appeal* sent me a cheque for writing exactly 104 words about the barn fire at Mr Troy McDonald's dairy farm. Two cows burned to death.

My most important story (215 words) was about our town's pride, Sidney Earl Putnam, when he was picked to join the Red Sox's Farm Team. Him I wrote about twice. Lots of people in Jenkinsville want me to write about things that the newspaper won't print. Mrs Esther Hoskins, for example, is always after me to write about the wonderful work that her missionary society is doing in Africa. Even when I tell her that the paper won't print it, she reminds me that I'm lacking in faith.

From the back of the store, I heard Little Henry beginning his up-from-nap cry. 'I'll get him,' I said, while breaking into a run. And since I got to him first, I won the prize of lifting this six-month-old up and over the crib and into my arms. Together Henry and I twirled around and around the room until I felt his wet diaper pressing against my shirt, and that's when I did the cowardly thing: I thrust Little Henry back into his mother's waiting arms.

As she changed him, Mrs Lee said something to me in her language; not a single word of it I understood. But just the same from her tone, I understood everything she was saying. And what she was saying was that I shouldn't ever be put off by a little pee.

Taking the smiling child into her arms, she did something and did it in a way that was so free, so easy, that it was like the most natural thing in the world to her, but it wasn't to me. It surprised — no, shocked me would be a better word for it. Yes, it shocked me. Because without trying to hide her breast, she ever so gently pushed her nipple into his waiting mouth.

Never before — not in my whole life had I ever seen a woman's unclothed breast. Nipple and all, and it was pretty. And if it's nipples you're interested in, then go to the town swimming pool in Wynne, because there are lots of fellows there and every one of them has a nipple. Actually, two nipples.

If Mrs Lee could speak English, or if I could speak Chinese, I'd ask her about it. Try to find out what the breast rules are for men and for women. Right off the only thing I can figure is that if the nipple is useless, then it's okay to show; but if the nipple is useful, then — Oh, my God — you've got to keep it hidden.

As she plunked his chubby little body into the sink's warm water, I gave a gentle tug at Henry's earlobe, saying, 'Ear.'

Mrs Lee then gave an equally gentle tug at her son's straight blue-black hair repeating, 'Ear.'

'No! No!' I said, while tugging at my own ear. Ear doesn't mean pulling, it means, 'Ear. Ear!' But after going back and forth while creating more (not less confusion), I reached into the sink to pull out a floating bar of white soap. Waving it over my head, I sang out, 'Soap! Soap!'

This time she smiled knowingly while poking the soap with her index finger. 'Soap!' she called out triumphantly. 'Soap! Soap! Soap!'

'Yes!' I answered as I saw skin tighten over her high cheekbones, giving her face a kind of sculptured beauty that I had never really seen before.

By September my friends may have returned from Baptist Training Camp, but it became clearer and clearer that the Baptist training camp had never really left them. They all had returned with a bolder, bondier kind of a bond. So there it was all this oneness for those who went to camp, but that bond never seemed to be stretchy enough to squeeze inside just one more girl. Me.

The girls brought back with them a whole new language of games, slangs, songs and campers' names that I had never heard before. As soon as a name was mentioned, it was a yea or sometimes a smile or even a clap if it was a person that they liked or a groan for those that they didn't. The names that brought the best bounce of enthusiasm were

Suby, Jumper and Claire, who all my friends liked, and then there was poor Pauline, who they didn't. They even gave Pauline an addition to her name that once made her cry. They got to calling her Putrid Pauline. Or sometimes they'd just drop the name Pauline altogether and just call her Putrid. As much as I could understand from the bits and pieces of all the Pauline mentions, it wasn't that she was such a bad person as it was that she had a bad mouth problem — or I should say bad breath problem.

So while it seemed to be a fun thing for them to talk about the bad thing that they did to Pauline, I knew it wouldn't be one bit okay for me to talk about the good things that I did for the Lees.

With my old friends who weren't all that friendly any more, I was feeling more and more like a piece of forgotten clothing. Something that still hangs in the closet, but isn't ever worn because, somewhere along the way, what you once liked enough to buy, you just stopped caring about. Not hated. Just stopped caring about. Leaving it just hanging there. Hanging all alone and neglected.

Maybe that's why I like being with the Lees. Helping them with their English and taking care of Little Henry always makes me feel as though, in spite of what other people might say about me, they really like me. And they know that I'm a good person. A person of value.

Then something happened in December that changed everything and everybody in Jenkinsville. But what happened didn't take place here. Not in our town, but in a place that's so very far away from here this place. Almost nobody had ever heard of this Pearl Harbor place before, but then almost nobody has ever heard of Jenkinsville either.

Anyway, it was a bunch of those sneaky Japanese planes that came roaring out of the clouds to drop bombs on our American ships, killing our sailors. These were peaceful ships that weren't doing anything to anybody but just minding their own business, out there in Hawaii.

After that, everybody in our town seemed to be busy shoving and pushing to become part of the soon-to-be great American victory over the Japs. Mayor Flint, for example, got on the phone to Sears to order a flagpole and an American flag that was the size of a small bedroom. Mary Caldwell organised the town's Victory Garden Project, and the big dog himself, Mr Jackson, headed the town's scrap-metal drive.

And exactly forty-two miles away, across the wide Mississippi River, Memphis's pride, the beautiful sunken Japanese Gardens were ploughed under. Then to the sounds of whoops, all the workmen took turns peeing on the now open earth.

Ask anybody and they'll tell you the same thing. There hasn't been this much excitement in our part of the world since Sidney Earl Putnam got picked to join the farm team of the Boston Red Socks. Course everybody in town got pretty bummed out quickly when they learned what happened to him after he went praying inside that revival meeting tent over in Wynne. What happened was that Sidney Earl up and got religion.

And he got it bad. Real bad! Problem was Sidney Earl told the Red Socks bosses that he would never again play on Sundays. No, no, no. Never again play on that day, that day being the Lord's Day. And that's when the Red Socks manager told Sidney Earl something, too: 'Goodbye!'

Now folks are once again bragging about Sidney Earl, saying he's is the first Jenkinsville boy to drive the forty-two miles to Memphis to enlist in the Marine Corp. He wasn't the only one, either. Boys who wouldn't know what side of a razor to use couldn't wait to become soldiers. Especially marines or pilots. Every guy wanted to be either one or the other.

Got to give credit where credit is due. Nobody is more patriotic than our Jenkinsville boys and that's for sure. There is though one thing that I wonder about. The religion thing. Do you suppose that the Marine Corp is going to give Sidney Earl his Sundays off? Naah.

All this patriotism is creating more bonding than even the Baptist Training Camp. Because the one thing that everybody (especially the men) talks about is how we're going to teach those sneaky little yellow-bellied Japs a lesson, once and for all. A lesson they'll never forget.

At the same time, they're teaching my father — a thirty-nine-year-old man with bad eyesight — a personal lesson that's making him angrier and more upset than usual. If that's at all possible. With my own ears, for example, I heard Mr Bubba Bradley ask, with a sneer on his face, 'Well, now, Harry, when are you joining up? Think you'd ever give up a little of your Jew-money to help America out?'

Although I was working hard on the scrap-metal drive, I didn't find enough metal to do all that much good for the war effort. I mean what are dozens of metal jar tops, rusty tin cans and the caboose of a toy train (also rusting) going to turn into? Not all that much.

When Saturday came around, I knew two things: I must have searched through half the back yards in town and the second thing I knew was that I wasn't as patriotic as I thought I'd be.

All that bending over gave me an achy back and that's when my patriotism cried out for a break. It had been five days since I'd danced with Little Henry and I missed him, and Mrs Lee especially. I was so happy to be teaching her English because, once she learns it, she has so very much more to teach me.

As soon as I crossed onto the cross street, I felt as though my energy had begun to be sucked right out of me. Something wasn't right. What wasn't right? It wasn't the sky. The sky was okay, a sweet watercolor blue. No storm warning. What's wrong with me, anyway? Everything is just fine. Just as it should be.

Nearing Chu Lee's, I saw what from here looked like a broken store window. Stepped closer. And there it was what I hoped it wasn't. A hole, bigger than a basketball, and from that hole a sunburst of splintered glass shimmered and sparkled.

Peering inside I had the second ugly shock. The Lees had packed up all their groceries and left.

People leave when they find better opportunities in other places. Nothing strange about that.

Yeah, well. Okay, maybe.

Inside me, two emotions were fighting each other for breathing room: anger and sadness. Anger that they'd take off without so much as a goodbye. No, not even so much as a wave and a 'See you later, alligator.'

And there was sadness because I'd never again dance with Little Henry, talk with Mrs Lee or smile with Mr Lee.

I then walked the two blocks to our store, Bergen's Department Store, hoping that my father wouldn't send me home to ask what Ruth is fixing for supper. Or worse, tell me to stop hanging around and go play with my friends. Why can't my parents get it through their thick heads that all my friends are already playing? Playing Jesus Loves Me games up in the Arkansas Ozarks?

Back inside the men's department, my father was selling Mr James Gilmore Jackson a three-piece suit while Mr Jackson was telling my father something that he definitely positively didn't want to hear. 'If you were just a little bit patriotic, Harry, you'd have been with us while we gave those Chinks a going-away party that they'll never forget! Only wish our boys at Pearl Harbor could have seen that!'

Mr Jackson's words dammed up my brain cells. It was as though I couldn't make a bit of sense out of any of the words that I had just heard. And then … and then the dam cracked open. Wide open. And I understood!

Without thinking, I charged into the space between my father and the plantation owner, while screaming, 'What did you do to them! Where are the Lees?'

For a moment, I thought that Mr Jackson looked scared. Maybe he was scared but maybe it wasn't so much fear as surprise. Surprise that anyone would dare yell at him. Him being the richest man in our town and all.

I watched as he searched my father's face for back-up. 'Harry, is this the way you Jew families teach respect to your young-uns?'

'Did you hurt them, Mr Jackson?' I watched as his gaze jerked away from my father and back to me. 'Did you hurt the Lees?'

His open palms reached out in my direction as though pleading for a bit of understanding. 'Hey, there now, there's nothing to get so excited about. It's not your fault. You're just a little young to know the bad things that those dirty Japs did to our brave sailors and soldiers at Pearl Harbor.'

'I'm old enough to know that the Chinks aren't Japanese. They're Chinese and they didn't have any more to do with

Pearl Harbor than you did! So where are the Lees, and what did you do to them?'

'Look, girl, don't you go pestering me. They weren't getting any business in this town so they moved away. Simple as that!'

'You can't fool me! I'm calling my editor, Mr Fitzgerald, at the *Memphis Commercial Appeal*. He'll send one of his best reporters over here to Jenkinsville, and he'll find out what happened. Find out where they are. Find out if the Lees are all right!'

'Hey, girl, you just wait a minute, 'cause you don't know who you're talking to!'

'Did you hurt them?'

'No! Nobody hurt nobody. But I'm going to tell you what I'm going to do. I'm going to send my boys over there, to where those Chinks are. We're going to get them all settled back in nice and cozy, so you talk to your editor over there in Memphis, he won't know what you're talking about. He'll just think you're nutty as a fruitcake.'

'Okay, do it, Mr Jackson,' I said. Turning on my heel, I walked quickly towards the door, because I didn't want him or anybody else to see that being called 'nutty as a fruitcake' was making me smile.

# Give peas a chance

*by Morris Gleitzman*

'Ben,' said Mum. 'Eat your veggies.'

Ben didn't hear her. He was too busy staring gloomily at the dead kids on TV.

'Come on, mate,' said Dad. 'A few carrots and zucchini won't kill you. Bung some tomato sauce on them and pretend they're sausages.'

Ben didn't hear him either. This was the third lot of dead kids just on tonight's news.

'Watch out, young man,' said Mum. 'If you don't eat those vegetables now, you might get them cold for breakfast tomorrow. With milk. And only one spoonful of sugar.'

Ben still didn't take his eyes off the TV.

The small blood-stained bodies were lying on a stone floor, arms and legs flopped in different positions like the kids were asleep. Except they weren't asleep, they were dead.

'Ben,' said Dad. 'Did you hear what your mother just told you?'

*303*

Angry men were standing next to the small bodies, yelling and waving guns. Ben could tell they were upset about the dead kids. But this didn't make him feel any better. The men looked like they were yelling for revenge, so by tomorrow night other kids in Iraq would probably have bullets in them too.

'Ben,' said Dad in a voice like a gun going off.

Ben realised the others were all looking at him. Mum wearily, Dad crossly and Claire with that you-are-such-a-der-brain expression big sisters liked so much.

Claire leaned towards him.

'You won't lose any weight skipping veggies,' she said. 'I went on a veggie-free diet last year. Waste of time. You end up eating extra ice-cream to get the vitamins.'

Ben sighed. How could a whole family not see what was happening to the world? Specially now they all had their new contact lenses.

'I don't understand, Ben,' said Mum. 'You like veggies.'

Ben had to admit she was right.

But that was before.

Dad tossed a two-dollar coin onto the table near Ben's plate.

Ben stared at it. Then he realised what Dad was doing. Giving him tomorrow's tuckshop money now. Hoping the thought of tomorrow's jam donut or cream lamington would be enough to help him force down tonight's veggies.

It wasn't.

'Sorry,' said Ben. 'I can't.'

He hadn't planned any of this. It was just sort of happening.

'Why not?' said Dad with that about-to-explode expression dads liked so much.

'Because,' said Ben. 'I'm not eating any more vegetables until people stop shooting each other.'

Later that evening after Mum and Dad calmed down, Ben explained that his strike wasn't just vegetable-based.

'I won't be tidying my room either,' he said quietly. 'Or clearing the table or taking the bins out or doing homework or being polite to relatives.'

Dad ran his big raw butcher's hands through his thinning hair.

Ben hoped all this wasn't going to make Dad's hair go even more thinning.

For a fleeting moment, Ben was tempted to tell Mum and Dad he was only joking. But he didn't, because he wasn't.

Now I've started this, he thought grimly, I have to keep going.

'This is crazy, Ben,' said Mum. 'People can't change the world even if they want to. Not unless they're Bono or that bloke who invented the iPod. You'll feel different in the morning. Have an early night, there's a good boy.'

'I'm not being a good boy any more,' said Ben. 'Not until grown-ups get rid of all the guns and bombs.'

'Why us?' moaned Dad. 'We haven't got any guns.'

Mum went out to the kitchen and came back. In one hand she had the gas gun for lighting the stove. In the other she had the kitchen waste-bin. She dropped the gas gun into the bin.

'There,' she said to Ben. 'Will you eat your veggies now?'

Ben shook his head.

'Those Iraq and Africa and Palestine people aren't killed by kitchen appliances,' he said.

Mum ran her slim office-manager's hands through her lightly-permed hair.

Ben hoped all this wasn't going to make Mum's hair go even more permed.


At bedtime, Claire came into Ben's room for a chat.

'You're making a big mistake, you know,' she said. 'You might think this is a clever way to get out of eating veggies and clearing the table and all that other stuff, but it's not.'

Ben could hear the distant sound of gunfire in the living room. Mum and Dad must be watching the late news.

'I tried something like it last week,' said Claire. 'I told Mum I wasn't going to stop biting my nails unless she let me wear nail polish. So she let me wear some and I forgot and my finger got glued to my mouth.'

Ben looked at his sister's frowning face and, he now saw, her slightly-green teeth.

'You must know why I'm doing this,' he said to her. 'You watch the news. Every night there's more and more people being killed in wars. Doesn't it make you upset?'

Claire thought about this.

'Not really,' she said. 'I don't look. Not when I'm eating.'

Ben wished he had that skill.

'When I see those dead people,' he said, 'it makes me think how I'd feel if it was you or Mum or Dad or my friends.'

Claire gave him the der-brain look.

'Don't worry,' she said. 'When the kids at school find out you're behaving like a complete psychiatric, you won't have any friends.'

The kids at school didn't think Ben was behaving like a complete psychiatric.

When he told them he was on strike and wouldn't be eating veggies or clearing the table or tidying his room or taking the bins out or being polite to rellies or doing homework, their part of the playground went quiet and they all looked sort of impressed.

And thoughtful.

'That is such a great excuse, guns and bombs,' said Skye Borlotti. 'When I want to get out of doing all that stuff, I can only think of things like headaches and pet allergies, and we haven't got any pets.'

'I'm gunna tell my parents they have to get rid of guns and bombs and spiders,' said Shane Moore. 'Our bathroom's a death-trap.'

Several of the other kids started discussing what they were going to add to the list.

Water pistols.

Sticks.

Aunties who kiss.

Ben was a bit worried some of the kids might be missing the point.

He explained about the thousands of people around the world who were killed each day by bullets and explosions, and what it must feel like to have a bullet or piece of shrapnel go through your head or your mum's head.

The kids all stared at him, even more thoughtful than before.

Shane started to ask how many people were killed by spider bites, then changed his mind.


That night, Ben sat in front of a large plate of steaming vegetables.

He peered at them.

The peas and broccoli looked new, but those carrots and zucchini looked like last night's.

'They are last night's,' said Dad. 'And if you don't eat this lot, they'll be on your plate with tomorrow night's lot.' He shrugged. 'Up to you how long this goes on for.'

Ben frowned as he chewed a mouthful of chop.

He didn't know how long it would go on for, but he was pretty sure the plate probably wouldn't be big enough.

Mum came in from the kitchen, also frowning.

'That was Jean on the phone,' she said. 'Jason's on strike. Veggies, bins, rellies, same nonsense as Ben.'

Dad got his about-to-explode look.

'Typical,' he said. 'There'd have to be one other clown and it'd have to be Jason.'

'Not one,' said Mum. 'Jean's the seventh school parent I've had ringing up complaining tonight.'

Dad stared at her in surprise.

Then Claire gave a yell.

'Look.'

She pointed to the TV. The news had started. On the screen was a headline. Ben had to read it three times to make sure he was seeing it right.

*Kids On Strike.*

'A text-message craze swept the country today,' said the newsreader. 'Thousands of children have gone on the offensive against what one nine-year-old described as weapons that hurt people.'

A girl Ben had never seen before appeared on the screen. She was standing in a milk bar with her arms folded. Behind the counter, looking on fondly, were her parents.

Ben hoped the girl wouldn't say anything about spiders or aunties who kiss.

She didn't.

'I'm not helping in the shop any more,' she said. 'Plus I'm not eating hamburgers, chips, toasted sandwiches or any other hot food or snacks. Not until there's world peace.'

The girl's mother looked even prouder.

Ben felt dazed.

Incredible.

He wanted to hug someone. But he didn't. The available people in the room were all staring at the TV, mouths open.

'Police are investigating,' said the newsreader. 'They say that with the aid of phone records, they will eventually trace the person or persons behind what some commentators are calling un-Australian behaviour.'

Ben had trouble swallowing his mouthful of chop.

Police? Investigating?

Mum, Dad and Claire were all staring at him now with grim faces.

'I tried to warn you,' said Claire.

Ben stayed home the next day.

'I don't want you running around at school causing more trouble,' said Dad as he left for work. 'Keep your head down here till it all blows over.'

'If a SWAT team busts in looking for you,' said Claire as she grabbed her school bag, 'you can hide in my wardrobe.'

'Don't answer the phone,' said Mum, zipping up her briefcase. 'Your veggies are in the microwave.'

Ben felt too excited to be hungry.

He spent the day on his computer, checking the news sites.

It wasn't blowing over.

Kids all around the country were staying home from school as part of the strike. Others were being driven to school by parents but refusing to get out of the car. Others were sitting in the playground, saying teachers would have to carry them into the classroom. Teachers were refusing because of their backs.

Grown-ups were getting very upset.

Ben felt sorry for them, particularly the vegetable shop owners who were saying they'd go broke if the major world powers didn't seriously rethink their armaments policies.

He knew the same thing could happen to Dad if kids started not eating meat.

Ben pushed the thought out of his mind. He clicked to another news site.

Incredible.

Kids were going on strike in New Zealand too.

And Japan.

Suddenly Ben felt a bit faint. He wondered if his blood sugar levels were being affected by the speed of the whole thing and how big it was getting.

He went to the kitchen and got a cold sausage from the fridge.

\* \* \*

'It'll blow over,' said Dad. 'Just watch.'

Ben looked at the pile of vegetables in front of him. Claire had just done a huge sneeze, but the five nights of veggies heaped on Ben's plate weren't even wobbling.

Ben realised Dad didn't mean the veggies.

'There were crazes when I was a kid,' Dad was saying. 'Pointy shoes. Disco. Smurfs. Hoola hoops. Mohawk hairdos. They all blew over.'

Mum gave Dad a look. She pointed to the TV screen, where a classroom full of Tibetan students were sitting at their desks, ignoring the bowls of yaks-milk porridge going cold in front of them.

'Didn't you hear what the news just said?' demanded Mum. 'Two hundred and thirty million kids in eighty-six countries have gone on strike. I don't think mohawk hairdos were ever quite that popular.'

Dad stared at the screen too.

His shoulders sagged.

He turned to Ben, not looking cross any more, just very worried.

'Why couldn't you have eaten your veggies?' he said pleadingly.

Ben didn't know what to say. He was feeling a bit stunned. He also hated seeing Mum and Dad unhappy, but that was partly why he was doing this, so it would be a happier world for them to grown old in.

The front door bell rang.

Claire went to answer it.

She came back looking frightened.

'It's the federal police,' she said.

After posing for photos with Ben on the steps of Parliament House, the Minister for Defence spoke briefly to the crowd of reporters.

'I salute the vision of this young Australian,' he said. 'The government shares his desire for a peaceful world. But unfortunately guns and missiles and our new fighter-bombers with their laser-tracking capability are a necessary evil. To have peace we must be well-armed.'

Ben took a deep breath and spoke up.

'Excuse me, your honour,' he said. 'But if nobody was armed, why would we need to be?'

The defence minister smiled for quite a long time.

'Young people get confused,' he said to the cameras. 'It's up to you, parents of Australia. Explain it to them.'

Ben saw that Mum was looking a bit doubtful.

'Could you just run through the main points?' she said to the defence minister.

The minister hesitated, then smiled some more.

'I know it's not easy,' he said to the cameras. 'I'm a parent too.'

Dad was looking thoughtful.

He nodded towards Ben.

'If you were his father,' Dad said to the minister, 'how would you get him to eat his veggies?'

For a horrible moment Ben thought the minister was going to announce a new law with on-the-spot fines for kids who wouldn't eat all their dinner.

Instead, Claire spoke up.

'Do you think any countries'll get rid of their guns?' she asked the defence minister, loudly so the reporters could hear.

The defence minister stopped grinning and shook his head.

'Not a chance,' he said.

The first country to get rid of its guns was Iceland.

Ben stared at the TV, struggling to stay calm, a piece of roast pork unchewed in his mouth.

Mum and Dad and Claire stopped chewing too.

'Unreal,' said Claire.

'We're doing it for our children,' said the Icelandic prime minister, standing next to a big drilling machine that was drilling into the ice. 'We've decided to bury our weapons in this glacier, so future generations of young Icelanders will be able to see them in the ice and think about how much better off we are without them.'

'And are you also doing it,' said one of a large group of journalists, 'so the current generation of young Icelanders will get out of bed and start eating fish again?'

'Yes,' said the Icelandic prime minister. 'That as well.'

Ben realised the rest of the family had stopped looking at the TV and were all looking at him.

So were the reporters outside the lounge room window.

Dad reached over and squeezed Ben's shoulder.

'Incredible,' he said in a stunned voice.

'Well done, love,' said Mum to Ben, sounding pretty stunned herself. 'Now will you eat your veggies?'

'Not yet,' said Ben.


Other countries tried to keep their guns.

'Hey,' yelled a reporter to Ben. 'Egypt has banned all pictures of shot and blown-up people on their TV. Any comment?'

Ben knew he wasn't meant to answer journalists who yelled at him through the lounge room window. But Mum was in the bathroom and he couldn't resist.

'If I was an Egyptian kid,' he yelled back, 'I'd draw a picture in coloured crayons of what happens when a toddler gets hit by a machine gun bullet and I'd stick the picture on my parents' TV screen.'

Two days later, the same journalist was yelling at Ben again.

'Two million Egyptian kids followed your suggestion,' he shouted. 'Any comment?'

'See what you've done now, Ben,' said Mum in an exasperated voice as she pulled the curtains. 'I told you not to talk to the media.'

* * *

The next country to get rid of its guns was Taiwan.

'Good on you, Taiwan,' said Dad as he turned up the sound on the TV.

Mum glanced at Ben's plate.

Ben pretended not to notice.

'We're doing it for our economy,' said the Taiwanese president, standing next to a brand new recycling plant for ferrous and non-ferrous metals. 'Melting down these guns will allow us to make many more MP3 players.'

'And are you also doing it,' said a journalist, 'so the young people of Taiwan will get out of bed and start buying MP3 players again?'

'Yes,' said the Taiwanese president. 'That as well.'

Ben helped Dad find Taiwan in the atlas.

'It's next to China,' said Mum.

Dad put a big tick with a texta on the map of Taiwan.

'Two down,' said Dad, studying the list of countries in the front of the atlas. 'A hundred and twenty-three to go.'

'I wish they'd hurry up,' said Mum, staring wearily at the huge pile of uneaten veggies on Ben's plate.

When China saw that Taiwan didn't have any guns, they decided to invade.

Millions of Chinese children lay down in front of the war planes and tanks. The Chinese authorities arrested the parents of every child involved. And the aunties, and the uncles, and the people who weren't really relatives but helped out with child-minding after school.

'Any comment?' yelled the reporters in Ben's front yard.

Ben didn't have any comment.

Not to the reporters.

Silently he worried that things might be getting a little out of control, and that it was all his fault.

'I'll send an email to the Chinese embassy,' said Claire. 'Remind them they've got the Olympics coming up.'

Soon the Chinese authorities started releasing people from jail.

Chinese children stayed on strike.

China started getting rid of its weapons.

'They had to,' said Claire to Ben. 'Most of their athletes are under eighteen. Plus who'll vacuum the Olympic stadiums if all the adults are in jail?'

'Thanks, Claire,' said Ben. 'I'm glad you're on our side.'


When the other countries saw China had got rid of its weapons, they did too.

America was last.

They made excuses and broke promises and pretended they didn't have enough recycling depots.

'That's bull,' said Mum indignantly. 'They can turn all their gun shops and missile silos into recycling depots.'

Ben grinned. Trust an office manager to get things organised.

Finally the US Congress persuaded the president to sign the disarmament bill by explaining the terrible damage that would be done to the US economy if American kids continued not to eat McDonald's.

'Come on, Ben,' said Mum. 'You've got no excuses now. Eat your veggies.'

Ben knew it was Mum from her voice. He couldn't actually see her because of the mountain of vegetables on the serving platter in front of him.

She sounded tired.

Ben wasn't surprised.

They were all tired after weeks of living in the media spotlight. Thank goodness the footy season had started and a couple of coaches had been sacked and the media had all gone to their front yards.

'Look,' said Claire, pointing to the TV screen.

Ben peered around his veggies.

On the TV news, the last gun from the last warship in the world was being melted down in San Diego.

'You heard your mother, Ben,' said Dad. 'You've got your own way, you've brought peace to the entire planet, now you have to keep your side of the bargain. Eat those veggies.'

Ben looked at Dad's proud grin and the relieved expression on Mum's face.

World peace felt good.

He stuck his fork into a big lump of much-microwaved broccoli, put it into his mouth and started chewing.

All next day at school, even while people were saying how nice it was to have him back, Ben couldn't stop thinking about how long it was going to take him to eat that pile of veggies.

About a year, probably.

Longer if he kept getting sick of their fridge-taste as quickly as he had last night.

But later, when Ben sat down at the dinner table, he stared in surprise.

The mountain of veggies had been divided into four smaller piles. Mum, Dad and Claire each had a pile on their plate. They were eating veggies as fast as they could.

'Thanks,' said Ben.

What a generous family.

'We're not doing it for you,' said Claire through a mouthful of spinach.

She pointed to the TV screen.

Ben stared. The news report was describing how two hours ago America had invaded Iran. On the screen, American warplanes and bombers hurtled over Tehran.

'But they haven't got any guns or bombs,' said Ben. 'How can they declare war?'

'Veggies,' said Dad grimly.

At first Ben didn't understand. Then he saw what the bombers were dropping from high altitude onto the panicked Iranian people.

Cauliflower.

Pumpkin.

Mashed potato with really big lumps in it.

'That is disgusting,' said Mum. 'Targeting kids like that.'

On the TV a fighter plane roared low over a block of flats. Every window exploded into shards of glass under a hail of frozen brussel sprouts and sweetcorn.

Ben stared in horror.

'Don't just sit there gawking,' said Claire. 'Eat your veggies.'

'The more we eat,' said Mum through a mouthful of carrot, 'the less there'll be to injure innocent civilians.'

Ben nodded.

He looked at his family, all doing their bit to make the world a better place.

Then he stuffed a big forkful of peas into his mouth and chewed as fast as he could.

# You can be greater than you know how to be

*by Talia Leman*

When Hurricane Katrina hit the Gulf Coast in 2005, I made a plan. I made the decision that, with Halloween around the corner, I was going to take advantage of that captive audience and trick-or-treat for coins instead of candy and give my money to hurricane relief organisations. It seemed a reasonable course of action for a ten-year-old.

I called my business TLC — an acronym which stood for Trick-or-Treat for the Levee Catastrophe. Except when it didn't. Sometimes it stood for Trick-or-Treat for Loose Change. And sometimes it stood for Trick-or-Treat for Loads of Cash. I took a flexible approach to branding.

I also determined that I would be the CEO of this effort — a title I took to mean chief executive optimist. Dutiful to my title, I set an early goal of raising $1 million.

By all accounts, things were coming along — I had a

nice *big* trick-or-treat bag and I chose a neighbourhood where the houses were really (really) close together.

Then my six-year-old brother got wind of what I was up to. He came up to me — clearly very upset — and said, 'I am "opposed" to what you are doing. I'd rather trick-or-treat for pirate relief.' Those were his exact words.

I didn't know what to do with that; it was very unexpected. But I decided to make room for it anyway — so I offered him a title, too. He became my official CON — chief operating nemesis. We even put him on our website in his favourite Darth Vader costume. He was thrilled.

And then something happened that turned my life around forever. The *Today Show* was visiting our little website, saw his photo and invited us on their program — CEO vs CON.

One day later I was fielding reports from kids all over the USA, tracking donations on a map with pushpins. One week later, a local grocery chain agreed to print 8.5 million trick-or-treat bags to be given out with my message on them in 226 stores in 13 States. Our governor held a press conference and UNICEF invited me to do media spots on CNN and NPR.

When it came time to draw our efforts to a close, I knew we had raised a considerable amount — but it was not $1 million. It wasn't even half a million. No ... it was, in fact, $10 million. Kids across the USA ranked in their giving power with the top five US corporate donors to Katrina — right up there with Walmart, Exxon and Amoco.

Through all of this, I became witness to a greatness in others that I never could have foreseen and, subsequently, to a success I never could have planned. It just happened. Which is a scary realisation.

If greatness often happens by accident — if it happens by surprise; if it's not a carefully orchestrated sequence of events — then how can we 'happen' upon it?

How can we do something greater than we know how to do — and become something greater than we know how to be?

I wasn't sure.

But what I was sure of is that someone had to harness that youth power for other disasters the world faces, and so I started an organisation called RandomKid — a unique non-profit that leverages the power of youth to solve real problems in the world. We provide all the tools and resources youth need to power up their ideas. I figured, if we can raise $10 million for hurricane relief, we can do anything.

Today RandomKid has unified the efforts of 12 million kids from 20 countries. And for every dollar we invest in a youth's idea, they turn it around into a 150–1000 per cent return for their cause. Together, youth have now placed safe water wells on four continents, built and refurbished schools both overseas and on our Gulf Coast, provided wind energy to bring water to once parched gardens, and so much more.

Despite all that success, do you know the most common question people ask me? It's why I decided to call the organisation RandomKid. It turns out to be a very important question. I tell them, quite simply, it's because I am a random kid. I tell them it's because if I see myself as anything more than a random kid, then how will those I seek to empower see the potential that they have? I tell them it's because when we believe in the power we each have, we have the greatest power of all.

What I hesitate to tell them is this — that RandomKid's success did not happen because of my ambitious Katrina goals or my lofty title. RandomKid's success happened because of ... did you catch it?

RandomKid's success happened because I made room for Darth Vader! It was the one step I took that seemed to have nothing to do with my success and it became the very thing that made me successful.

So, then, how can we do something greater than we know how to do and become something greater than we know how to be, when it is often serendipity that gets us there?

I now know the answer.

It happens when we make room for the plan we *didn't* have — when we are free enough and brave enough to take a step sideways to a place where unexpected things might happen. And do you know why that is? Because the great miracles of life, by definition, can *only* appear in those

unexpected places. By making room for the unexpected —
for passions that don't make sense, for playfulness that has
no purpose, for ideas that are not your own, for people
who are not like you, for a path you didn't define, for a
dream you were afraid to dream, for a future you didn't
imagine …

You can sometimes follow your heart to a larger destiny,
be captured by a grander idea, realise a power you never
knew, choose a path that raises you higher, dream that
impossible dream, believe yourself into a new way of being
and create a future defined by miracles and marked with a
greatness you never thought possible.

The answer is we don't have to know how. We can just
head in the direction of what pulls us forward, and we will
get there.

# A global citizen

*by Hugh Evans*

My passion for poverty eradication was sparked at the age
of fourteen when I was invited to visit the Philippines and
spend time in the slums of Manila.

World Vision organised the trip. I'd been able to raise
significant funds through the 40 Hour Famine and was
rewarded with the chance to see its work on the front line.

Unable to afford the journey on the savings from my
paper round, I turned to my local Rotary Club in North
Balwyn, Victoria, for help. There I found not only the
financial assistance I needed but also the support and
encouragement of an inspiring group of people who saw
the value of a young person widening their world view.

In Manila I was struck by the injustice of a world in
which birthplace determines your life prospects.

I was taken to Smokey Mountain, a makeshift
community built on and around a massive rubbish dump.
The very infrastructure of this community revolves around

scavenging. The children literally run after the garbage trucks to find food and things that they could recycle. It is about as far from the comfort of suburban Australian life as you can get.

That night I was placed in the care of a boy named Sonny Boy. We were the same age, but Sonny Boy had tattoos all over his forearm. He was about to become the leader of his gang and the tattoos were part of his initiation. Sonny Boy took me to his house and together we cooked a meal with some food that I'd brought with me.

Coming from Australia I was so naive: I thought we'd go to some kind of bedroom to sleep. However, when it was time to sleep we simply moved the pots and pans and lay down on the cleared concrete slab, which was about half the size of my bedroom at home — Sonny Boy, the rest of his family and I: seven of us in a line.

I'll never forget lying there that night, with the smell of rubbish, and cockroaches crawling around us. I didn't sleep a wink. If there is one moment that has the ability to change someone's life forever, that was mine.

When you've been exposed to abject poverty, you know that once you have seen it, experienced it, endured it, you can't pretend it doesn't exist. You're forced to confront an uncomfortable truth: the poor, those living on less than a dollar a day, are people just like us who deserve the same rights and opportunities we take for granted. I was no different from my new friend, and it wasn't fair that simply by virtue of the country in which I was born, I had access to the basic necessities of life while Sonny Boy did not.

After I returned home statistics — such as 21,000 children dying every day from preventable diseases — took on meaning. They were no longer just facts in news reports; I'd seen the human face of those statistics and to be honest, at such a young age I felt helpless and disillusioned.

Following a trip to South Africa in 2002 as World Vision's inaugural Youth Ambassador, I co-founded the Oaktree Foundation, Australia's first youth-run aid organisation, with a mission to bring young people together to see an end to global poverty. Since 2003, Oaktree has helped fund development projects providing education opportunities to more than 40,000 young people in developing countries around the world.

I had begun to understand that we don't have to stand idly by and lament the horrors of extreme poverty; we don't have to just accept the statistics. I believe strongly that the mass mobilisation of individuals can effect real change in the world.

I began working to grow the Make Poverty History campaign in Australia, helping — with Dan Adams and John Conner — to run the 2006 Make Poverty History Concert, a free event held in Melbourne to coincide with the G20 Summit.

The idea was to reach out and campaign for the achievement of the Millennium Development Goals, the United Nations' eight-point plan to halve the number of people living in extreme poverty by 2015. We had a whole bunch of great Australian artists that no one outside our borders had ever heard of. Then one day our dream for a concert of global significance became a reality: Bono from U2 called, and everything changed. The event went on to become Australia's largest ever youth-run concert.

The following year's Federal election led to the ZeroSeven Road Trip and a campaign to increase Australia's foreign aid to 0.7 per cent of GDP. Simply asking the government to increase foreign aid wasn't going to get a result; we needed to prove this was an issue that resonated with the electorate. So, working with our partners, we mobilised people all over Australia. We even lit up the Sydney Opera House to spread the message.

And we did it. Just before the election, the incoming government announced an additional $4 billion in aid for the world's poorest countries by the year 2015. Make Poverty History showed us what was possible when people are galvanised around an issue.

Since then I've been involved in other international campaigns that have furthered the cause of ending extreme poverty. The Live Below the Line campaign, which encourages participants to attempt to eat on less than

$1.25 a day for five days, raises more than $1.6 million per year. The End of Polio campaign has made a significant contribution to eradicating this terrible disease in the developing world and among the world's poorest citizens, which in turn will help break the poverty cycle.

But while progress has been made to achieve the Millennium Development Goals, an estimated 1.3 billion people still live in extreme poverty, on less than the equivalent of $1.50 per day.

By giving every child a chance to thrive, our generation can end extreme poverty. We need to ensure that we have political will; we need to ensure that our voices are heard. We have the tools at our disposal and the plans in place. We've got to act now, and we've got to act together to end extreme poverty and help the world's poorest people to live lives of progress and promise.

# Literacy

*by Andy Griffiths*

Over the years I've written many stories about out-of-control children, runaway bums and exploding cows, but no matter how silly and lurid the subject matter, underlying everything that I've written has been a serious and passionate desire to communicate my love of reading to new readers by creating books that they can't resist — books that hook them on the first page and keep them reading right to the end.

So I was deeply disturbed to discover a few years ago that only one in five children living in remote Indigenous communities can read at the accepted minimum standard.

It's very easy for us in the cities to take literacy — and access to books — for granted.

Literacy is the key not only to the enjoyment and knowledge that books can provide, but it's also a crucial factor underlying health outcomes.

Literacy also gives us a measure of independence and self-determination — things that people in remote communities need every bit as much as anybody else if they are to take control of their lives, interact with the wider community and be able to have meaningful participation in making decisions that are right for them and their people.

There are a range of reasons for the poor literacy levels in these communities. One reason is that their parents, by and large, aren't writers or readers. They are story-tellers and fluent readers of country, but there are no newspapers, bedtime books, street signs or other things that children growing up in print-soaked cultures take for granted.

The first time many of them encounter a book — or even English — is on the first day of school. And that's if they're lucky. Kids in these communities can be 'cut off' from the outside world by long distances for most of the year; they are many hours' drive from the nearest regional town and can become literally isolated by floods for many months of the year. They cannot get to bookshops, or libraries in regional centres.

I'll never forget the time I told a group of students in Daly River the sad story of my dog Sooty's heroic life-long quest to bite the tyres of passing cars and how he ended up getting run over in the process. I love to end it with the gratuitous — and I have to confess completely made-up — detail about how his 'guts came out of his mouth' — always a trusty inducer of delighted groans of disgust from most audiences ... but not in Daly River. The kids just shrugged and one said, 'That's nothing! Last week a crocodile got run over by a semi-trailer … and we got photos!' (I probably don't need to tell you that the crocodile's guts were *actually* coming out of its mouth.)

As a visitor to communities I'm continually reminded of how much I don't know. One girl once told me that during the floods lots of animals float into their houses, including snakes.

'What do you do when you get a snake in your house?' I asked.

'Get a stick and get it out!' she said, looking at me as if I were an idiot.

I quickly learned to turn the story-telling sessions around and got the kids to tell me their stories and encouraged them to write them down and illustrate them in their own simple books. I invited them to fill their books with both words and pictures with dramatic, funny or ordinary stories based on their own lives.

Over the years they've written stories about the simple pleasures of playing with friends, riding motorbikes, picking berries, hunting for emu eggs and wild pigs, as well as tales of terrifying turkeys, angry spirits, farcical football matches and crocodiles with an unfortunate — but entirely understandable — preference for eating naked people.

Twenty-five years ago, I could never have predicted that my writing would give me the opportunity to undertake regular trips into the silent and spacious heart of Australia's outback to conduct writing sessions with children in some of our country's most remote Indigenous communities.

But life — thankfully — is full of surprises.

It's still early days in developing Indigenous Literacy. We've really only just dipped our toes into what's possible and look forward to many more opportunities for sharing stories. But even more importantly, even beyond words and stories, our efforts are opening up the possibility of trust. After reassuring one woman that there are no hidden strings or catches in the assistance that the Indigenous Literacy Foundation* offers, she asked, 'You mean people in the cities *know* about us? And they *care?*'

Yes, we do.

*The Indigenous Literacy Foundation, or ILF, was created by Suzy Wilson in 2004 and aims to supply culturally appropriate and educationally useful books to Indigenous communities around Australia. For more information, visit www.indigenousliteracyfoundation.org.au

# Sources

Graeme Base : 'From the shadows', poem and illustrations first
    published in *The Age*, 2009. Copyright © Graeme Base
    2009

Gary Crew: 'What we eat', first publication. Copyright © Gary
    Crew 2013

Deborah Ellis: 'Travels with teddy', first publication. Copyright
    © Deborah Ellis 2013

Hugh Evans: 'A global citizen', first publication. Copyright ©
    Hugh Evans 2013

Kate Forsyth: 'In the tower', poem first published in 'Enchanted
    conversation: a fairytale magazine' online blog, May
    2012. Copyright © Kate Forsyth 2012

Rose Foster: 'The two-month turnaround', first publication.
    Copyright © Rose Foster 2013

Janine Fraser: 'wikipedia leaks war list by death toll', first
    publication. Copyright © Janine Fraser 2013

Jackie French: extract from her novel *Refuge*, published by
    HarperCollins Publishers Australia, 2013. Copyright ©
    Jackie French 2013

Susanne Gervay: 'Meatloaf soldiers', first publication. Copyright
    © Susanne Gervay 2013

# About the contributors

**Graeme Base** is an award-winning children's author and illustrator whose 1986 alphabet book, *Animalia*, earned international acclaim. To date, *Animalia* has sold nearly three million copies worldwide and has been adapted to an animated TV series, for which Graeme co-wrote the theme song. Since his first book, *My Grandma Lives in Gooligulch* (1983), he has gone on to publish fifteen books, including such favourites as *The Eleventh Hour*, *Jungle Drums* and *Uno's Garden*. His most recent book, *Little Elephants*, is a charming and poignant tale of a herd of tiny elephants who rescue an impoverished mother and her son. Graeme lives in Melbourne with his wife and three children.

**Gary Crew** developed a keen interest in reading from a young age, due to a childhood illness that prevented him from partaking in outdoor activities. He left school at sixteen to become a draftsman, and worked in the field for ten years, before attending university to train to be an English teacher. It was as a teacher that his prolific twenty-five-year writing career began, resulting in over seventy works for children and young adults. He has won the coveted Children's Book Council of Australia Book of the Year award four times, among numerous other accolades, making him one of Australia's most awarded children's / young adults authors. Gary is now an Associate Professor (Creative Writing) at the University of the Sunshine Coast.

**Deborah Ellis**, a multi award-winning Canadian author, joined the Peace Movement as a teenager and later became a mental-health counsellor. In the 1990s she spent time in Afghani refugee camps in Pakistan, an experience that inspired several books: *Women of the Afghan War*, an adult non-fiction work, and the 'Breadwinner' trilogy, for teenage readers. Deborah's fiction deals with issues of social justice. Among them are *The Heaven Shop*, in which a family of orphans in Malawi struggle with the fallout of HIV/AIDS; *I am a Taxi*, which looks at poverty and the cocaine industry; and *No Safe Place*, whose main characters are children who fall into the hands of people smugglers.

**Hugh Evans** was fourteen when he began his humanitarian work, visiting the Philippines as an ambassador for World Vision. After travelling extensively to poverty-stricken countries such as India and South Africa, he became the founder and director of the Oaktree Foundation, Australia's first youth-run aid organisation, aiming to combat global poverty. Oaktree has provided educational opportunities to thousands of people, in such countries as Ghana, Papua New Guinea and East Timor. In 2004, the Australia Day Council awarded Hugh the Young Australian of the Year award. In 2005, he was named by the Junior Chamber International as one of twelve Outstanding Young People of the World. He is now CEO of the Global Poverty Project.

**Kate Forsyth** is an internationally bestselling author of more than twenty books, including picture books, poetry and novels for both children and adults. She has won or been nominated for several awards, including a CYBIL award in the US. She is also the only author to win five Aurealis awards in a single year, for her Chain of Charms series. Kate's books have been published in fourteen countries around the world, including the UK, the US, Russia, Germany, Japan, Turkey and Spain. She is currently undertaking a doctorate in fairytale retellings at the University of Technology, Sydney.

**Rose Foster** grew up in Melbourne, Australia. After she finished high school, Rose embarked upon tertiary studies at Swinburne University of Technology, but found herself constantly pulled in another direction — writing for young adults. Her stunning debut, *The Industry*, is the first instalment in a series of psychological thrillers. She is currently studying creative writing at RMIT University.

**Janine Fraser** is an award-winning poet and children's author. She has published ten books of junior fiction. The Sarindi series, published by HarperCollins, tells the story of a boy called Sarindi who lives in the city of Yogyakarta, Indonesia. *Abdullah's Butterfly*, also published by HarperCollins, is set in the Highlands of Malaysia. Janine's interests in people, place and travel find their expression in much of her writing. *Portraits in a Glasshouse* is her first book of poetry.

**Jackie French** is one of Australia's most lauded and beloved children's authors, and her writing career spans twenty years, more than 140 books, thirty-six languages and over sixty awards in Australia and overseas. Jackie is one of the few writers to win both literary and children's choice awards. Her work includes *Hitler's Daughter*, which won the CBCA Book of the Year for Younger Readers award in 2000, and *Diary of a Wombat*, created with illustrator Bruce Whatley, which is one of Australia's best loved picture books and remains on bestseller lists across the world, with a still increasing number of awards and translations. Jackie and her husband, Bryan, live in the Araluen Valley in New South Wales.

**Susanne Gervay** is an award-winning Australian author of children's and young adult literature, as well as a specialist in child development. Her much-loved and bestselling *I am Jack* has become a classic on school bullying, and has been adapted into a play by the Monkey Baa Theatre. Susanne's books are endorsed by organisations including the Cancer Council, the Alannah & Madeline Foundation, the Children's Hospital Westmead, Room to Read, and Life Education Australia. She is head of the Society of Children's Book Writers and Illustrators (SCBWI) Australia East & New Zealand, and has been awarded an OAM for Children's Literature and professional organisations, as well as the Lady Cutler Award for Distinguished Services to Children's Literature.

**Libby Gleeson** is an Australian children's author whose works are published widely throughout the world. Shortlisted for the Children's Book Council of Australia awards fourteen times, Libby won the award for Fiction for Younger Readers in 1997 with *Hannah and the Tomorrow Room*, the Picture Book of the Year in 2002 for *An Ordinary Day*, illustrated by Armin Greder, and Early Childhood Book of the Year in 2007, for *Amy and Louis*, illustrated by Freya Blackwood. *The Great Bear* won the Bologna Ragazzi in 2000, the only Australian title to have won this prestigious award. In 2011 she published *I Am Thomas*, illustrated by Armin Greder, and *Look! A Book!* , illustrated by Freya Blackwood. In 2012 she published a novel, *Red*. Libby is an adjunct Associate Professor in the Department of Education and Social Work at the University of Sydney. In 2007 she received a Member of the Order of Australia Award for services to literature and literacy education.

**Morris Gleitzman** is one of Australia's funniest and most successful children's authors. Born in England, Morris migrated to Australia aged sixteen. He has held a menagerie of colourful positions, including paperboy, bottle-shop shelf-stacker, department store Santa, fashion-design assistant and sugar-mill employee. A regular contributor to *The Age*, the *Sydney Morning Herald* and *Good Weekend*, Morris has written stage material for people such as Rolf Harris, Pamela Stephenson and the Governor General of Australia. Morris's international bestselling novel *Two Weeks with the Queen* was adapted into a play by Mary Morris. All of Morris's other books have been shortlisted for or have won numerous children's book prizes. His stories have been published in seventeen countries and include such titles as *The Other Facts of Life*, *Second Child*, *Misery Guts* and *Gift of the Gab*.

**Danielle Gram** was sixteen when she and her friend Jill McManigal co-founded Kids for Peace, a not-for-profit organisation that educates children about other cultures while teaching them to become service-oriented leaders, peace builders and environmental activists in their communities. Kids for Peace has over seventy-five chapters across eighteen countries and keeps growing. While an undergraduate at Harvard, Danielle joined the Harvard Humanitarian Initiative, a think-tank for humanitarian response. She has taken her Kids for Peace message to places torn apart by crises and conflict, such as Haiti, Sudan and the Democratic Republic of Congo, and has adapted the program to the needs of former child soldiers, refugees and abused women and children.

**Neil Grant** was born in Glasgow, Scotland, moved to Australia at the age of thirteen and finished high school at the International School of Kuala Lumpur. He has travelled extensively and had a series of unlikely occupations, including instrument steriliser, cook, brickie's labourer, roof-tile reclaimer, carrot picker and tree planter. But Neil has always been a writer. In 2000, he was awarded a Victorian Writers' Centre Mentorship for his young-adult surf novel *Rhino Chasers*. His second novel, *Indigo Dreaming*, was shortlisted for the Melbourne Prize in 2006. To research his 2012 novel *The Ink Bridge* — about the friendship between a young Afghani refugee and a troubled Australian boy — Neil travelled through Afghanistan in 2009; it was awarded a Queensland Literary Award for Young Adult Literature in 2012.

**Bette Greene** is the author of several books for children and young adults, including *Summer of My German Soldier*, *The Drowning of Stephan Jones*, and the Newbery Honor book *Philip Hall Likes Me, I Reckon Maybe*. Bette was raised in a small town in Arkansas, where she stuck out as a Jewish girl in the American South during the Great Depression and World War II. Her books focus on themes of injustice and alienation. Her book *Summer of My German Soldier* was heavily based on her childhood. Bette currently resides in Boston, Massachusetts.

**Andy Griffiths** is one of Australia's most popular children's writers. He is the author of over twenty books which have been *New York Times* bestsellers, won over fifty children's choice awards, been adapted as a television cartoon series and sold over five million copies worldwide. He's best known as the author of the hugely popular 'Just!' series and *The Day My Bum Went Psycho*. In 2008 he became the first Australian author to win six children's choice awards in one year for *Just Shocking!*. Andy is also an ambassador with the Indigenous Literacy Foundation, which promotes literacy in Indigenous communities, and the Pyjama Foundation, which provides literacy-based mentoring programs to children in foster care.

**Libby Hathorn** is a poet and award-winning author of some fifty books for children and young adults. Her stories have been adapted to screen as well as to stage, both plays and opera, and translated into several languages. Her novel *Thunderwith* was made into a movie by Hallmark Hall of Fame and starred Judy Davis. Her latest picture book is *A Boy Like Me: A Story About Peace* and her upcoming novel *Eventual Poppy Day* is set largely in World War I. She devotes much of her time to writing and teaching poetry and has current projects with the Powerhouse Discovery Centre and the State Library of NSW. She is co-editor of *Women's Work: A Collection of Contemporary Women's Poetry*.

**Rosanne Hawke** lives in rural South Australia in an old Cornish-style farmhouse. She has written over twenty books for young people, including *Shahana: Through my Eyes, Marrying Ameera, Soraya, The Storyteller, Mustara* and *Mountain Wolf*. Many of her books have been shortlisted or named as Notable Books in the CBCA Awards. *Taj and the Great Camel Trek* won the 2012 South Australian Festival Award for Children's Literature. Rosanne has been a teacher, and for almost ten years was an aid worker in Pakistan and the United Arab Emirates. She is a Carclew, Asialink, Varuna, and May Gibbs Fellow, and a Bard of Cornwall. She has a PhD in Creative Writing from the University of Adelaide and is Senior Lecturer in Creative Writing at Tabor Adelaide.

**Jack Heath** wrote his first book, *The Lab*, at the age of thirteen, and had a publishing contract for it at eighteen. Since then he has written six action books for young adults and been shortlisted for the Aurealis Sci-fi Book of the Year award, the Nottinghamshire Brilliant Book award and the National Year of Reading 'Our Story' Collection. In 2009, he was named the ACT Young Australian of the Year. Jack has also taught creative writing at the Canberra Institute of Technology, and been featured in the Shanghai World Expo. He continues to teach and lecture at schools and festivals. His book *Money Run* is published in nine countries. He continues to teach and lecture at schools and festivals.

**Talia Leman** is the CEO and a founder of RandomKid, a non-for-profit organisation that seeks to educate, mobilise, unify and empower youth to directly impact local and global needs. Appointed as UNICEF's first National Youth Ambassador, Talia has worked with kids from twenty countries and together these kids have reported close to US$11,000,000 through RandomKid-guided initiatives. Talia is the winner of numerous international and national awards for her philanthropic work, including the National Jefferson Award for global change, alongside co-recipients Marlo Thomas and Ruth Bader Ginsberg. She was the subject of a *New York Times* article entitled 'Talia for President'. She is also the author of *A Random Book about the Power of ANYone*.

**Alison Lester**'s picture books, which she writes and illustrates, celebrate the differences that make each child special, with a focus on children learning to believe in themselves. Among her many awards are the 2005 CBCA Picture Book of the Year award for *Are We There Yet?*, and the 2012 CBCA Eve Pownall Book of the Year award for *One Small Island*. In 2012 Alison was shortlisted for the prestigious Melbourne Prize for Literature. Alison is heavily involved in community art projects and spends part of every year travelling to schools in remote Indigenous areas, encouraging children and adults to write and draw about their own lives. She was recently named Australia's inaugural Children's Laureate, alongside Boori Monty Pryor.

**Michael Leunig** is an Australian cartoonist, writer, painter, philosopher and poet. His commentary on political, cultural and emotional life spans more than forty years and has often explored the idea of an innocent and sacred personal world. The fragile ecosystem of human nature and its relationship to the wider natural world is a related and recurrent theme. His newspaper work appears regularly in the Melbourne *Age* and the *Sydney Morning Herald*. He describes his approach as regressive, humorous, messy, mystical, primal and vaudevillian — producing work which is open to many interpretations and has been widely adapted in education, music, theatre, psychotherapy and spiritual life.

**Melina Marchetta** made an impressive debut as an author with the 1992 publication of *Looking for Alibrandi*, a novel for young adults that won numerous accolades and awards and sold in fourteen countries. She went on to write the award-winning script for the movie of the book, and several other books for young people. Melina grew up in Sydney, where she still lives, and is of Italian descent. For ten years she juggled writing with her career as a teacher of English and History in secondary schools, but now writes full time. Her published work includes a children's book and fantasy novels. Melina's books have been published in seventeen languages.

**Michael Morpurgo** is a British author, poet and playwright who has penned over a hundred books, including the internationally bestselling *War Horse*. Among the highly prestigious honours he has received over his career are Children's Laureate, Order of the British Empire and several honorary doctorates. In 1976 Michael and his wife, Clare, started the charity Farms for City Children, which provides inner-city children with the opportunity to work actively and purposefully on farms in the heart of the countryside, to enrich their experience. Michael is also patron to many charities, including (to name but a few) the Prince of Wales Art and Kids Foundation, the Down Syndrome Educational Trust and the Browning Society.

**Anna Perera** was born in London to an Irish mother and Sri Lankan father. She worked as an English teacher in secondary schools in London before running a unit for excluded boys. She gained an MA in Writing for Children and had six children's books published, including the critically acclaimed *Guantanamo Boy*, which was shortlisted for the Costa Children's Book Award and nominated for the Carnegie Medal and numerous other awards. She learned about the plight of children held at Guantanamo Bay at a benefit event held by the human rights charity Reprieve. Anna says the story found her. Her latest young adult novel, *The Glass Collector*, is set in Cairo and tells the story of a Zabbaleen teenager who collects and recycles the city's waste. It was also nominated for the Carnegie Medal and other awards.

**James Phelan** is a Melbourne-based writer. He has studied and taught writing at a post-graduate level, and has been a full-time novelist since the age of twenty five. His first book was the author interview collection *Literati: Australian Contemporary Literary Figures Discuss Fear, Frustrations and Fame.* His thriller novels featuring investigative journalist Lachlan Fox include *Fox Hunt, Patriot Act, Blood Oil, Liquid Gold* and *Red Ice.* His ALONE trilogy of young adult post-apocalyptic novels are titled *Chasers, Survivor* and *Quarantine.* He is currently working on a new adult thriller, a thirteen-book young adult series called The Final Thirteen, and several other projects.

**Anna Snoekstra** is a Melbourne-based writer and filmmaker and is a screenwriting graduate of RMIT. Her short films have been screened at the Melbourne Underground Film Festival and the Melbourne Fringe Festival, and she has directed two music videos. Her recently completed first novel, *Grey Fields,* is set in Victoria and is a modern take on Australian gothic. A long-time blogger, Anna regularly contributes film and television reviews for 'The Spinning Wheel', and writes for a range of online publications.

**David Nyuol Vincent** is a former child soldier and peace activist. One of the thousands of 'Lost Children', David was separated from his family, given a gun and trained to fight during the conflict in Sudan. In 2004 David was granted a humanitarian visa to come to Australia, where he completed a Bachelor of Arts at the University of Melbourne and has spent the years since gaining extensive experience working with young people in community development. David co-founded the Sudanese Summit, an annual event aimed at empowering South Sudanese youth to become agents of change and has also created the Peace Palette, a cross-cultural NGO working towards the empowerment of communities through the use of their local skills and knowledge. David was appointed as a People of Australia Ambassador and one of Melbourne's Top 100 most influential, inspirational, provocative and creative people for 2011. David's first book, a biography entitled *The Boy Who Wouldn't Die*, was released in 2012.

**Bruce Whatley** is one of Australia's most respected author–illustrators. He has illustrated over sixty picture books, published both in Australia and overseas. His first book, *The Ugliest Dog in the World*, became an instant classic, and was a Notable Book in the CBCA Book of the Year awards in 1993. Throughout his career Bruce has had several successful collaborations with esteemed authors, including Andrew Daddo, Ahn Do, Libby Hathorn, his wife, Rosie Smith, and, in particular, Jackie French, with whom he created the runaway bestseller *Diary of a Wombat*. He has recently completed a PhD on the implications of ambidextrous image-making. Bruce and his wife live on the south coast of New South Wales.

**Lili Wilkinson** was first published at the age of thirteen, in *Voiceworks* magazine. After studying Creative Arts at Melbourne University, she managed a website called 'Inside a Dog', about books for teenagers, and worked on the Inky Awards and the Inkys Creative Reading Prize as part of her role at the Centre for Youth Literature at the State Library of Victoria. Since then she has written seven novels for young adults, and has been published in Australia, the UK, the US, Germany, Italy, Turkey and China. Currently Lili is working on her PhD and writing full time. Her latest book, *Love-shy*, features a schoolgirl investigative journalist in search of a story. Lili lives in Melbourne.

# Acknowledgments

This book has come a long way. It began as a simple idea dreamt up in a school classroom and, through the dedication, generosity and enthusiasm of the many wonderful people I have had the pleasure of working with, has become something special.

I would like to thank HarperCollins Australia for their readiness to get involved, their support throughout the whole process and their belief in the cause and this final product. In particular, I would like to thank Lisa Berryman, Anne Reilly and Pauline O'Carolan for the many hours of hard work, the emails and the phone calls involved in getting this book ready.

I would like to thank all of the contributors who donated stories, illustrations or articles — Graeme Base, Gary Crew, Deborah Ellis, Hugh Evans, Kate Forsyth, Rose Foster, Janine Fraser, Jackie French, Susanne Gervay, Libby Gleeson, Morris Gleitzman, Danielle Gram, Neil

Grant, Bette Greene, Andy Griffiths, Libby Hathorn, Rosanne Hawke, Jack Heath, Talia Leman, Alison Lester, Michael Leunig, Melina Marchetta, Michael Morpurgo, Anna Perera, James Phelan, Anna Snoekstra, David Nyuol Vincent, Lili Wilkinson and Bruce Whatley.

My sincere thanks go out to Mum, Dad, the Kennedy family, Doug Macleod, Rebecca Lim, Tamora Pierce, Jessica Grills, Nan McNab, as well as all of the generous people who donated to UNICEF through the Everyday Hero Fundraising Page, in support of the book and this project.

All of the wonderful people at UNICEF Australia deserve appreciation —a huge thank you, in particular to Norman Gillespie, Monique Hughes and Mia Cox. I would also like to thank Penguin Group and Allen & Unwin Publishing for their incredibly generous offers of the use of several excerpts free of charge. My thanks also to Michael Leunig, who generously contributed not only three cartoons but also the beautiful illustration that graces the cover of this book.

And finally I would like to thank the reader, you. For in purchasing this book, you have not only supported the life-changing work of UNICEF Australia, but you have also demonstrated an interest in the lives of the people that this book is about — and that is the first step to a better world.